# DAN THE BARBARIAN

### (GOLD GIRLS AND GLORY #1)

## HONDO JINX

WWW.HONDOJINX.COM

Cover design by eBook Launch

Edited by Karen Bennett and Cheshire Phoenix

If you would like to know when my next book is released, SIGN UP HERE.

## THE WORST DAY

With a mighty roar, Wulfgar Skull-Smasher surged forward, swinging his massive two-handed sword at the towering troll.

The party's other adventurers yelped with surprise.

"What the hell, Dan?" Kurt said.

Dan Marshall laughed. He was a hack-and-slash player to the core. "You guys think too much. Thinking kills action!" He sent the yellow twenty-sided die rattling across the coffee table.

"Twenty!" Dan shouted triumphantly. "Double damage!"

At nineteen, Dan shared the square jaw and dark hair of his fearsome Towers & Trolls character, Wulfgar, but the similarities pretty much ended there. At six feet and 190 pounds, Dan was far from puny, but he was no six-foot-six, 250-pound barbarian.

Dan rolled three six-sided dice. "Max damage, baby!"

Willis, Dan's diminutive roommate and old school Towers & Trolls TM, shook his head, unable to conceal his grin. "The blade shears straight through the troll's neck, and its head flies through the air, spurting blood."

"Speaking of decapitation, Dan," Kurt said, pointing at the clock above the sink overflowing with dirty dishes, "don't you have class now?"

"Oh shit!" Dan said, hopping to his feet. "I'm late!"

He grabbed his backpack, rushed out the door, and tripped in the hallway. He fell hard, and his unzipped backpack vomited its contents onto the filthy maroon carpet.

*Why am I always so clumsy?* Dan thought.

Muttering curses, he started shoving stuff into the backpack. Of all classes, he was running late for Geoscience 02 with Dr. Lynch, a professor as old and inflexible as granite.

*If I'm late, she'll probably take points off my paper.*

Then the door opened.

Not his door.

*The* door.

As in the door across the hall, where his secret crush, Holly, lived.

Holly was drop-dead gorgeous, with long blond hair, a curvy figure straight out of a Boris Vallejo cover, and a pair of glasses that managed to make her look both super smart and uber-hot, like a cross between a Greek goddess and a geek goddess. Dan and his friends practically worshipped her, but to his knowledge, Holly didn't even really know that they existed.

Now she stood, blond, busty, and bespectacled, in a tight purple t-shirt that read *My Best Friend Is a Tree*, looking down at him uncertainly. "Are you okay?"

"Um…" Dan said, frozen by her beauty. As a gamer, he was bold and adventurous, leaping fiercely into combat. In the real world, however…

"Sorry," he said lamely, and felt the warmth of his face blushing.

He jumped up and started running again. He almost fell

going down the stairs then banged out the main door and sprinted across the yard, heading for campus.

*Sorry?* he thought and felt like slapping himself. *You finally get Holly's attention, and that's what you say to her... sorry?*

Despite the self-loathing he felt for mishandling his first ever face-to-face with Holly, he had to smile at the perfect October day. Penn State was beautiful year-round, but the best season was fall, with its crisp air, bright leaves, and—

*Wham!*

Dan's head jerked hard. He lost his balance and fell to the ground, confused. What happened? Had someone hit him?

He heard laughter, *mean* laughter, several voices all laughing together. A second later, he noticed the football rocking back and forth on the sidewalk nearby and understood.

Grady Lambert.

Dan turned toward the laughter and saw Grady and half a dozen of his "brothers" standing in front of their frat house, which just happened to be straight across the street from Dan's apartment. Talk about bad luck.

Grady was a curse.

They had met in fifth grade, when their respective elementary schools consolidated. Up until that point, Dan's life had been all right. Not *great*, exactly, but pretty good.

Dan was poor, like the other kids at his elementary school, and country as a corn crib. He and his classmates wore hand-me-down clothes and brown-bagged white bread sandwiches to school. No big deal. They were all pretty much the same.

Dan's father worked blue-collar at a factory in town. The man worked hard, drank hard, and spent his free time hunting and fishing.

Dan's mom worried about money all the time and did an amazing job running the household and taking care of Dan;

his kid sister, Hannah; and his wild but awesome older brother, Kip.

From an early age, Dan had a long list of chores around the house and worked at the farm down the road, picking crops and haying it in the summer and lending a hand in the milking shed seven days a week. He'd done well in school, and everybody liked him.

But two things happened in the brutally hot August of his eleventh year that would change his life forever.

Dan's brother died, and Dan started middle school.

Someone had sideswiped Kip on Johnson Hill. Kip lost control, went off the road, and plowed into a tree at seventy miles per hour.

Dan was gutted. He loved his brother.

Still reeling from Kip's tragic death, Dan climbed aboard a bus and rode across the river to town. After that, Dan always felt behind, somehow. Sure, he knew more about the woods, hunting, fishing, and farming than the town kids did, but none of that mattered in middle school.

He wasn't stupid. He just didn't know the things that the town kids knew. He rode the Cow Catcher, as the town kids called his school bus, and like most of the other country kids, went to school smelling like cow shit and wore beat-up work boots and old clothes that made the town kids snicker.

Suddenly, Dan had gone from being a kid to being a hick. He retracted into himself, shell-shocked into shyness.

The king of the town kids was Grady Lambert, whose dad was a white-collar, college-educated manager at the factory where Dan's dad worked. Grady strutted like a fighting rooster, with his fancy clothes and movie star hair. He smelled like cologne, not cow shit, and was great at sports and confident in the classroom. All the girls loved him, which was weird to Dan, since Grady was mean as hell.

None of this would have mattered to Dan, but he was

almost as big as Grady, and for some reason, that made Grady hate him. And because Dan was shy and awkward, Grady targeted him mercilessly.

Dan's friends urged him to fight back. *You're stronger than Grady,* they said, pointing to muscles Dan had inherited from his father and built, working the farm. *Hit him once, hard, and he'll leave you alone forever.*

But Dan never did, knowing that if he got suspended from school it would break his mother's heart. And we would never do that to her, not when she was hurting so badly from losing Kip.

The trouble is, some assholes, they keep pushing and pushing until you punch them in the face. Grady and his cool crowd friends dumped Dan's books, tripped him in the hall, made fun of his hand-me-down clothes and the cow-shit smell that followed him to school from the milking shed every day, and worst of all, called him—

"Danielle!" Grady said. "Oh, Danielle, are you all right?"

Dan felt a rush of anger and humiliation. Instantly, it was like being back in middle school.

Of all the colleges in the world, his tormentor had to come here. And of all the frats on campus, Grady had to rush *Alpha Alpha Alpha*, which just so happened to sit directly across from Dan's shoddy apartment house.

A curse. That was the only possible explanation. Grady was a real-world curse.

Dan said nothing and started to gather his things, which had again spilled from his battered backpack. He had to hurry, or he was going to be late to Dr. Lynch's class.

"You should really watch where you're going, Danielle," one of Grady's friends said, and the whole crew burst out laughing as if the guy had actually said something funny.

Dan reached for the last paper, his assignment for Dr. Lynch, due in twenty-five minutes. However, as his fingers

5

closed on the homework, a sneakered foot slammed down on the paper.

"Hey," Dan said. "Get off."

The foot twisted back and forth, wrinkling the assignment, and lifted away. Grady stood there with his muscular arms crossed over his broad chest, his pretty-boy face smirking down at Dan. "Oh, I'm so sorry. Did I step on your homework, Danielle?"

"Grow up," Dan said, grabbing the paper. It was all messed up now, badly wrinkled and stamped with a muddy sneaker print.

He wanted so badly to jump up and smash that smirk right off Grady's face.

But Grady was super athletic and had taken karate lessons. Besides, everyone knew that frat boys never fought alone. Even if Dan miraculously landed a lucky punch, Grady's buddies would knock Dan down and stomp him.

So instead of leaping boldly into combat, Dan Marshall, AKA Wulfgar Skull-Smasher, shouldered his backpack and scampered away like some level zero peasant.

2

## THE WORST DAY GETS EVEN WORSE

Twenty minutes later, sprinting up the elm-lined path known as the Pattee Mall, Dan spotted the Sparks Building uphill on the left. He only had a few minutes, but that was all he needed.

*Yes!* he thought. *I'm actually going to—*

"Look out!" a girl's voice cried, and Dan realized that a bicycle was flying straight at him.

He lurched to one side.

The girl zoomed off the path. Her bike wobbled and fell to the ground, and the girl spilled across the grass in a tumbling roll.

"Are you okay?" Dan asked, running to where she lay on the ground.

*Crap, crap, crap...*

He really didn't have time for this, but he wasn't about to leave the poor girl lying there.

The girl pushed off the ground. She had thick, chestnut-colored hair, the muscular build of a gymnast and, Dan couldn't help but notice, an A+ ass.

"I'm okay," she said with an embarrassed sounding laugh, and rubbed her shapely hip. "Ow."

Dan helped her to her feet and practically gasped when he saw her face.

She was beautiful. Not petite and ultra-feminine, like Holly. This girl was taller, maybe five-seven, with bright emerald-green eyes.

She could've been a model if it weren't for her slightly crooked nose, which had obviously been broken in the past, and which somehow made her even more beautiful to Dan.

He stood there for a second, gaping at her like an idiot.

She smiled. Her teeth were small and very white, with pronounced canines.

"Sorry for almost hitting you," she said. Laughing, she reached out and gave his bicep a squeeze. "Good thing I didn't. Would've been like hitting a stone wall."

Dan felt his face go beet red. "It's okay," he said, and leaned over to pick up her bicycle.

"Aw, thanks," she said. She threw her arms around him and gave him a hug. "You're sweet."

Dan froze, shocked by her embrace and very much aware of her firm breasts pushing into him, the warmth of her cheek against his neck, and the nice, floral smell of her hair.

"I..." he stammered, but his overloaded brain couldn't seem to form words.

"And you have a really nice butt," she said, and squeezed his ass with both hands.

He couldn't believe it. "What?" he laughed.

She stepped back, popped onto her tiptoes, and kissed his cheek. "Thanks," she said, "gotta run."

He stood there, stunned, and watched as she hopped gracefully onto the bike and started coasting downhill.

He probably would've stood there, mesmerized, until she

completely disappeared, if the shouting hadn't snapped him out of his trance.

"Stop that girl!" a short guy with glasses hollered at Dan. "She stole my bike!"

Confused, Dan turned to see the girl, who had paused fifty feet down the path. She smiled, shrugged, and held out a small, brown rectangle.

*Looks like a wallet,* Dan thought. Then, remembering the feel of her hands grabbing his butt, he thought, *Looks like* my *wallet.*

"Sorry," the beautiful girl said, pulling out and pocketing the cash before dropping the wallet to the ground. "You really do have a nice ass, though."

Then she zipped away, laughter trailing behind her like a colorful streamer.

## 3

## HEAT AND PRESSURE

**D**an skidded to a stop outside Room 213 of the Sparks Building. Fighting to catch his breath, he hurriedly straightened his clothes, finger-combed his tangled mop of dark hair, and flattened his demolished paper.

He was late.

He'd sprinted all the way from his apartment, and he was still late, all because he'd stopped to help that girl.

That *thief*.

He'd worked his ass off for that money, washing dishes at the Nittany Lion Inn three nights a week when he could have been studying or playing T&T or actually trying to have some kind of social life. To make matters worse, rent was due next week, and she'd taken every last dollar.

What made him even angrier, however, was the fact that he couldn't be purely mad at the girl.

He kept remembering the feel of her against him, her smell, and the sound of her laughter. Most maddening of all, he kept remembering her parting comment about his ass—

and how, despite just getting ripped off, he'd felt a rush of excitement at her words.

*How frigging lame am I to crush on a girl who just ruined my life?* he thought.

Now he was late to a class he was barely passing, a class taught by the meanest teacher in the universe. For a second, he stared at the heavy wooden classroom door, heart thudding with apprehension.

Faintly, he could hear Dr. Lynch lecturing beyond the wooden door, her ancient voice like a hissing snake muffled beneath a blanket of fluttering moths.

"Heat and pressure," Dr. Lynch's voice hissed. "Pressure and heat."

Dan put a hand on the door but hesitated.

*Just slip inside*, he told himself, *silently as a thief. Maybe they won't even notice you.*

He summoned his courage, opened the door as quietly as possible, and tiptoed into the classroom.

The snake stopped hissing.

Everyone turned to look at Dan.

*So much for stealth...*

Framed in a crown of white hair, Dr. Lynch's wizened face looked up from the podium and fixed Dan with a death stare.

"Sorry," Dan stammered, his blood turning to ice.

Dr. Lynch raised her scrawny arm slowly and pointed a gnarled finger in his direction. Her rheumy eyes blazed with cold fire. "Late," she said, her voice as dry and merciless as that of a necromancer casting the final word of a death incantation.

"Sorry," Dan said again, and started toward an empty seat in the back.

"Do you have your assignment?" Dr. Lynch rasped.

"Yes, Dr. Lynch," Dan said, "I'm sor-"

"Bring it to me," she said.

"Okay," he said, feeling a surge of hope. He struggled with his bag, clutching it to his chest and unzipping it to retrieve his homework. Several pens, a half-eaten Snickers bar, and a dog-eared copy of John Norman's *Raiders of Gor* fell to the floor.

Nearby students stifled laughter.

Dan set his bag beside these items and hurried to Dr. Lynch's podium. He held out the dirty, wrinkled paper in a shaking hand.

Dr. Lynch held the assignment at arm's length, pinched between two bony fingers. She fixed him with her blazing eyes. "You are late," she said. "This paper is late."

"I know," he said quickly, trying to plead his case before she passed some harsh judgment. "I'm sorry that I'm late. A girl wrecked a bicycle, so I stopped to help her, but—"

"This isn't English class, and I'm not interested in your stories," Dr. Lynch said. "This is geology, the study of heat and pressure and *time*. This essay is late, and I do not accept late work."

"I know," he said. Desperate, he went for broke, leaning in and lowering his voice. "I'm sorry, but please, cut me a break this once. If I don't keep a 3.0, I'll lose my scholarship, and without that, I won't be able to stay in school."

Dan could feel his eyes starting to burn and realized that he was close to tears, a surprising realization. He hadn't cried since he was eleven and his older brother, Kip, had died.

Dan fought now to hold it together, knowing that tears to someone like Dr. Lynch would be like fresh blood to a vicious dog. "Please," he said. "My whole future depends on this."

Then Dr. Lynch shocked him, doing the last thing he would have ever expected, something he'd never seen her do before, something he wouldn't have thought her even capable of doing.

She smiled.

Dr. Lynch's teeth were small and tightly packed into red gums receding from the enamel. Her breath hit him full in the face, a horrible rotten smell that made his gorge rise.

*She must be sick*, he thought. *Like really sick.*

Maybe that was why Dr. Lynch always seemed so harsh. Maybe she was in a lot of pain.

*Maybe she isn't even mean,* he thought. *Maybe she's just hurting.*

"Late," Dr. Lynch rasped, and tore Dan's paper in half.

## 4

## THINGS GET WEIRD

Dan wanted to head home and play T&T. Forget Dan Marshall, level zero sophomore, and become Wulfgar Skull-Smasher, level seven barbarian instead.

But no.

He couldn't pretend that everything was okay.

If he lost his scholarship, he would never be able to afford college. He would be forced to move back home, where he would be lucky to land a job at one of the factories in town or the slaughterhouse over in Wyalusing. He would have no degree, no high-paying job, nothing but a boatload of debt and two boatloads of regret.

So no. He couldn't just "pull a Dan," lose himself in the game, and put off his troubles.

This was it. His last chance.

He walked uphill to the library and rode the elevator up to the fourth floor and the Rare Books Collection, where he liked to study. During breaks, he could look through old books and check out the glass display cases that housed cool stuff that often seemed straight out of a T&T adventure.

First, he rewrote the GeoSci paper. He would go to Dr. Lynch's office and beg for mercy. Grovel, if need be.

He sighed and glanced out the window.

Outside, day gave way to dusk. Up and down the Pattee Mall, lights twinkled to life. Overhead, the sky had turned electric blue.

*Time for a break*, he thought. He stood, stretched, and walked away from the table, his legs tingling from sitting too long.

His stomach was growling, but he didn't have money for the vending machines, so he decided to feast his eyes instead. He beelined it past the librarians' desk to one of the pedestals holding a glass display case.

Nearing the display, he smiled at the sparkling, gem-encrusted decanter inside.

*Cool,* he thought. *Looks like something out of 1001 Arabian Nights.*

Then he stumbled.

Epically.

He grunted with surprise and fell, thick arms pinwheeling. The moment slowed in that particularly sadistic way that terrifying moments so often do. Dan saw the display case coming closer and closer and had time to think, *Oh no... oh shit... I'm going to hit it,* but his body couldn't keep pace with his mind. He was trapped in a nightmare, able to see exactly what was about to happen, able even to think it through, but completely incapable of doing anything to stop it.

He hit the display, knocked it over, and watched in paralyzed terror as the glass case and the doubtlessly priceless vase inside fell in slow motion toward the library floor.

The display case shattered with a horrifying explosion of noise. Glass shards flew everywhere. The ancient bottle hit the floor and bounced into the air, where the glittering stopper came loose and... stopped.

The cap stopped in mid-air. So did the bottle.

In fact, everything stopped.

The librarian's voice cut off in mid-gasp, the startled cries of the handful of people studying nearby shut off instantly, and right before Dan's eyes, the bottle, stopper, and spraying glass froze in the air as if someone had hit a cosmic pause button.

*Everything* stopped.

Everything except Dan, that is.

"What the hell?" he asked the frozen world. He looked around. No one moved. Everything was silent. Except...

He heard a faint hiss then, and looking down, he saw a strange purple mist rising from the uncapped decanter.

"Whoa!" Dan blurted.

The purple mist poured out faster and faster. It hovered above the frozen bottle and slowly condensed, seeming to grow into a solid form.

Dan took a step backward. He was terrified but also too amazed and curious to run.

The mist formed into the shape of a huge man, easily eight feet tall and packed with muscle. As the man's features coalesced, the purple mist thinned, spinning round and round the huge figure.

The spinning mist lowered, revealing a golden turban, a huge head with a handsome bronze face punctuated by dark, amused eyes. The swirling vapor dropped lower still, revealing more of the huge man, until it reached his waist, where it stabilized, whirling slowly in a purple tornado that stretched from the mouth of the gem-encrusted bottle to the golden belt of the humongous man.

Above this belt rose a muscular, bronze-skinned giant dressed in a golden vest. His mustachioed face split into a wide grin that shone as brightly as a scimitar flashing with desert sunlight.

"Thanks for releasing me, kid," the man said. "Zohaz the Magnificent at your service." And with this, he gave a little bow.

For a few seconds, Dan could only stare. He was absolutely flabbergasted. "You're a genie," he said.

"Bingo! You college kids sure are smart. So anyway, let's get down to business. I don't mean to be rude, but I've been trapped in that bottle for nineteen years, so I don't want to spend the whole night getting to know you, all right? As thanks for freeing me, I will grant you one wish."

"Only one?"

"Yes."

"I thought genies granted three wishes. That's the way it always is in books."

"Don't believe everything you read," Zohaz the Magnificent said, glancing at the door. "Look, do you want the wish, or should I be on my way?"

Dan felt a spike of panic. Of course, he wanted the wish.

He spent every day wishing. Wishing his life was better, wishing he was done with school, wishing he had money, wishing he had a girlfriend, wishing he could just play RPGs instead of trudging through an empty life that was more boring than a *Family Ties* marathon.

But which wish should he choose?

"Hey," the genie said. "I hate to seem ungrateful, but I've been bottled up for a long time, so... places to go, people to kill, you know what I mean?"

"Oh, sorry," Dan said, wringing his hands. "Yeah, I want the wish. Of course, I want it. I just want to choose the right thing, you know?"

The genie rolled his eyes and edged toward the door. "Come on, kid. It's now or never. What do you want?

Straight A's? A bunch of money? A girl like that?" He nodded across the room, where a stunningly beautiful redhead hunched over a book, frozen in time.

Dan was panicking now. Here he was, with the world in his hands, his greatest moment, and he was more afraid of making a mistake than he was excited to choose something great.

Straight A's? Yeah, right. That would be a waste.

A million dollars? Or a billion? That would be cool. He could quit school and just play games forever, but was that really what he wanted?

His eyes slid back to the redhead and his heart sped up. How much better life would be with a girlfriend like that, a girl magically bound to you. Or even better, a girl like his neighbor, Holly, or even that thief, if she wouldn't steal from him. They could study together and laugh a lot and have sex whenever he wanted….

The genie sighed. "That's it, kid. Time's up."

"Wait."

"Ten seconds or I'm gone."

"All right, all right," Dan said. All of these choices were too one-dimensional.

"Ten, nine…" the genie counted.

Dan's mind raced. As a billionaire, he'd just play games all the time, which would certainly beat his current life, but he wanted more than that from existence. With a hot girlfriend, he would still be a stressed-out college kid, washing dishes for minimum wage, up to his eyeballs in student debt, and pretty much doomed to losing his scholarship.

"Five, four…"

Dan didn't just want something cool. He wanted a cool *life*, one where he was strong and could fight for gold, girls, and glory.

"Three, two, one…"

## 5

## THE WISH

"Make my life like a T&T adventure," Dan said. Then he panicked again, remembering that genies often messed with sloppily framed questions. "I want my life to be like that, where I'm strong and women like me, and I have abilities and can level up and have adventures and get gold, girls, and glory."

A broad smile spread across the genie's face, and his eyes twinkled with pleasure, mischief, or both. "Excellent," Zohaz the Magnificent said, his deep voice drawing out the word, almost savoring it. "It shall be done."

Dan laughed with nervous excitement. Could this be real?

"What class?" Zohaz the Magnificent asked.

"Huh?"

"What character class?"

"I don't know," Dan said. "What are my choices?"

The genie sighed. "Here we go again. You waste your whole life playing Towers & Trolls, and you're going to ask me which classes you can pick? Heroes are decisive, noob. Pick a class, or I'll pick for you. You want to be a scribe?"

"No," Dan said, shaking his head emphatically. Again, his mind raced.

Being a wizard would be cool, but they had such low hit points. Besides, genies were famous for using irony to turn a wish into a curse. What if he couldn't find spell components?

What class, then?

In high school, he had often played a thief, but what good would that do him? His nineteen-year-old, decidedly male brain imagined scaling a female dorm, sneaking inside, and hiding in shadows, but he rejected this outright. He had higher aspirations than being a tenth-level Peeping Tom.

He wanted a life of adventure. He wanted to stride boldly into danger and laugh as he crushed his enemies.

"Barbarian," he blurted.

Zohaz the Magnificent nodded. "So be it. You are a first-level barbarian with zero experience points."

*First level?* Dan thought, feeling a little deflated. He couldn't exactly strut as a first-level barbarian. "I said I wanted to be a *powerful* character."

Zohaz the Magnificent shook his head, eyes glimmering again. This time, the glimmer was definitely mischievous. "You said," –and though the genie's mouth kept moving, it was Dan's voice coming out now– *"Make my life like a T&T adventure. I want my life to be like that, where I'm strong, and women like me, and I have abilities and can level up and have adventures and get gold, girls, and glory."*

Dan growled with frustration. Why hadn't he wished to be tenth level? So stupid! He could've had 100 hit points and a barbarian horde to do his bidding. He could wipe out Garth and *Alpha Alpha Alpha* frat boys without breaking a sweat. "Will I become powerful?"

The genie shrugged. "That's up to you. Your wish has been granted. You now have special abilities and the opportunity to level up."

"Special abilities and the opportunity to level up?" Dan said, and snorted derisively. "You sound like a guidance counselor."

Zohaz the Magnificent's big hand settled on Dan's shoulder. "I gotta jet, kid. Nineteen years, I was cooped up in that gloomy old jug. Can you imagine?"

The genie laughed. "Actually, I suppose you can. After all, you've been cooped up in your gloomy life for just as long. I don't know what you're going to do with your new freedom, but I'm going to visit those who imprisoned me and then fly off to someplace warm and sunny to work on my tan."

"Wait," Dan said. "How does this all work? How do I—"

"You will meet a mentor."

"A mentor?" Dan said, scrambling to gather as much information as he could before the opportunity passed. He had a long history of figuring out too late that he should have asked clarifying questions when he'd had the chance. "What mentor?"

"You will meet him tonight, at your home."

"What if I need to talk to you? Is there some magical phrase or something?"

"I'm a genie, kid, not a plumber," Zohaz the Magnificent said. He gave Dan's shoulder a light squeeze. "You've made your choice. Now embrace it. Go all in. That's what you want, right? A life of adventure?"

Dan nodded.

"Well, there you have it. No one can give you a life of adventure. You have to go out and take it. Don't make the same mistake I see all the time. People wish to change their lives, but when the gate opens, they don't believe in themselves enough to step through. A world full of adventure is meaningless if you lack the courage to become an adventurer."

Dan nodded again. "I'll do it," he said. "I really will." But even he could hear the self-doubt in his own voice. Whom was he trying to convince—the genie or himself?

"That concludes our business," Zohaz the Magnificent said, and gave a slight bow. He reached into his vest, pulled out a pair of Wayfarer shades, and put them on with a broad smile. "I have necks to break and rays to catch."

"Thanks," Dan said, but before the word even left his mouth, Zohaz the Magnificent vanished with a pop, which might have been kind of cool if the real world hadn't come loudly back to life at that same moment.

First came the tremendous shattering sound of the display case as it finished smashing against the floor. The gem-encrusted bottle shattered next, but that sound was muffled by a chorus of gasps and startled yelps from library workers and patrons who had suddenly come back to life and were turning now to stare at Dan.

## 6

## EVERYTHING CHANGES

Someone let out a loud, shrill scream.

Dan swiveled in that direction and saw the pretty redhead, her face far from pretty now, twisted as it was into a mask of horror. She was screaming like a startled banshee—and pointing straight at Dan.

"Stay right there, young man," a librarian squawked at Dan from her desk. Then she was picking up the phone... to call security, no doubt.

*Well, you wanted adventure*, Dan thought. *Now you have it.* But getting tackled by campus security wasn't exactly what he'd meant by adventure.

Without even grabbing his backpack, books, or rewritten essay, he charged out the door and hurried down the stairwell. Normally, his clumsiness would've sent him tumbling down the stairs, but luckily, he raced down all four flights without so much as a wobble.

He strolled out of the library into a beautiful October night. The tree-lined pathways bustled with students, mostly scuffing along in small packs. Overhead in the electric blue sky, stars twinkled between wispy rags of cloud. On the horizon shone a gibbous moon straight out of a Conan novel.

But he couldn't stand here, admiring the night. Campus security would be here any second.

He hurried down the steps, losing himself in the flow of students walking downhill.

What the hell had happened back there?

It had all seemed so real, but now that he was outside, breathing the cool night air, he realized that Zohaz the Magnificent must've been some kind of hallucination.

He'd never had hallucinations before, wasn't on drugs, and didn't have a fever, but maybe all the stress of this unbelievable day had gotten the best of him.

That had to be it.

He looked up as he was passing the Sparks Building and slammed to a stop in the middle of the path.

Halloween had come early to the Sparks Building, which suddenly looked ancient and spooky. A pair of stone gargoyles sat atop the steps. Heavy vines wrapped its signature columns. Near the top of these pillars hung a gauzy cloud, like massive cobwebs.

Behind this thin and eerie veil, dark shapes moved, scampering, half-seen, along the upper reaches like... well, like giant spiders. But those shadowy shapes couldn't be actual spiders. They were big as cats... hell, big as dogs.

Something even bigger slammed into Dan, and he stumbled but didn't fall.

"What the Hades are you doing standing there, asshole?" the huge, bald guy who'd run into to him bellowed.

He was taller than Dan and bigger, too, with muscles that looked like they were carved out of marble. This was easy to see, since the guy wasn't wearing a shirt.

The only thing covering his bodybuilder pecs was a strip of leather that apparently kept the massive battle axe strapped to his muscular back. Below this, he wore blue jeans tucked into tall leather boots and a wide belt, from which hung a nasty scrap of something that very much looked like a human scalp.

Dan just blinked at the guy.

*Holy shit.*

Did this mean what he thought it meant?

To either side of them, students passed, barely taking notice, as if this sort of thing happened all the time.

The guy pushed Dan's shoulder. "I'm talking to you, asshole."

"Sorry, dude," Dan said. Without even thinking about it, he dropped his right foot back, blading his body from the guy and making himself a smaller target.

The guy's girlfriend tugged at his thick arm. "Come on, Erik, let's go to the Skeller and have some fun."

At first, Dan thought that she was ugly. But then he realized that she wasn't human.

The girl's brow was low and heavy, the eyes beneath small, dark, and pig-like, set to either side of a stubby upturned nose. Her mouth was wide, and her lips were full, savage, and somehow alluringly sensuous.

She had a fantastic body, muscular but curvy. Her breasts, squeezed between the straps of a backpack, strained against the fabric of a Penn State t-shirt, which she hadn't bothered to tuck into her leather pants, alongside which hung the stubby scabbard of what could only be a broad-bladed short sword.

"He's not worth your time," she told her glowering boyfriend. "Look at him. He doesn't even have a weapon. He's just a peasant."

The guy snorted with contempt, spat at Dan's feet, and followed his girlfriend, whom Dan very much suspected to be a half-orc, down the hill toward town and the Skeller.

Dan just stood there for a second, watching the students flow past. In most cases, *flow* was definitely the right word, as most of them wore long, fluttering cloaks, a good percentage of which were blue and white with Penn State logos.

The students themselves were a weird mash-up of the people he was used to seeing here and characters from a T&T adventure. They wore jeans and sweatpants, sneakers and backpacks, t-shirts and cotton hoodies, but also leather boots, leather armor, and leather belts holding hand axes, daggers, and swords.

The guys looked more muscular than usual, and the girls looked hotter and also more muscular. He saw dwarves, even smaller students that he assumed were halflings, and a slender, beautiful girl, whose huge eyes and pointed ears meant that she had to be an elf. Beside the elf strode a girl with cruel eyes, dressed all in black, with a hunched and horrible creature that could only be a quasit riding on her shoulder.

Usually, students shuffled along campus walkways, mumbling quietly. Tonight, however, a weird energy crackled in the air.

People were animated. Conversations were loud. Laughter was bold and raucous. Here and there, lusty voices rose in song. It felt like anything was possible.

This was still Penn State, but a very different Penn State. A Penn State with elves and half-orcs, where people wore weapons and didn't even blink if some shirtless psychopath might lop off a peasant's head.

"Holy shit," Dan said aloud. "It worked. My wish came true."

His stomach lurched, caught in a tug of war between *wow* and *what the hell*.

Zohaz the Magnificent had transformed Dan's life into something like a T&T adventure.

Which meant *what*, exactly?

Dan had no idea. He couldn't even tell if the rush of emotion that he was feeling was excitement or white-knuckled, eyes-flung-wide, hair-standing-on-end-just-before-it-turns-white terror.

At that moment, he knew only one thing: if he was going to survive long enough to enjoy this adventure, he had to get home and meet his mentor.

# WHAT HAVE I DONE?

Dan hurried downhill toward home but slowed his pace when he left campus.

Crossing College Ave, which was now a cobblestone road, he saw no cars, only horses and wagons and pedestrians, but as he crossed to the other side, he heard a horn blow and looked down the street to see Penn State's blue and white bus, the Campus Loop, coming down the street.

*So,* he thought, *no cars or trucks... but a bus?*

How did things work in this new world? What were the rules?

Town was crazy. It felt like a football Saturday night on steroids. Swaggering packs of heavily armed drunks shouted and sang and cursed, lifting tankards overhead, sloshing dark grog over the world.

Dan entered the westbound river of revelers and bobbed along toward home.

Long lines waited outside the bars. The bouncers carding people wore chainmail and permafrowns. Most of these doormen, he noticed, were half-orcs. In addition to the weapons strapped to their backs and belts, these doormen all wore heavy plate gauntlets.

*Man,* Dan thought, *I'd hate to get punched by them.*

Someone coming the other way bumped into Dan's shoulder, then spun, giving him the stink eye.

Dan looked away. He was used to guys doing stupid stuff like that on crazy weekends, bumping into him, trying to start something, but those guys didn't have longswords at their sides.

He kept moving.

When the crowd slowed, bottlenecking around a pair of bloody combatants wrestling on the sidewalk, a female called from above, "Hey, baby!"

Dan looked up to see a pretty girl leaning out of a second-story window, smiling down at him. "Hey, handsome," she called. She bit her lip and pulled down her lacy halter top, revealing small yet perfect breasts. "Want a date?"

Dan gulped, feeling a rush of heat. Then, noticing the red-tinged light of the room behind the teasing girl, he thought, *That's a whorehouse.*

And not just a whorehouse. A whorehouse straight out of the imagination of his roommate and tower master, Willis.

*Hey, handsome. Want a date?* the girl had asked, a line straight out of Willis's campaign.

When Dan had made his wish—*Make my life like a T&T adventure*—had Zohaz the Magnificent crafted this world specifically from adventures Dan had played? Was the world around him now stitched together with Willis's TM style?

And if so, what would that mean?

Good times, fun quests, beautiful women who loved sex, and men who were willing to fight to the death over pretty much anything. Abrupt and frequent violence, twisty and complex plots, unthinkably evil villains with legions of back-stabbing minions. And monsters. Lots of monsters.

Then the crowd was moving again, and Dan was pulled along past a body stretched in a pool of blood on the pavement. The other combatant, bloodied but victorious, was rifling through the pockets of his unconscious opponent.

At least Dan thought the guy was unconscious.

Either that, or…

He turned right at South Garner. Across the street, McClanahan's, the one-stop shop for Penn State students, was still McClanahan's, but mannequins in the windows wore a mish-mash of college gear, armor, and what looked like a leatherworker's spring S&M collection, little strips of black leather barely concealing the figures' breasts and privates.

Signs in the window advertised current sales, as usual. Instead of ramen noodles on the cheap, however, the store was currently offering specials like *Cure Light Wounds-only 85 gold pieces!* and *This week only: potions, buy 2, get one free!*

The line outside of The Lion's Den was huge, filled with muscular, shirtless guys and hot girls dressed like McClanahan's S&M mannequins. The guys and girls bopped in place, dancing to the incredibly loud hip hop music thumping from within the bar.

The fenced outdoor patio at the back of the Den throbbed, jam packed with a crowd of enraptured drunks dancing close, their hard bodies rubbing together. Their lithe bodies glimmered with sweat beneath flashing red and blue lights overhead.

Then Dan noticed the elevated dance cage at the center of the patio and slammed to a stop. His jaw dropped.

Dancing within the cage was the most beautiful woman he had ever seen.

Though, she wasn't exactly a woman. Not a *human* woman, anyway.

Dressed in a gauzy, diaphanous shift, the dancer had

green skin and a lithe ballerina's body that undulated like a thing made not of flesh but of water.

Dan stared, unable to breathe.

The dancer gyrated her hips slowly, looked over the crowd, making direct eye contact with Dan, and licked her lips.

Dan grew hard in an instant.

Still staring at him, the dancer reached a long, shapely arm through the bars of her cage and curled her finger in a come-hither gesture.

Before Dan knew what he was doing, he was scaling the low metal fence, crazy with lust.

Then, just as abruptly, he slammed to the sidewalk.

The crowd flowed around him, laughing and shouting down at him and calling him an asshole.

"Get in line like everybody else, punk," the hulking half-orc bouncer who'd shoved him said, leaning over the fence.

*Punk*, Dan thought.

The only people he knew who used that word were Willis and the NPCs that Willis created. How many times had short and skinny Willis imitated some hulking NPC, doing his best to make his high-pitched voice gruff, saying, "You want to make something of it, punk?"

Were Dan's suspicions right, then? Was this new reality governed by Willis's TM style?

If so, it would mean getting laid a lot, getting attacked frequently, and pretty much immediately getting sucked into a dungeon expedition, a siege, a wilderness adventure, or a more complex city-bound campaign, with Dan battling some evil overlord and his henchmen.

And what else?

It would mean good things, like a loose interpretation or rejection of nitpicky rules and regulations, such as level limitations or class restrictions based on race, and instant attainment of hit points and abilities when leveling up.

But it would also mean that magical items were rare and characters leveled up slowly.

"Get lost, punk!" the bouncer shouted.

Dan picked himself up and moved on down the street, careful not to look back at the dancer. Whatever she was, she'd had him under some kind of spell.

If he looked back, she would lure him once more over the fence, and Dan would end up with a mouthful of shattered teeth.

So he kept moving uphill, crossed over Calder Way, which had transformed into a twisting, torchlit alley of seedy looking shops, and passed the big parking lot, which now filled with horses and wagons. Strangely enough, through the big plate glass windows of Playland, things looked pretty much as they had before he'd made his wish, with rows of flashing arcade games.

So weird.

*Lay low*, he told himself. *Figure this place out.*

Of course, if this was Willis World, he wouldn't be allowed to lay low for long. Slow play always resulted in random encounters.

These encounters often felt like the wrath of a bored TM, a punishment that taught players to stay active. If Dan didn't find trouble, trouble would find him.

*Hurry home, then*, he told himself. *Find your mentor before you get killed in some random encounter.*

Leaving the throbbing heart of town for the quieter backstreets, Dan was instantly on edge.

Things were darker here, quieter. Normally, that was a nice change of pace on the long walk home, but now he stayed on point, ready to run if someone–or some*thing*–stepped from the shadows.

Luckily, however, he made it all the way back to his block without trouble. As soon as he sighed with relief, however, he went rigid with fresh apprehension.

Across the street from his apartment house, on the front lawn of the *Alpha Alpha Alpha* fraternity house, shadowy figures danced around a huge bonfire that was so bright it made him squint.

"Look!" an inhumanly deep voice growled from that direction, and a huge shadow, easily seven feet tall, dispatched itself from beside the bonfire, marching in his direction. Other shadows followed quickly in its wake.

The tall shadow reached the street, its features becoming clearer. The thing, which he now saw to be not a human but a humanoid covered in reddish-orange fur, wore studded leather armor with *AAA* emblazoned on the chest.

It pointed a long, muscular arm in Dan's direction. A menacing grin packed with sharp teeth gleamed on its short snout.

"It's Danielle," the Grady-thing said, and his frat brothers, also tall and doglike, erupted into crazy, keening, hyena laughter.

Dan's blood ran cold. *They're gnolls,* he realized. *Grady and his frat brothers are gnolls.*

With that realization, Dan sprinted away from their insane laughter and ducked into the relative safety of his apartment house.

Peering out the door's little window at the monsters leaping and laughing in the street, Dan thought, *What have I done? What in the world have I gotten myself into?*

## 8

## OH, HOLLY...

Dan slipped inside his apartment, closed and locked the door behind him, and leaned back against it, letting his eyes close and his mind cool down.

In the next room, he heard voices and laughter, probably the guys gaming in there. The thought made him grin. His friends were so obsessed that they still played T&T inside of a T&T world.

Hearing a noise in the hall, he turned and looked out the peephole.

The door across the hall opened, and Holly stepped out, only... *wow*.

Holly had gone from incredibly gorgeous to *impossibly* gorgeous. Her pale blonde hair shimmered even in the low light of the hallway, falling in a golden cascade all the way to her ass.

Her face was still familiar, but the features were more angular and refined, the high cheekbones sweeping sharply back to pointed ears. Most striking of all, however, were her bright violet eyes.

Holly wore a matching cloak of fine violet silk. The

garment fit snugly against her slender body, covering her neck and shoulders before opening again to bare the tops of her tremendous breasts, beneath which her abdomen was encased in a cummerbund of braided golden metal that matched glowing golden bracers on her wrists.

Beneath the cummerbund, a thin strip of black silk encircled her narrow waist. She wore black leather pants and black leather boots, and black leather covered her shapely arms.

In her hands, she held a slender staff, which, like the bracers, glowed softly with magical enchantment.

Dan's eyes narrowed at the sight of magical items, and he growled instinctively.

*What the hell?*

Then he grinned.

*Ah yes,* he thought. *I'm a barbarian, and barbarians hate magic.*

But he sure didn't hate Holly.

She was an elf. And not just any elf. A grey elf. The most noble, intelligent, and reclusive of all the elves.

Only she wasn't alone.

Some guy followed her out of the apartment, closing the door behind them. He was short but thick with muscle. He wore ring mail and had a small metal buckler strapped to one forearm. His opposite hand rested on the ornate pommel of a sheathed longsword.

Holly's violet eyes stared at him intensely. Her face was serious. "You're certain?"

"My brother will be there," the guy said. "How could he forget? It's the biggest event of the year."

"Noon," she said. "It's very important to me."

"You worry too much," he said with a lazy smile and laid a hand on her shoulder.

Holly brushed the hand away. "And you are too familiar."

*Not her boyfriend, then,* Dan thought, and his eyes fell again to her half-exposed breasts. She was shorter now, just a hair over five feet, he'd guess, but her boobs were even bigger and rounder than they had been in the real world. It was incredible, completely—

"Hey, punk," a high-pitched voice said, startling him from behind, "is Holly out there?"

The voice was familiar but wrong. Willis's voice, but way too high, as if his roommate had inhaled a dozen helium balloons.

Dan turned and shouted with surprise. "Willis!"

"Dan," Willis said. In real life, Willis was short… but now he was only three feet tall with ruddy, nut brown skin and a thistle patch of unkempt sandy hair. His eyes were glittering black orbs.

"You're a gnome!" Dan said.

"And you're an asshole," Willis said. "Now quit hogging the view and pop me up to the peephole, dude."

Too stunned to refuse, Dan picked up his tiny roommate–the guy weighed no more than a sack of groceries–and hoisted him up to the peephole.

"Aw, crap," Willis squeaked. "She's gone."

Dan put him down.

Willis hooked a tiny thumb toward the living room, from which came sounds of laughter. "The game's still in session. You in or what?"

Dan followed Willis into the other room, where he encountered a familiar scene, his friends gathered around a table covered in books, graph paper, dice, lead figures, two-liter soda bottles, and an empty pizza box.

"Dan!" Rick shouted.

"Uh oh," Jerry said. "Hide the prostitutes."

Dan smiled. A dose of familiarity was nice.

But then, nearing the table, he got a closer look at the game they were playing.

"Advanced Drudgery & Dullards," he read aloud.

"You know it, baby!" Jerry said.

"It's been pretty eventful since you left for class," Willis squeaked, climbing onto a tall stool.

*"Oh, shit, I'm late!"* Jerry mocked.

Dan barely heard them. On the cover of *The Drudgery Master's Guide*, a sleepy-looking guy in a tan suit stood at a crosswalk, holding a briefcase.

"As I was saying before I was so rudely interrupted," Willis continued, pushing toward Dan a sheet of graph paper that appeared to map not a dungeon or a castle but a corporate office full of cubicles, "a lot has happened. Rick filled out his monthly expense reports and tried to file them, but the system went down, so now he's stuck at the watercooler."

Willis nodded toward Jerry, who was grinning excitedly. "Ol' J-Money put in for a promotion."

"You know what that means," Jerry said, and bounced his thick eyebrows up and down. "I'll get +1 on my roll when I propose to a girl."

"*If* you get the promotion," Willis said, giving his player a don't-be-so-certain look.

"Here," Rick said, handing Dan a sheet of paper and a potbellied lead figure wearing glasses and a cheap business suit.

Dan looked down at the Drudgery & Dullards character sheet.

*Player's name: Dan*
    *Character's name: Bob*
    *Strength: 8*

*Intelligence: 13*
*Wisdom: 11*
*Dexterity: 10*
*Constitution: 11*
*Charisma: 8*
*Character class: third-level accountant / tenth-level procrastinator*

DAN BLINKED AT THE SHEET FOR A FEW SECONDS. IT WAS ALL too much.

"I can't play," he said robotically, and turned to leave.

"Dude!" they called after him. "Come on, man! We need you!"

Dan marched straight to his room, closed the door behind him, and let out a shuddering breath.

"Just have to catch your breath," he told himself. "Just have to chill out for a minute, get your balance."

He paced his small room.

His room was still messy, and the walls were still covered with photos from home and posters of hot girls in bikinis, only the girls now wore leather or fur.

He saw no weapons, no armor, nothing that said *barbarian.*

He felt a surge of disappointment. Zohaz the Magnificent had lied.

Oh, the genie had changed the world around Dan, but the rest of it? Dan being strong and girls liking him, adventures and all that? A big, fat lie.

He turned and faced the mirror.

Same old Dan.

Sure, he had a square jaw, a thick neck, and broad shoulders, just like a million other country boys, but he was no hulking barbarian. "Maybe that guy on campus was right. Maybe I'm just a peasant."

Then a deep voice from the other side of the room startled him, roaring, "To Hades with that!"

9

## MEETING THE MENTOR

**D**an shouted with surprise and spun around, but the room was empty. "Hello?" he called, feeling stupid. "Who's there?"

Silence.

He saw no one.

Had he just imagined the voice?

*Be careful*, he thought. *This is a T&T world now. It could be someone invisible.*

He raised his fists and took a tentative step forward. Then he saw what was leaning inside his open closet.

"Whoa… a sword."

And not just any sword. A huge two-handed sword in a no-frills scabbard, just like the one he used in Towers & Trolls.

Still seeing no one in his room, he retrieved the massive sword and grinned. For all its massive size, the sword was light.

He buckled the scabbard onto his belt and drew the sword. The draw was quick and easy, far too smooth and effortless for a sword this length.

*Just like in Willis's campaigns,* he thought. Willis even let you wear and draw a two-handed sword from your back, physics be damned.

The large pommel was a perfect fit for his big, calloused hands. He gave it a little swing, and his grin graduated into a full-blown smile. The blade was perfectly balanced.

"All right, asshole," the sword said in the deep voice that had spoken moments earlier, "let's get this party started!"

Dan squawked with surprise, dropped the sword, and backpedaled to the wall.

Rich laughter filled the room. The sword was laughing at him! "Some warrior you are, kid!"

"You startled me," Dan said. He stared at the sword for a second. He saw no mouth. The weapon's voice came out of nowhere. Normally, he might've freaked, but after the day he'd had, he recovered quickly. "All right if I pick you up?"

"You'd better pick me up if you want to survive in this world," the sword said.

"So you're… what… a talking sword?"

"You're sharp."

"Was that a sword joke?"

"Maybe," the sword said. "Look, kid, I'd shake your hand if I had one to offer, but I don't. I'm Wulfgar Skull-Smasher, fearless barbarian, famous drunkard, and insatiable sex God!"

"You're my T&T character?"

"I was," Wulfgar grumbled. "Now, as you can see, I've changed forms. But I'm more than the sword. I'm your mentor. How are you liking the new world so far?"

Remembering Garth, a seven-foot-tall hyena with a hundred-dollar haircut, Dan shook his head. "I don't know. Towers & Trolls is fun, but this is real, you know? I mean, it's really dangerous out there."

"What the fuck, dude?" the sword shouted. "Are you really Dan?"

Dan hissed and looked at the door. "Hey, man, not so loud."

"Don't be such a worrywart," Wulfgar said. "Those pansies can't hear me. Only you can hear me."

"Oh."

"Let's get down to business," the sword said. "Your glorious mentor is ready. Hit me with questions."

A flood of questions roared through Dan's skull. Ironically, however, there were so many, it was hard to choose one.

"I'm waiting," Wulfgar said in an impatient, singsong voice.

"Okay," Dan blurted, "what happens if I, you know, die?"

The sword laughed. "Everybody dies."

"You know what I mean."

"Are you asking if you get to go back to Boring Land if somebody chops your head off?"

"Yeah," Dan said with a shrug, "or maybe I get to start over or something? Make a new character?"

The sword was silent for a moment. "I'm not sure."

"Wow," Dan said sarcastically. "Some mentor you're turning out to be."

"In that capacity, I'd recommend that you assume the worst and avoid getting killed."

Dan let out a low whistle. "There seem to be a lot of ways to die here."

"A lot of ways to live, you mean!" Wulfgar thundered. "Stop pussyfooting around. See, this was your problem back in the real world. You're too fucking timid. You gotta get out there and live a little. Did you even notice the girls on your walk here? They're hotter than ever—*way* hotter! You don't believe me, look out that window."

Dan pulled the curtain aside, looked out the window, and moaned. Holly stood on the lawn, talking to the stocky guy in ring mail. "Holly," he groaned.

"Yeah, that's her, but she's even hotter now!" Wulfgar said. "That rack! That face! Shit, can you imagine those purple eyes staring up at you while you give her the old—"

"All right," Dan interrupted, letting the curtain fall. "I get you, but I've never been very good at talking to girls."

Wulfgar growled with frustration. "Wake the fuck up, asshole! This is your opportunity to start over. Don't tell me how old-world Dan used to be. Tell me what you're going to be like now. Better yet, don't tell me. Show me. You made the wish. Now make the life!"

Despite the anxiety whirling within him, Dan felt a little surge of excitement.

*A clean start...*

"You're acting like some kind of victim," Wulfgar said. "This is your wish come true, remember? Your fantasy world. These girls are fierce creatures, with hot blood, ready to fight or fuck whoever and whenever they see fit. Now grow a set of balls, get out there, and talk to Holly."

Dan balled and un-balled his fists. What would he even say to her? "I don't know," he said. "She's talking to someone."

"Fuck that guy," Wulfgar said. "He doesn't like you talking to her, wash me to the hilt in blood!"

Dan laughed nervously, thinking, *Yeah, but what if he cuts me in half instead?*

Wulfgar sighed. "Look, if you're really too much of a pussy to enjoy your own fantasy, Zohaz the Magnificent did give you an out. But if you're going to use it, you gotta use it right now. All you have to do is grab your character sheet and jump into that Drudgery & Dullards game. Do that, and all of this will fade away. No more Wulfgar, no more hot chicks, no more adventure. You can have your boring, old, shitty life back."

This time, it was Dan's turn to sigh. At least he had an option to go back.

This was crazy. Should he stay, or should he go?

*If I stay*, he thought, *all my fantasies could come true. Girls, gold, and glory. On the other hand, I might get beaten to death on College Ave.*

He paced back and forth. If he did go back, it would only be to avoid risk and danger. He wouldn't be going back *for* something. His real life sucked. And unless he pulled some kind of miracle, he was going to lose his scholarship soon.

He imagined sitting at the dinner table at home, not on a visit from school but *permanently*, imagined looking down at his food and wondering how much it cost, wondering if his father was having the same thoughts, calculating the number of hours he had to work at the factory to feed his disappointment of a son, washed up at nineteen.

Of course, Dan would get a job as quickly as he could. Guys at the slaughterhouse, where he would be lucky to get a job, got paid well, but they all had horrible nightmares. Over the years, slaughterhouse work took its toll.

People got cut, got pulled into machinery, fell off the steel ramps while power washing. But you didn't even need to have an accident to mess yourself up. Guys in the boning room, their index fingers got crooked from holding the knife and making the same cut over and over and over. They called it *trigger finger*.

"Time's running out," Wulfgar said. "It's now or never, half-stepper. Decision time. You've got five minutes to walk out there, join the game, and book a one-way ticket back to Boring-ville. Otherwise, you're stuck here with your old pal Wulfgar and everything else. The good, the bad, and the ugly.

And believe me, you haven't seen ugly until you've seen a zombie crawling with maggots."

Dan paced faster. What should he do? He didn't want to go back to his old life, but what chances did a first-level character have in a world like this?

Outside, a scream knifed through the night air.

Dan raced to the window, pulled aside the curtain, and gasped.

*Holly!*

The stocky guy in ring mail hustled away into the darkness, screaming.

In the yard outside, Holly swung her staff in a luminescent arc, trying to fend off four attackers in midnight blue cloaks, all of them edging toward her, blades in hand.

## 10

## SWEET, SWEET BLOOD

Dan threw open the window and punched the screen from its frame.

"Take me with you," Wulfgar growled.

Dan grabbed the sword, climbed out of the second-story window, and dropped to the ground. His legs, feeling strong and steady, absorbed the shock and launched him in a mad sprint toward Holly and her attackers.

Red-hot rage roared up in him. He'd never before felt anything like this urge, this *need*, to destroy. Fueled with bloodlust, he bellowed a barbaric battle cry.

Some small part of him knew that shouting was stupid. The element of surprise and all that...

But the rest of him didn't give a damn. It didn't matter if they knew that he was coming. He was going to butcher them for threatening Holly.

Startled, the robed men turned to face him, blades at the ready.

Holly's glowing staff cracked hard into one of the hooded heads, and that guy collapsed in a heap.

Instinctively, Dan jumped into the air, hoisting his massive two-handed sword high overhead.

"Time to die, assholes!" the sword bellowed.

Dan flew through the air... flew and flew and flew, soaring a good twenty feet before his boots smashed into the chest of one of the men with the loud crack of breaking bones.

The guy jerked backward and slammed to the ground. His short sword spun away.

Dan hit the ground shoulder first and rolled with it, tumbling past Holly and popping onto his feet. He felt strong and dextrous and absolutely out of his mind with battle rage.

Something thudded into his thigh. Then he was aware of one of the robed men dancing away.

What had the guy done, kicked him?

Now the asshole jabbed at him with a dagger of black metal.

Dan dropped back, avoiding the blade. Then, as the guy drew back his arm, Dan stepped back in, swinging Wulfgar in a wide arc that caught the guy just below the ribs, sliced through robe and flesh and bone, and cut the man nearly in half. The remains fell into a dark-robed, strangely shaped heap.

"Sweet, sweet blood!" Wulfgar roared. "That's the stuff. Give me more. I'm fucking thirsty!"

Dan stepped up beside Holly, who faced the last of her attackers.

"You should have let us take you," the robed man told her. A nasty grin shone from within the dark recesses of his hood. "Catch you later." He flicked his wrist as if tossing something to the ground.

There was a sharp cracking sound, and a pillar of pitch black smoke spangled with hissing sparks billowed up around the man.

Dan's lips peeled back from his snarling teeth, and the hair at the back of his neck stood on edge. "Magic!" He sneered with primal loathing and swung Wulfgar straight through the smoking column.

But where he had expected to feel the glorious sensation of his two-handed sword cleaving the man in half, he felt nothing.

Nothing at all. Only air.

He lifted the sword overhead, ready to drive it downward through like an executioner's axe.

"Don't bother," Holly said, panting softly. "He's gone."

"Gone?" Dan said, and shuddered with revulsion. In a flash, he understood something about his new self. He *hated* magic. The hatred was bone deep, instinctual, as real as anything he'd carried here from the other world.

*That's because you're a barbarian*, he realized.

Strange, that. He wasn't just *playing* a character class; he was *feeling* its traits.

Holly stepped over the man she had hit from behind. By the unnatural shape of his head, the guy was clearly dead.

She approached the only survivor still here, the groaning man whom Dan had leveled with his high-flying dropkick.

The man pushed unsteadily off the ground and stared in the direction of his blade.

Holly crouched beside him, drew a short dagger from the silky folds of her purple cloak, and held the point to the man's armpit. "Don't bother," she said.

She must have pricked him with the point, because the man gave out a pitiful yelp. But he didn't make a move toward his weapon. She definitely had his attention.

Dan trotted over, Wulfgar at the ready.

"Yowza!" Wulgar shouted, as Dan looked down at the crouching girl. "Have you ever seen a rack like that?"

Dan hadn't, and the view was amazing from where he

stood above her, but he shoved the sword back into its scabbard, reducing the foul-mouthed blade's dialogue to a muffled clamor.

Luckily, Holly hadn't heard Wulfgar.

She ripped back the man's hood, grabbed a fistful of light brown hair, and shoved hard, knocking the guy flat again and smashing his face into the ground. She drove a knee into his spine, pinning him to the ground, yanked his head back, and pressed the blade to his exposed throat.

"Who are you?" Holly demanded. "Why did you try to kidnap me?"

"You're the only grey elf on campus," the man said. "Perfect gift for the Mother of Darkness." His lips wriggled into a sickly smile. Dry, nasty laughter chortled out of him. "You can't stop the darkness!"

"Neither can you," Holly said, and drew her blade across his throat. He bucked and gurgled but died quickly.

Holly cleaned her hands and blade on the dead man's robe, then looked up and gave Dan a smile. "Thanks, neighbor," she said, and offered her hand. "I'm Holly."

"Dan," he said, and shook her hand.

Her purple eyes traveled up and down his body, and the corners of her mouth curled upward.

"No offense," Holly said, "but I'd always thought you were a peasant. I had no idea that you were a barbarian." She gave him another once-over, bit her lip, and said, "Let's search the corpses before the city guard shows up."

Dan blinked. "Okay," he said and walked over to the guy that he had cut pretty much in half.

Part of him knew that this was very, very weird. He and the cute, formerly geeky girl from across the hall had just killed a few people on the lawn behind their apartment house, and now she was telling him to loot the corpses as matter-of-factly as she might suggest ordering a pizza.

As if killing was no big deal.

And truth be told, it didn't feel like a big deal.

Sure, battle had been exciting. In fact, he'd worked himself up into a pretty good frenzy.

But now it was over, and he didn't feel a drop of remorse.

Holly was right. Search the bastards before the cops arrived. Just like in T&T.

"You're wounded," Holly said, pointing to his thigh.

"I am?" Dan grunted, and looked down. His jeans were torn midthigh. Below this, his leg was covered in blood that looked black in the moonlight.

He remembered getting hit, thinking the guy had kicked him, but now he understood that the guy had actually stabbed him.

In his frenzy, Dan hadn't even noticed.

It was weird, realizing that he'd been stabbed, but even now, despite the blood, he only felt a dull throb.

He shrugged. "Whatever."

Grinning, Holly rolled her eyes. "Barbarians."

The guy Dan searched didn't have much. Just one of those weird black daggers and a leather purse containing two silver pieces, a handful of coppers, and a student ID. "Aaron Haze Biscoe the 3rd," Dan read aloud. "This asshole is a math student."

"Not anymore, he isn't," Holly said, pocketing the things she'd found. "Let's go inside and do something about that cut."

## HOLLY'S APARTMENT

**B**y the time they went inside and climbed the stairs, Dan's thigh had started to hurt. His Wranglers clung to his leg, wet and warm and sticky. His boot squished with every step, full of blood.

*Have to make a poultice*, he thought, the unfamiliar word *poultice* coming into his head effortlessly, and he pictured a heated compress of herbs and roots, swamp berries and pale flowers, everything mashed together and wrapped with strands of coarse grass that he somehow knew he could find only on a shaded hillside in a clearing between trees. Spruce, if possible.

*How do I know all of this?*

Holly opened the door and ushered him into her apartment, a thing old-world Dan had dreamed of countless times.

"Home sweet home," she said, and locked the door behind them.

The apartment looked like a scene from some enchanted forest, with plants and flowers everywhere. Leafy vines grew up the walls and wove through the upper reaches of the numerous potted trees that lined the room's outer edges. Strung along these vines and throughout the trees were strands of twinkling white lights. Above these, the ceiling was painted to resemble a night sky. Below, the carpet was brilliant green, a rectangle of living grass. The air smelled fresh and clean and summer sweet.

"Wow," he said. "This place is awesome."

"Thanks," Holly said. Then she pushed him up against the door, yanked his head down to hers, and kissed him.

Dan was shocked, but he got over it quickly.

He didn't have much experience with girls. He'd kissed a few but kissing them had never felt anything like this.

This was *awesome*.

Holly held his face in her hands, and her mouth, wet and warm and eager, moved against his, lighting a fire within him, burning away the shyness that had plagued old-world Dan, replacing it with raw, barbaric desire.

Then Holly broke the kiss and stepped back with a devious smile. "There," she said. "Now I've properly thanked you for helping me earlier."

Holly unclasped her violet robe and hung it on a peg near the door. She looked absolutely stunning in a skintight black jumpsuit with a plunging neckline and open back.

"Come back here," Dan said, reaching for her, but she evaded his hand and walked into the kitchen.

Looking back over her shoulder with a sexy grin, she said, "Wait there."

He did as he was told, enjoying the view. Her ass looked fantastic in the skintight black fabric. He was reeling. He'd just kissed his dream girl!

When she disappeared into a pantry closet, he glanced around. Holly's staff leaned against a small table atop which sat a thick tome bound in bark: *Intermediate Druidic Spells*.

He narrowed his eyes and sneered at the book. *Magic...*

Holly returned, carrying a sprig of bright green mistletoe. "Yes, I'm a druid," she said, "and luckily for you, I know healing magic."

She slapped his shoulder playfully. "Relax, you silly barbarian. What god do you worship?"

Dan gave his stock answer from years of playing Towers & Trolls, "Crom," and instantly realized that Crom wasn't even an actual T&T god!

Dan had borrowed the deity from his beloved Conan books, and Willis had let it slide.

To his surprise, Holly merely nodded as if the answer made total sense.

"Your god is in the earth," she said. "We druids worship the earth, the trees, the moon and sun and stars. We draw power from the four winds and rushing rivers and the quavering songs of crickets on the last morning before the year's first hard frost."

As Holly spoke, she ran the mistletoe up and down his leg to either side of the wound. "We aren't like wizards. Our energy is of the world."

Then Holly began singing softly in a strange, beautiful language that had to be Elvish. A second later, a warm breeze sighed through the open window, rattling the leaves of the trees and stirring her long blond hair.

The breeze wasn't just warm. It was too warm. A summer breeze blowing in out of a crisp October night.

*She's casting some kind of spell*, he thought. He considered telling her to stop, but then a pleasant sensation passed over his leg. The throbbing pain died away, and as Dan watched, the wound closed and faded, leaving only a slight scar.

"Wow," he said, and ran a hand over the place where the puncture wound had been. It wasn't even tender now. "Thanks. I'm completely healed."

"Good," Holly said. "Now I don't have to worry about hurting you."

She smiled, her purple eyes flashing. "You know, I always thought you were handsome, but I didn't think you were interested in me. I mean, every time I saw you in the hall, you hurried away."

"I was too shy to say anything to you," he confessed.

"A shy barbarian? You really are full of surprises!" She grabbed his belt and tugged him toward the living room.

## DREAM GIRL

**D**an ducked beneath a low-hanging branch and followed Holly onto the grassy carpet of the living room.

"Take off your boots," Holly said. "Feel the grass on your bare feet."

He kicked off his boots. The grass didn't just feel real. It *was* real. It felt soft and springy beneath his feet.

Holly's eyes glowed with excitement. "Better take off that shirt, too. We should make sure that you don't have any other injuries that you didn't happen to notice."

Dan peeled off his shirt and threw it aside.

Holly walked around him slowly, trailing her fingertips along his chest and shoulder and back. "Your upper body looks fine," she said, and unhooked his belt.

"Can't be too safe, though. I had better check everything." Holly unzipped his jeans and pulled them down and then stood there staring at him with her mouth open in an amazed smile. "You really are a barbarian!"

That's when Dan realized that he wasn't wearing any underwear. "Sorry," he said. "Guess I forgot my underwear."

"I'm not talking about that," Holly said. "I'm talking about that," and she pointed between his legs.

Dan looked down and grunted. He'd never been small, but now he was somewhere between huge and gargantuan. *The Arcane Unearthed* hadn't mentioned this character class bonus.

"And no need to apologize," Holly said, her violet eyes gleaming. "I'm certainly not complaining."

"Well," he said, "we'd better make sure that you didn't get injured out there, either."

Holly smirked and unfastened a clasp behind her neck.

Dan reached out with both hands and peeled the jumpsuit down, stripping her to the waist.

Topless, she was the most gorgeous thing he had ever seen. In all of his wildest fantasies, no woman had ever been this lovely.

"You are the most beautiful woman I've ever seen," Dan said.

"Thanks," Holly said. "You look incredible yourself."

She gave him a hungry smile, pushed down with both hands, and wriggled out of her jumpsuit with an incredibly sexy little shimmy. And then Holly, the girl of his dreams, was standing before him, completely naked.

He couldn't believe it, and yet he no longer felt like Dan the timid farm boy. He felt strong, confident, and happy; excited in the moment but not nervous. Sure, this was weird, jumping straight into sex, but they were in a new world, a T&T world, where this sort of thing was possible.

Holly opened her arms to him, and he went to her and lowered her to the grass and kissed her long and deep. Her hands moved over his neck and shoulders and back, exploring him as their warm, hard bodies pressed against one another.

Dan kissed her neck, loving the heat and sound and tickle of her breath in his ear.

He kissed her collarbone and moved lower to worship her perfect breasts with his mouth and hands, taking a nipple into his mouth and sucking as he massaged the other breast and kneaded the nipple gently between his thumb and forefinger.

Holly squirmed beneath him, her breaths quickening with desire. She pushed his head further down. He trailed kisses down her taut abdomen, inhaling the good, fresh smell of her, an aroma like honeysuckle in high summer, and then she pressed his face between her open legs and drenched him with her sweet essence.

This was crazy, he knew. Just minutes ago, they were fighting for their lives, and now he was going down on the girl of his dreams.

How was it even possible? This sort of thing could only happen in poorly written books or a T&T adventure.

But then his inner barbarian rose up, grabbed hold of these quibbling old-world thoughts, swung them by their skinny legs, and dashed their brains against the stone tower of his raging desire.

Dan shoved his hands beneath Holly's tight ass, squeezing its perfection as his mouth and tongue explored her sex, kissing and licking and teasing. She tasted wonderful.

He'd never done this with a girl, but it didn't matter. It wasn't rocket science, and Holly was clearly enjoying his efforts. Gripping his hair in her hands, she pushed her hips up against his mouth in pulsing little thrusts.

When she began to quiver with pleasure, Dan quit teasing, pressed his mouth firmly into her swollen mound, and met her pulsing thrusts beat for beat, rhythmically lapping her soft folds with his tongue.

"Yes," Holly moaned. "Yes, just like that."

Her breath grew faster and faster. Then it gasped inward, and her hands tightened in his hair. For several heartbeats, she was locked in a paralysis of mounting pleasure.

Then she cried out in Elvish and bucked against him for several seconds before collapsing back to the grass, shivering with completion.

Dan kept kissing, softly now, until she tugged weakly at him and pulled him back on top of her.

Holly kissed him deeply, then stared up at him with her glowing violet eyes. "That was wonderful," she said, and her hands left his face and smoothed down over his back to grip his ass. "I want you, Dan."

"I want you, too," he said, his voice husky with desire.

She reached down and smiled. "I can tell." Then she guided him to her entrance, gasping when his tip pressed against her silky folds. Her eyes went wide. "Start slow, please," she said.

He kissed her and slid himself gently partway into her.

Holly gasped again.

Dan paused, not wanting to hurt her, but she was so wet and warm, tight and wonderful around him, it was all he could do to hold off.

Then she smiled and bit her lip and nodded, pulling him deeper into her. In and out, deeper with each stroke, inch by inch, he filled her.

Madness. Sweet madness. Never, in all of his fantasies, had he imagined that anything could feel this amazing. He filled her, and she gripped him, wet and warm and oh so tight.

Holly urged him on, and his inner barbarian responded, building until he was thrusting into her, fast and hard, both of them panting and groaning like animals, their bodies glistening with sweat. Sweet hot pressure built within him, built and built until Holly cried out beneath him, and they writhed against each other, riding a long, mutual climax into euphoria.

He kissed her then pushed up to stare down into her purple eyes. A sweaty strand of golden hair stuck to her forehead. She looked incredibly happy and more beautiful than ever.

"Wow," he said, still breathing hard, and laughed. "That was actually… um…"

She tilted her head, staring up at him with questioning eyes.

"That was my first time," he confessed.

Holly laughed. It was a beautiful sound, pure light and warmth, no edges, no criticism. "Really? Well, you could have fooled me."

They kissed and laughed, locking gazes as each touched the other. Dan slid his fingers through Holly's soft, golden hair. Holly traced the lines of his jaw and kneaded the thick muscles at the back of his neck.

"Am I supposed to be this hungry?" he asked as they disentangled. "I'm starving!"

"I have to go to the Diner and meet a friend," she said. "You should come along."

"A friend, huh? Not a boyfriend, I hope."

She grinned. "Is my big, strong barbarian jealous? No, not a boyfriend."

He kissed her and stood. "I'll come, then," he said. "I mean, I would've come anyway. Just wanted to know whether or not I had to kill somebody."

"Where do you think you're going?" she asked, still stretched out on the grass, an image of impossible beauty.

He nodded toward the door. "Figure I'd better go across the hall and change my jeans."

She shook her head and curled her finger in a come-hither motion. "Oh no, you don't, mister. Not yet. Get back down here. Before we leave, we're going to do that again. Now that the first one's out of the way, we can slow down and really enjoy it."

But then the sound of blasting trumpets filled the room.

## 13

## STATS

Dan roared with surprise and turned his body to shield Holly and face the intruders.

Only there weren't any intruders. None that he could see, anyway. The loud music came from all directions, out of thin air.

That's when he noticed that Holly wasn't reacting at all. She was locked in place.

Time had frozen again, like it had when Zohaz the Magnificent appeared.

"Crom!" Dan uttered, and his lip curled into a snarl. More witchcraft!

The trumpets blared out a final flourish then cut. The room filled with deep laughter.

Not Zohaz the Magnificent.

Wulfgar.

"Congratulations, asshole!" the sword bellowed.

Dan turned to his side. The sword was still sheathed. "How can I hear you if you're still in the scabbard?"

"Different Wulfgar," the voice said. "You're now hearing

the voice of super cool, omniscient, disembodied Wulfgar coming atcha intermission-style, bearing news from none other than the big guy himself, Zohaz the Magnificent."

"All right," Dan said, instinctively reaching for his pants.

"You might want to leave those off and stay where you are, kid," Wulfgar's voice said. "Once I'm done here, time's going to come rushing back in. Your girlfriend will freak if you're suddenly halfway across the room, wearing those raggedy-ass bloody jeans."

"Good point," Dan said. "What's the news?"

"Congratulations, punk. You leveled up!"

Dan smiled. Halfway.

Leveling up now didn't make sense. Barbarians needed six thousand experience points to make second level, a *crazy* number, three times the number it took for a fighter to jump to second level.

"Wait," Dan said, wanting to understand this new world. "How? Don't get me wrong, I want to level up, but all I did was kill one robed asshole and drop kick another. So Holly and I split the points for the second guy. Right?"

"Yup," Wulfgar's voice said. "Call it one-and-a-half kills."

"Unless one of them was secretly a purple worm in disguise, the math isn't working for me."

"Nope," Wulfgar said. "They were first-level fighters. That's it. You earned twenty-three experience points for killing them."

"That's not quite six thousand," Dan said. "How did I level up?"

The sword's voice snorted with contempt. "Never look a gift horse in the mouth, kid. Zohaz was feeling magnificent *and* magnanimous. He gave you six thousand experience points for finally getting laid."

"Wait a second," Dan said. He couldn't believe it. "I just got six thousand experience points for having sex?"

"Who's ever heard of a nineteen-year-old barbarian virgin? Getting laid was a huge step in the right direction."

"Wow," Dan said, and a huge smile came onto his face. "That's awesome. Honestly, I'm kind of surprised. This world feels like one cooked up by my old TM, Willis."

Wulfgar's voice said, "Makes sense, given your wish. You wanted your life to be more like the T&T adventures you played. If Willis ran those games…"

"Right," Dan said. "But Willis was stingy with experience points. It took a long time to advance levels."

Then Dan thought of something, and his smile faded. "In fact, the only time that Willis let me jump a level quickly was when he knew that an adventure was so dangerous that I would die without the extra hit points. Is that what's going on here?"

"You worry too much," Wulfgar's voice said. "Speaking of hit points, more good news. You don't have to roll. You automatically get the max. So, with constitution bonuses, you're up to 36 hit points!"

Dan nodded thoughtfully.

"You don't seem particularly pleased for someone who just jumped a level and got a mountain of hit points all for having sex with a smoking hot elf."

"Yeah," Dan said, "well, that's because I'm pretty certain that the only reason I'm getting all these hit points is because I'd die if I didn't. So yeah, pardon me if I'm not overly excited about getting chopped to pieces."

"Oh, don't be such a drama queen," Wulfgar's voice said. "You're supposed to be a second-level barbarian, for Crom's sake, not a fourteenth-level pussy. Stop your whining and get down to business!"

"That's easy for you to—"

"Have a look at this, tough guy," Wulfgar interrupted.

A gigantic scroll appeared, hovering in the air five feet

away, and unfurled like a window shade drawn by an invisible hand.

Dan was looking at a character sheet.

*His* character sheet.

*Name: Dan the Barbarian*
*Strength: 18(92)*
*Intelligence: 9*
*Wisdom: 8*
*Dexterity: 17*
*Constitution: 17*
*Charisma: 16*

*Strength bonuses: + 2 attacking / +5 damage*
*Dexterity: +6 armor rating, unless bulky armor is worn; +3 initiative, reaction, and missile attacks*
*Constitution: +6 hit points per level*

Dan grinned. These awesome stats had been taken straight from his character sheet for Wulfgar Skull-Smasher. He was stronger than an NFL fullback, super agile, crazy healthy, and way more charismatic than he had been in the real world.

He saw only one problem. "How am I supposed to handle college with an intelligence of 9 and a wisdom of 8?"

"Not my problem," Wulfgar said. "Besides, don't flatter yourself. You weren't exactly the sharpest sword in the armory back in the real world."

"Hey," Dan said, "I was pretty smart. In third grade, my teacher said—"

"Save it, dummy," Wulfgar said. "We're almost out of time."

Dan went back to reading the sheet.

CLASS: BARBARIAN
   Level: 2
   Hit points: 36
   Experience: 6023
   Alignment: Chaotic good

"CHAOTIC GOOD, HUH?" HE SAID. "I'D ALWAYS WONDERED about that."

"Hurry up and read, or you're going to run out of time," Wulfgar's voice said.

Dan kept reading.

BARBARIAN SAVING THROW BONUSES: +4 VS. POISON; +3 VS. paralysis, death magic, petrification, and polymorph; +2 versus magical rods, staffs, or wands; +2 versus breath weapons.

PRIMARY BARBARIAN ABILITIES:
   Scale cliffs and climb trees
   Hide in wooded settings
   Surprise opponents
   Prevent blind attacks
   Jumping
   Detect illusion
   Detect magic
   Leadership

*Secondary barbarian abilities:*
  *Wilderness craft and survival*
  *Primitive first aid*
  *Hunting and tracking*

*Tertiary barbarian abilities:*
  *Long-distance running*
  *Small boat building and use*
  *Imitate animal sounds*
  *Snare and trap building*
  *Sexual stamina*

*Native territory: The Endless Mountains*

*Weapons of proficiency:*
  *Hand axe*
  *Spear*
  *Knife*
  *Two-handed sword*
  *Battle Axe*
  *Short bow*

"Not bad," Dan said, feeling pretty good about his new abilities.

"Yeah, don't get too excited, dummy," Wulfgar said. "You move your lips when you read now."

"Really?" Dan said, trying to remember if he had actually done that or if Wulfgar was just messing with him. "Are you—"

But then the scroll disappeared with a pop, time came rushing back in, and Dan had just enough time to reposition himself before Holly was pulling his lips down to meet hers.

# OLD MEMORIES OF A NEW PAST

Holly was right. The second time was better than the first. The third time was even better.

Around midnight, they finally left Holly's apartment to get some food and meet her friend. "It's a good thing we're going," Dan said. "I'm so hungry, I might eat you."

"Don't tease me," Holly said, and stuck out her tongue.

Winding through the back streets, they held hands and talked about their lives.

Holly's family lived in the forests just outside State College. She was excited to be here, living in town and experiencing college life, but she missed the woods and her family, especially her little sister, who was so crazy for the forest that she hadn't even started druidic training yet.

"Lily is an absolute savage," she said. "She's out in the forest all the time. We won't see her for days. Weeks, even."

Holly laughed, and Dan could tell that she missed her sister. This realization made him like Holly even more.

"Lily disappears into the woods," Holly said. "She can spend days scouting around, listening to the wind and the streams, studying the patterns in moss or the brindle of a stone outcropping. She speaks with faeries and tree folk and every animal she meets. Her hair is always such a wild tangle and jagged, too, from where I've had to cut out burs, and she always smells of flowers and honey and creek water."

"Sounds a lot like my little sister," Dan said. At eleven, Hannah still loved chasing butterflies more than chasing boys. Or at least old-world Hannah had. What would she be like now that she came from barbarian stock?

A rush of hope flooded him.

What about Kip? In this new world, could…

But something in him hardened. No. Even here, dead was dead. His brother was gone.

"Where are you from, anyway?" Holly asked.

"Northeast of here," Dan said. "The Endless Mountains."

"That's wild country, right?"

As Dan talked, a rush of brilliant images flooded his head. In them, he recognized steep green hillsides, beautiful valleys dotted with farms, and the muddy Susquehanna, all of which were familiar from his old-world life. But new images, real as memories, showed him other sights, too.

He remembered a lakeside village in autumn. Clustered tents, smoking fires, and the good smell of freshly killed game roasting on the spit. Men, women, and children mingling, sharing food, and laughing, everyone well-fed and happy. His people, the Free.

In the next memory, a very young Dan moved slowly through a forest muffled in snow. His stomach growled, and his breath huffed out before him like the ghost of warmer, more bountiful days.

Beside him, silent as owls, stalked his father, uncle, and several neighbors. All of them were bearded, winter-drawn, and feral looking, dressed in animal hides and armed with spears, moving slowly through the forest, following a bright red blood trail turning pink atop a path of churned snow.

His father raised a fist, and the men stopped, spears at the ready. Then a tremendous roar shattered the silence, and in the memory, Dan raised his own spear and offered a barbaric battle cry in his high-pitched boy's voice, as a massive black bear charged out of the briars, attacking the men.

In the final flash of new memory, Dan was a little older, perhaps eleven or twelve years old, drifting down the Susquehanna early one morning in a small canoe he had helped his father build. He could sense his father in the canoe behind him, paddling softly as they drifted through banks of heavy fog coming off the river.

Then Dan spotted the savage, a male, standing in the shallows thirty feet away at the river's edge, still as a statue, holding a sharpened stick overhead, trying to spear fish.

A river Pict.

The Pict was short and barrel-chested with long, wiry arms and bowed, muscular legs, his flesh the reddish-brown of river clay. He was naked, save for a twisted rag of breechcloth and a necklace of colorful beads obviously obtained from the men of the White Fortress upriver, where wealthy gnolls gave such trinkets in trade for scalps of the Free.

The Pict's face was primitive and brutish, the head blunt and squat, the hair a wild thatch of unruly black bristles, the eyes small and dark and narrowed in concentration, the nose small and pig-like, the mouth a long, wide slash drooping open like the mouth of a catfish.

In the memory, Dan's father whispered to him, the canoe veered silently toward shore, and Dan rose to stand in the prow, a movement so smooth and practiced that the boat didn't even wobble. He drew back his spear, and...

"That was the first man I ever killed," he said, realizing that he'd been talking for a long time, telling her all about these past events that he was only now discovering. "My father told me that this Pict was the one who had killed my brother, Kip." He shrugged and laughed emptily. "My dad told me the same thing every time we saw a Pict after that. *That's the one who killed your brother.*"

Holly gave his hand a squeeze. "Oh, Dan. I'm sorry. I know where you're coming from, though. Sadly." And she surprised him then, explaining that she, too, had lost a brother, her oldest sibling, Nettle, who'd been killed by slavers in the forest near her grove. Nettle's death had turned her other brother, Briar, into a bloodthirsty killing machine who lived for revenge.

Dan comforted Holly, and in that quiet moment, he felt something strange, their shared tragedy drawing them even closer.

"How did you turn out to be such a great guy," Holly asked, "growing up in such a brutal place?"

Dan laughed. "Brutal? Who said it was brutal?" And then he realized then that he missed his family and the Endless Mountains, violence and all. Just like that, he ached with homesickness for a place he'd never actually been.

*Or have I?*

*What are all of those memories if I've never been there?*

*Am I still Dan? Or am I living now inside a different Dan?*

But then he pushed these strange thoughts out of his head. They were heavy and blurred over with something like river fog. Besides, why should he bother thinking when he was walking beside the most beautiful girl in the world and about to fill his stomach with something good to eat?

Then, up ahead in the darkness, he spotted a lovely sight, glowing in the night like an altar.

"Hey," Holly said, tugging him to the left, "the Diner is this way."

"Later," he said, eyes locked on the bright arches glowing golden in the darkness. "I'm getting a Big Mac first."

*Thank Crom, McDonald's existed here, too!*

Drunks packed the sidewalk outside, laughing and shouting, friends shoving friends, all of them stealing sideways glances, looking for action.

Some of the drunks started looking their way, grinning and whispering.

"Let's just come back tomorrow," Holly whispered as they drew closer. "This place isn't worth the trouble this late at night."

"We'll just keep to ourselves," Dan said, meaning it. "I really want a Big Mac and a Coke."

Then a rakishly handsome, foppish warrior type with finely sculpted muscles and an expensive looking brass breastplate emblazoned with frat letters, stepped in front of them, leering at Holly. "Hey, sugar tits," he said, "is it true that grey elves have the tightest—"

Whatever he'd meant to say, he never got it out. Getting knocked the fuck out tends to make finishing disrespectful sentences difficult.

Dan caught him with a two-punch combination: a blistering right hand that nailed him square in the nose, shattering it and putting him to sleep on his feet, and a sharp left hook that landed a fraction of a second later, snapping the asshole's jaw before he could even drop to the sidewalk.

Dan opened the door for Holly.

Behind him, confusion burbled. Then he heard the sounds of several swords rasping free of their scabbards.

Dan turned and saw a semicircle of jumpy-looking frat boys eyeing him, swords in hand.

None of them were laughing now, none of them were saying shit to him or his girl, and none of them were stepping forward. They were privileged kids, sent here by wealthy parents to party and get laid and earn degrees that all boiled down to making money in towns and strongholds. Guys like them swaggered all over campus, barking and bluffing, feeling safe in their numbers, but they couldn't piece together a set of balls between the lot of them.

With no expression on his face, Dan said, "I'm going inside to have a burger. If you guys are still here when I come back out, I'll kill every last motherfucking one of you."

## 15

## THE DINER

I nside, Holly rolled her eyes. "Barbarian."

"I didn't want any trouble," he said, "but nobody talks to my girl like that."

"Oh?" Holly said with a playful look in her purple eyes. "Is that what I am, your girl?"

"Yup," he said, putting his arm around her shoulders, "and you love it."

Holly laughed and slipped her arm around his waist. "Works for me—especially if that means you'll buy me a six piece chicken McNugget and a small order of fries."

"Done," he said, "but let's just share a large fry."

For a silver piece and two coppers, he got their food and a couple of 32-ounce beers, which came in familiar McDonald's soft drink cups.

They laughed and flirted through the meal. Holly's small foot kept running up the inside of Dan's leg.

"Keep fooling around like that," he said, gathering their trash, "and I'll throw you over my shoulder, take you home, and give you the barbarian special."

"Big talker," she laughed. "We'll see who ends up on top

after I get you back to my lair."

They tossed their trash and started out the door. Dan scanned the street through the glass. No surprise. The punks had cleared out. He held the door for Holly.

"Thanks," she said. "Before we head home and I take advantage of you, come with me to the Diner. My friend is going to be bummed."

"Why?" he asked, taking her hand and heading west down College Ave.

"Remember that guy who bailed when those jerks tried to kidnap me?"

Dan nodded.

"He was on our Campus Quest team," she said. "He was supposed to be our fighter, if you can believe it."

Dan snorted. "Some fighter. Guess he didn't want to scratch his fancy armor. What's Campus Quest?"

"Ha ha, very funny," Holly said sarcastically. Then she did a double take. "Wait, you're serious? I mean, I know you're a barbarian, but *everybody* knows about Campus Quest."

Now it was Dan's turn to roll his eyes. "Enough already. Just tell me what it is."

"It's the biggest event of the year," she said. Then a sly smile came onto her face. "I assumed that you were already on a Campus Quest team."

Dan shook his head.

Holly's smile grew wider. "Well then, my big, strong barbarian, are you up for an adventure?"

As they strolled, she told him all about Campus Quest.

On opening day, hundreds of four-person teams competed in adventure challenges on the HUB Lawn. Only the best teams qualified and stayed in the competition.

There were four stages in all, each stage harder than the last. The finals were a really big deal, held at Beaver Stadium, with 80,000 screaming fans in attendance and the whole thing televised on national TV.

"All right," he said. "Sounds good to me."

Holly gave him a serious look. "It's dangerous," she said. "Especially if you make it past day one. People die."

Dan shrugged. "I'm in."

Part of him was aware that this was all pretty coincidental, Holly happening to need a fighter right when he entered her life. The timing of it all was straight out of T&T, where most adventures started with incredibly ham-fisted coincidences.

Honestly, though, Dan didn't give a shit. He was up for an adventure and definitely up for hanging with Holly.

"Cool," she said, smiled brightly, and pulled his head down to give him a long, slow, sweet kiss.

Then they reached State College's iconic, all-night hangout spot, Ye Olde College Diner, famous far and wide for its delicious sticky buns or "stickies."

Dan's mouth watered, just thinking of stickies. He'd only come to the Diner once before.

Whenever Dan's friends invited him, he begged off, making excuses, too embarrassed to admit that he couldn't afford stickies, with or without ice cream. As a dishwasher, he scarfed down free food at the Nittany Lion Inn. Beyond that, he had a meagerly funded dining hall meal card and enough money for ramen noodles. That was about it.

He hoped that his remaining silver piece and handful of coppers would cover the bill. With that thought, he suppressed a growl.

Here he was, transported to a fantasy world, and he was still worried about money. He hated being poor. Hated not being able to get a sticky or go to the Creamery or buy one of the nice Penn State sweatshirts that everybody wore around campus.

*Well*, he told himself as they entered the Diner, *you don't have to be poor here. In a T&T world, you can do something about it.*

The Diner was way different in this new world.

Beyond the expected glass display case and lunch counter, the place was normal enough, stretching away in familiar fashion, a narrow establishment with booths lining both walls and the smells of sweet sticky buns and percolating coffee filling the air.

But everything else was completely different.

The lights were turned down low, and a haze of multicolored smoke hung above the booths, many of which had hookahs in plain view atop their tables. A mix of humans, elves, half-orcs, and dwarves filled the booths, most of them hunched forward in dark cloaks, whispering conspiratorially. Dan saw the Diner's signatures stickies, most of them paired with scoops of vanilla ice cream and tall glasses of dark beer.

"Looking for your friend?" a smiling hostess asked Holly.

Holly said that she was, and the hostess told them to follow her. As they walked down the narrow, smoky aisle between the booths, eyes flicked up, quick as daggers, to study them. Cagey, suspicious eyes.

"There she is," the hostess said, pointing. "Back booth, as usual."

Holly thanked her, and they kept walking.

A young woman sat in the last booth, wearing a dark cloak. The hood covered her face, but she was *definitely* female. That much was obvious, based on her shapely figure, which was clad in a low-cut, skintight black leather bodysuit.

She didn't have quite as much in the chest as Holly, but then again, who did? Besides, what the mysterious girl's breasts lacked in size, they made up for with sheer perfection.

Packed into the booth around her were what looked like a bunch of gnomes, mostly in black hoodies.

No, Dan realized, drawing closer. Not gnomes. Children.

The mysterious girl gestured to the kids and said, "Scatter."

The kids, a mix of boys and girls in their teens and tweens, hopped up without a word and slipped away past Dan and Holly.

"Holly," the girl said warmly from within the shadowy confines of her hood. "The sexiest elf on the planet."

They embraced.

The mysterious girl sat back down with her back against the rear wall, facing the front of the Diner.

Holly slid in across her. Dan slid in beside Holly.

"Who's this?" the girl asked.

"This is Dan," Holly said with a grin, "my new sex slave."

Dan snorted. "Your new master, you mean."

"We're still working out the details," Holly said. "One way or the other, Nadia, meet Dan. Dan, Nadia."

Nadia slid her hand across the table into Dan's. Her grip was surprisingly firm.

"Nice to meet you, handsome," Nadia said, and he saw a bright smile flash within the hood.

"Nice to meet you, too, um… mysterious hooded girl who might be pretty."

Nadia laughed. "You'll have to forgive me. Occupational hazard. I try to keep a low profile."

"Nadia is a thief," Holly said.

"Wow," Nadia said, sounding sarcastic. "You really don't do subtle, do you?"

Then the waitress was standing beside them, offering menus.

"I'm full," Holly said, waving her off.

*That makes one of us*, Dan thought.

He popped open a menu, hoping he could afford some-thing. He could. Barely. A sticky and a cup of coffee would wipe him out. He ordered, and the waitress left.

"So, Dan," Nadia said, "are you the one that helped Holly kill those guys outside her apartment?"

Dan leaned back in his seat. "How did you know about that?"

Holly rolled her eyes. "Nadia is more than a thief. She's also a show-off."

Nadia spread her hands. "I make it my business to know everything that happens in this town. So what happened, anyway?"

"It was crazy," Holly said. "These four guys tried to kidnap me. They came out from behind trees when I went outside. I had just met with that guy Randy. He said that he and his brother would join the team."

"Good," Nadia said. "That's taken care of then."

Holly shook her head. "As soon as those guys stepped out from behind the trees and drew steel, Randy let out a shriek and ran away like a terrified little kid."

"Are you serious?" Nadia said. "What a jackass."

Holly nodded toward Dan. "Well, we have a new fighter, anyway."

"Excellent," Nadia said. "But I don't want anything to do with Randy's brother now. Which means…"

"We need a new spellcaster."

At the mention of magic, Dan's hands tightened into fists.

"I'll ask around," Nadia said, "see what I can find out. In the meantime, Holly darling, I'm worried about you. Your attackers were waiting for you, and from what I hear, one of them got away."

Holly fumbled inside her cloak. "I wanted to ask you about this," she said, and placed a black dagger atop the table.

"Oh, shit," Nadia said, and pulled the weapon off the table

just as the waitress returned. Then, to the waitress, she said, "That was fast."

"One sticky and a cup of coffee," the waitress said, setting down Dan's order.

"Thanks," Dan said.

The waitress asked, "You ladies sure you don't need anything? No? Well, if you change your minds, just let me know."

Once the waitress had left, Nadia examined the black dagger, keeping it hidden under the table. "Don't let anybody see you carrying this thing," she said.

"Carrying it?" Holly said, and made a face. "I don't ever want to touch that dagger again. Toss it, sell it, I don't care. But I don't want the thing. What is it, anyway?"

"This dagger is called a Sliver of Darkness," Nadia said.

"Darkness, huh?" Dan said, chewing a bite of delicious sticky bun. "That one guy kept talking about darkness. The Mother of Darkness and all that."

Holly nodded, sipping Dan's coffee.

"Not good," Nadia said. "You're dealing with an apocalyptic death cult. The Acolytes of Eternal Darkness."

Dan snorted. "They're not even trying to hide the fact that they're total assholes, huh?"

"I know they sound ridiculous," Nadia said, "but be careful. They're serious as an aneurysm. They're dedicated to oblivion, committed to putting out the lights forever."

Holly's purple eyes flashed with sudden anger. "How can people be so stupid? Light and darkness are balanced, just like good and evil, order and chaos. People go trying to mess up the nature of things." She cut herself off, shaking her head and grumbling with frustration.

"Spoken like a druid," Nadia said, and Dan could hear the laughter in her voice. But then Nadia got serious again. "Just don't take these guys lightly. I'm afraid that you haven't seen the last of them. You need a place to stay?"

"No," Holly said, and gave Dan's arm a squeeze. "He isn't just my sex toy. He's also my bodyguard."

Dan grinned. "A body that perfect deserves protection."

Holly squeezed his arm again. "Oh yeah?" she asked, a mischievous smile coming onto her face. "And what about Nadia? What do you think of her body?"

The question would have shocked old-world Dan. He probably would've spit out his food in surprise.

But he was done with all that nervous half-stepping. If Holly wanted to ask, he would tell her the truth. He stared across the table at the thief's fit, leather-clad physique and perfect bosom. "She has a gorgeous body."

The bright smile appeared again in the darkness of the hood. "Well, then," Nadia said, her voice going sultry, "maybe you'll have to guard it sometime, if Holly will let me borrow you for a few hours."

The thief stood, looking very gorgeous indeed.

"Unfortunately," Nadia said, "I have to leave now. Places to go, people to rob, you know the deal. And I have to see about finding us a wizard in what, two days?"

Holly and Dan stood.

The girls hugged goodbye.

Nadia touched Dan's shoulder. "Nice meeting you—oh!" She slipped and fell forward into him.

Dan caught her before she could fall to the floor. Her body felt firm and fit. An alluring, somehow familiar floral aroma filled Dan's nostrils.

"Thanks," Nadia said. "I am so clumsy."

She gave his arms a squeeze. "Hmm, I could definitely use a bodyguard with muscles like these."

Dan chuckled.

Nadia's hands slipped around behind him and squeezed his ass. "Oh," she said, "nice butt, too."

Old-world Dan would've been shocked.

Had been, in fact.

But new Dan, Dan the Barbarian, grabbed Nadia's wrist and pulled her hand—and his wallet—into view.

Nadia dropped the wallet and laughed. "How did that get there?"

"Wait a second," Dan said, and pulled back her hood, revealing a beautiful face with a slightly crooked nose and bright emerald-green eyes. "You!"

Nadia put her hood up again, ducked under his arm, and slipped away.

"See you, Holly," Nadia called, then pointed to the floor at Dan's feet. "Keep an eye on that wallet of yours. This place is full of thieves."

Then she stuck out her tongue and left, trailing laughter.

## 16

## CAMPUS LIFE

The next morning came early. But that was the only bad thing Dan could say about it.

He woke in Holly's bed. She was between his legs, naked and lovely as a dryad, her head bobbing up and down on his morning erection.

Later, after they had finished, she kicked him out of her apartment. "If you're hanging around here, I'll never make it to class," she said.

She gave him a long, sweet kiss and then shoved him into the hallway with a laugh. "Meet me for lunch at Pollock Dining Hall."

Dan smiled at the door for a moment after Holly closed it. She was really something.

Stepping into his own apartment, things felt strange, simply because his life had changed so much in the last twenty-four hours.

It was crazy. Not just the T&T transformation. Holly, too.

She was more than sex to him. A lot more. After not even twenty-four hours, he knew that as fact. And he was one hundred percent confident that she felt the same way.

Maybe the ease with which they had slid into an actual relationship was another function of the T&T world. Maybe in this world it was possible to skip the bullshit and get straight down to liking each other.

Ultimately, he didn't care why things were the way they were, so long as they stayed this way. He was just happy and couldn't wait to see her again.

Willis appeared in the kitchen doorway, mouth hanging open in exaggerated shock. "Dude," he said.

Dan smiled at him. "Dude," he responded.

"Duuude," Willis said, his high-pitched voice drawing out the word. "Did you just come from across the hall? It sounded like you just came from across the hall."

"I did," Dan said.

"Duuuuude," Willis said, this time drawing it out with obvious glee. "From Holly's place?"

"Yup," Dan said matter-of-factly.

"Duuuuuuuude!" Willis all but shrieked. His skinny arm flew up. "High five!"

Dan reached down and slapped palms with his tiny friend.

Grinning like a madman, Willis scrunched his nose rapidly several times, his habitual way of working his spectacles higher up the bridge. "Did you just bang the hottest girl in the galaxy?"

Dan frowned at him. "That's between me and her," he said. "Besides, I gotta go to class."

At least he *thought* he had to go to class. With everything else changing so much, he realized that he needed to check his schedule.

"You dog!" Willis said. "You dirty, magnificent dog!"

Dan went into his room and closed the door. He unzipped his backpack and found his schedule. It took him a second to remember which class he was supposed to have this morning… Intro to Shakespeare.

Why had it taken him a while to remember? Was it because he'd just had the most amazing night ever and had slept only a few hours? Or were his intelligence and wisdom dwindling away, just as his strength and dexterity were swelling?

He checked his schedule and smiled.

No Shakespeare, no sociology, and best of all, no GeoSci with Dr. Lynch!

Instead, his schedule showed Swordplay 303, Wilderness Survival, Intro to Dungeoneering, Unarmed Combat, Battlefield Tactics and Strategy, and Treasure Identification.

"Yes!" he shouted, pumping a fist in the air.

His first class started in an hour, giving him just enough time to grab a quick shower, heat up a pack of ramen noodles, and head out the door.

He kicked off his boots, unbuckled his belt, and dropped his pants. The scabbard thumped off the floor, and Wulfgar slid out a few inches.

"What the fuck?" the sword roared. "Gotta be honest, dude. I'm not digging the whole leave-your-mentor-in-his-sheath-all-the-time thing."

"Sorry about that," Dan said, peeling off his shirt and grabbing the towel from the bedpost. "I've been kind of busy."

"You and every other buddy fucker in the universe," Wulfgar said. "We were thick as thieves until you got laid. Then it's *Wulfgar who?*"

Dan laughed. "Are you really whining like a little bitch right now? I never would've expected this from you, man."

Wulfgar laughed. "Well, I'll give you one thing. You're funnier after you get laid. But don't let me damn you with faint praise. Go hit the showers, you filthy ape!"

The morning kicked ass.

Back in the real world, Dan had always felt like he was a step or two behind the other college students. It was like the disadvantage he'd felt in comparison to the town kids in middle school, only worse.

The kids in his college classes weren't necessarily smarter than Dan, but he was from a little hick town in the middle of nowhere, and most of them were from fancy suburban schools.

There was a difference.

That difference showed in the way they carried themselves, the things they talked about, and the way they answered so confidently in class. Old-world Dan had felt self-conscious and shy.

But those days were apparently over. In sword fighting class, he dominated. The instructor was cool, a grizzled veteran named Harper.

"Given the choice," Harper told them, "don't slash... stab!"

He demonstrated, plunging the point of his sword into a practice dummy, then explained that puncture wounds made people retract into themselves, made them feel like quitting. Slashing attacks, on the other hand, made people crazy with desperation, made them go wild and fight back.

"Besides," Harper said with a grin, "when you stab instead of slash, you increase your chances of poking holes in those nice, juicy organs."

Dan had been all right with Macbeth and Hamlet back in the real world, but this was way, way more interesting.

And in this world, he didn't just hide in the back. Harper called on him frequently. More than any other student, in fact.

Dan answered questions, helped with demonstrations, and always earned Harper's praise during drills. Harper also took the time to correct Dan's technique, which was great.

Strangest of all, Dan's classmates looked up to him now. Quite a change from the past.

Wilderness Survival was even easier. When they started working with camouflage techniques, the instructor stopped several times and asked Dan for his input.

Dan was happily surprised to realize that he actually knew this stuff. All of it. For the first time in his life, having grown up in the sticks was a good thing.

If his new-world classes were all like this, he'd be set!

Of course, he had no way of knowing then what lay in store for him.

# 17

## AN UNWELCOME VISITOR

D an got to the dining hall a few minutes early and waited outside. He saw Holly coming down the path toward him. She hadn't seen him yet.

Holly looked absolutely stunning, dressed in work boots, faded jeans, and a long-sleeved white top, her golden hair shimmering in the sunlight and her purple cloak billowing out around her as she strode along.

Then she looked up, saw him standing there, and lit up with a beaming smile that made her even more beautiful.

Holly gave a little wave, and he walked down to meet her, and just as he would have expected, there was zero bullshit. She jumped up, wrapping her arms and legs around him in an acrobatic hug, and gave him a long, passionate kiss for all the world to see.

Hand in hand, they entered the cafeteria. They grabbed trays and got into line together and talked about their mornings.

Holly was studying veterinary science. She already knew a lot from growing up in the wilderness, where she protected the animals and did her best to help any of them if they were injured or sick, but the classes were interesting, and she was excited to take new knowledge back to her grove.

"Whatcha want?" a deep voice asked.

Dan looked up. He'd been so focused on Holly that he hadn't noticed the servers until he was face-to-face with them.

The lunch ladies were hulking hobgoblins in blood-red smocks and black leather aprons splattered with slop. Grayish fur covered their arms and the backs of their hands, as well as their necks and the tops of their heads, which he could see through their flimsy little hairnets.

The lunch lady who had spoken to him had a bright red face and yellow eyes. Her heavy jaw jutted forth, the pronounced underbite studded with dirty yellow teeth.

"Come on, come on, lover boy," the hobgoblin said, her voice gruff. "What do you want?"

Surprisingly, the food looked pretty much the same as it had back in the old world: boiled vegetables, mashed potatoes, and a choice between dried-up chicken and a dubious, brown stew.

Dan took his chances with the stew.

At the beverage center, he was in for another surprise. Alongside the soda and juice, students lined up at a row of self-serve beer taps. Dan snagged a pair of large plastic tumblers and filled them both to the brim with dark beer, then joined Holly at a table.

They talked about everything and nothing, their conversation lighthearted and effortless. Then they took care of their trays and trash and went outside together.

They both had a while before their next class, so they walked over to the HUB to check the bulletin boards, where people posted all types of stuff, from wagon-pooling to apartment sublets to announcements for strange new clubs.

Holly wanted to check for any flyers advertising spellcasters looking to get in on Campus Quest.

Dan grumbled, but Holly explained that every team needed a wizard. The way that the challenges were set up, each team needed to display a variety of strengths. Combat, critical thinking, thieving skills, and yes, spellcasting.

Even if they could only find a relatively weak mage to join their team, Holly would be happy, but she was worried that this late in the game they were going to come up empty. And sure enough, though they found dozens of Campus Quest flyers advertising wizards, all of the little contact tabs at the bottom had been ripped away.

"Oh well," Holly said, but Dan could see that she was disappointed. For one reason or another, this Campus Quest thing was really important to her. "Maybe Nadia will find somebody. If anybody can do it, she will."

He was about to say something about how he hoped that Nadia would find his rent money, too, but Holly narrowed her eyes and pointed across the room to where midday crowds were coming and going through the doors.

"Hey," she said, "is that an acolyte?"

Dan spun around, instantly ready. "Son-of-a-bitch," he growled, seeing the skinny guy in a midnight blue robe standing near the door, staring at them.

Dan dropped his hand to Wulfgar's hilt and took a step forward, but the skinny guy grinned at them, squeezed into the crowd and left the building.

Dan craned his neck, trying to see which way the asshole had gone but only caught a quick glimpse of the dark robe before it disappeared.

## TAKEDOWN

**D**an roared, going for a tackle.

Then his leg jerked away beneath him, and he was pulled completely off balance. Before he could even regain his footing, two hundred and seventy pounds of muscle slammed into him and drove him to the mat.

Hard.

Again!

A second later, his Unarmed Combat classmate, Rob, who just happened to wrestle heavyweight for Penn State, was up and moving again, a friendly smile back on his face.

Dan jumped to his feet.

The takedown had knocked the wind out of him, but he didn't care. He had to get the best of Rob at least once before class was over.

Rob moved gracefully for such a big guy, circling Dan in a lateral shuffle like a boxer, first to the right, then back to the left, then right again.

He wasn't even breathing hard!

"Take your time," Rob said. "You're telegraphing every attack. Know what I mean? Keep a poker face. Feint a little."

Rob demonstrated, pawing the open air and taking a quick step toward Dan before scooting back out of range and juking away again to the side.

Dan nodded, breathing hard, and started feinting, doing his best to keep his face set. No more snarling, no more bulging eyes, no more battle cries.

"That's better," Rob said, "but don't get lazy. Don't leave your arm out there."

As the huge wrestler said this, he snatched Dan's forearm, tugged it forward, and pulled him off balance.

Dan yanked his arm free and snapped back instinctively, standing straight.

Half a second later, he was down on the mat again, staring up at the big lights on the White Building's ceiling high overhead. When he'd stood up, Rob had shot in with a double-leg takedown.

Even though it was frustrating as hell, getting his ass kicked again and again, Dan had to admit that Rob was cool.

Their instructor, a former mercenary who also doubled as the Penn State boxing coach, had paired Rob and Dan after seeing how badly Dan demolished classmates of his own size. Honestly, after yesterday's cakewalk classes, it was good to know that he would be learning a ton here.

After class, Rob slapped him on the back. "Good work, man."

"Thanks," Dan said. He was exhausted, drenched in sweat, and really thirsty. "You're amazing. I appreciate the tips."

Rob grinned. "You start taking me down, the tips stop. What do you weigh?"

Dan shrugged. "A buck ninety, maybe two hundred." He'd weighed one-ninety in the old world. Since then, he'd put on some muscle, more each day, it seemed, but he'd lost fat, too, so he really wasn't sure what he weighed.

Rob whistled. "You're strong for one-ninety, man. Like,

freakishly strong. You know one-ninety's a weight class, right? You should come to practice with me sometime. Teach you a takedown or two, a few escapes, a couple of pinning combinations, you'd wreck people. But you'd have to work on that temper!"

Dan laughed. "Thanks, man. Maybe next season. My nights are kind of busy right now."

Busy, indeed.

Last night, he'd worked until midnight, disappointed to learn that yes, he was still a dishwasher even in this fantasy world.

Then he'd come home, showered off the coleslaw stink of the restaurant, and crossed the hall to see Holly.

At some point, he'd lost count of how many times that they'd made love. They'd done it on her grassy living room floor, in her bed, in her shower, up against the wall....

They couldn't get enough of each other.

Holly's kinky side was definitely showing. Despite all of her lighthearted smack talk, she loved it when he dominated her. Nothing too rough or crazy, but she was turned on by his size and strength.

Dan was turned on by everything about her.

But now he was running on four hours of sleep and dying of thirst. He said goodbye to Rob and headed for the dining hall. He planned on taking a long lunch and drinking approximately ten gallons of water before heading to his last two Monday, Wednesday, Friday classes, Battlefield Strategy and Tactics and Treasure Identification.

He went through the lunch line, where the red-faced hobgoblin from yesterday served him potato wedges, a pile of green beans boiled to the color of pale spring grass, and a mound of lumpy, tan "chicken surprise" every bit as dubious as yesterday's stew.

"Chicken surprise," Dan said. "What's the surprise?"

The hobgoblin grinned a yellow smile. "Surprise is, that ain't chicken." She barked laughter and asked the next student what they wanted.

After filling up four tall glasses of water, he found an empty table in the corner and started his meal by pounding two full glasses.

He wished Holly was here, but their lunch schedules didn't coincide today.

After yesterday's run-in with the acolyte, he hated the idea of her being alone on campus, but his concern only made her laugh. "You're sweet," she had said, and kissed his cheek, "but I can take care of myself."

He knew that she could, and that glowing staff of hers was no joke, but that was the bitch of falling for someone. You couldn't help worrying about them.

He was halfway through the chicken surprise, which, like the stew, turned out to be pretty good, when a tray slapped down on the table across from him.

"Hello, handsome," Nadia said, her green eyes gleaming.

He almost didn't recognize her. She looked completely different than she had at the Diner, and way more like she had that day back in the real world. No cloak, no shadows, no mystery.

Nadia's chestnut hair was pulled back in a ponytail. Over a bright Dance-a-Thon shirt, she wore a cheery plaid shirt knotted at the midriff. She looked like a crisp, shiny goody two-shoes who belonged not to the Thieves' Guild but to some service sorority that split its time between curing cancer and teaching blind puppies how to read.

"Good news," Nadia said. "I might've found a wizard."

"Good," he said. "Holly's really worried that she won't be able to compete."

"I'm meeting the guy at his dorm tomorrow morning. You and Holly should come." She glanced quickly to the side and gestured to a pack of approaching girls. Freshmen, by the look of their young faces, makeup, and nicely polished leather armor.

"All right," Dan said, "We'll—"

"Now," Nadia interrupted, "not another word about any of this, or I'll cut you." Then she turned with a big smile and welcomed the girls, who filled in seats around them.

Nadia introduced the girls one by one, but Dan was so floored by her innocent and bubbly routine that he didn't even catch their names.

"Daniel is an old friend," Nadia said.

The freshmen grinned as if they thought that was just super.

Dan looked back and forth between Nadia and the others in stunned silence.

"And I am their scary RA," Nadia said.

The girls laughed. "Yeah, right," one of them said. "Nadia's the greatest. We'd be lost without her!"

Dan leaned back, flabbergasted. "Wait… you're an RA?"

"Why yes, Daniel, I am," Nadia said, smiling more brightly than ever but shooting him daggers with her eyes. Meanwhile, her boot kicked him in the shin. "It's hard to fit in between classes and gymnastics, but I really wanted to give back, you know?"

Dan burst into laughter and stood up with his tray. "Well, if you really want to give back—"

"So good seeing you, Daniel!" Nadia said, cutting him off, and the girls launched into a gaggle of goodbyes.

Dan laughed all the way out the door.

## FIRE AND BRIMSTONE

On the steps of the Willard Building, the Willard Preacher had been replaced by an emaciated half elf in rough-spun robes, who was preaching no less fervently to a crowd of lingering students. As they had back in the old world, some of the students listened respectfully, some laughed, and some heckled viciously.

The preacher railed on, unperturbed. "Oblivion stands upon the doorstep, ladies and gentlemen!"

"That's what you said last Friday," a heckler called.

A smattering of halfhearted laughter rippled through the onlookers, most of whom didn't look all that concerned.

But something in the preacher's intensity stopped Dan.

"No," the preacher said, leveling a bony finger in the direction of his antagonist. "In the past, I told you that troubled times were approaching.

"But now," he said, panning his fiery gaze across the slouching crowd until his eyes found Dan, "dark days are upon us! As you worship gold pieces and study blasphemous texts and befoul your bodies, wallowing in sin, the forces of evil are rising up to blot out the very sun!"

An involuntary shudder rattled through Dan and he hurried away toward class.

*Don't freak out,* he told himself. Priests always railed about impending doom. Just because the preacher had spoken in terms of evil blotting out the sun, that didn't mean that he'd been talking about the Acolytes of Eternal Darkness.

Of course, in a T&T adventure, little coincidences like that were always more than coincidences.

At that moment, a cloud passed over the sun, dimming and cooling the day.

Dan marched on doggedly to class. Not that his next class made him feel any better.

The schedule said *Treasure Identification*, which sounded pretty cool, but class was being held in 213 Sparks, the very same classroom where he'd had GeoSci 02 with Dr. Lynch, who'd seemed hellbent on destroying his old life.

*Relax*, he told himself, climbing the broad stone stairs. New world, new classes, new teachers.

High above, where he'd thought that he'd seen spiderwebs that first night in this new world, he saw only the same old names chiseled into the stones between the building's famous Ionic columns: *Dante, Aristotle, Goethe*.

He went inside, climbed the stairs to the second floor, and entered 213 Sparks for the first time since his old life had come apart in so many shreds as Dr. Lynch tore his essay to pieces in front of him.

He breathed a sigh of relief as soon as he realized that the classroom was completely different. No grid of student chairs, no podium, and–*praise Crom!*–no Dr. Lynch in sight.

Long tables filled the dimly lit room. Atop these tables sat a strange cornucopia of armor, weaponry, jewelry, and every manner of treasure and trinket, from curious statuettes to ornate mirrors to what looked like a gem-encrusted toilet brush.

But then anxiety washed over him.

There was no one in here. Sure, he was a few minutes early, but he didn't see even a single student.

Had he made a mistake?

Maybe he'd misread the schedule. Maybe this was where the class met for labs or something. Maybe there was a regular class, with lectures and stuff, in some other classroom.

He groaned.

This was exactly the kind of thing that old Dan used to do. So much so, in fact, that old-world Dan had constantly worried about missing something: directions, assignments, program requirements, everything. He'd been that way all through middle and high school, and college had been even worse.

*Relax,* he told himself. *If there's another classroom and it's just down the hall, you'll still make it to class on time.*

He unzipped his backpack and checked his schedule.

He had the right time, the right building, and the right room. But he also noticed an asterisk beside the class number. The bottom of the page was cut off by his sloppy folding job.

He unfolded it. There was the asterisk, and beside it, an explanation: *IND STD.*

*Industry Standard?*

Then he understood. No, not Industry Standard.

Independent Study.

He was the only student in the class.

And for now, at least, the only person. His teacher was nowhere in sight.

Class officially started in two minutes.

This was going to be weird. He'd never been in an independent study before. If the teacher was cool, class could be awesome. But if the teacher was horrible...

*No,* he thought. *Don't even think that way. Besides, maybe I'll get lucky and the teacher won't show.*

He drifted alongside a table, his eyes passing dully over various dusty knickknacks, passing time until class started.

Then, reaching the end of the table, he slammed to a stop.

Staring up at him was a shriveled human head with long, silver hair.

No, not human, he realized, overcoming his shock and taking in the fine features and pointed ears.

An elven head, female and long dead, her eyes sewn shut and her mouth drawn down in a frown of eternal agony.

A wave of sorrow and revulsion passed over him.

Who had she been?

How had she died?

And what in the world was her head doing here, propped up on a table between a brass letter opener and a crown made of yellowed bones?

"I'm sorry," he told the head. "I'm sorry this happened to you."

That's when the head opened its mouth and spoke.

# SPEAKING WITH THE DEAD

"Thank you, Dan," the head said, not with the creepy, dried-up whisper he would have expected from a thing long dead but in a clear, lively, almost musical voice.

But he still jerked back, because even a musical voice is shocking when it comes out of a decapitated head. "You can talk?"

"Yes. And I have much to tell you, Dan."

"How do you know my name?"

"I know more than your name," the head said. "I know you, your soul, your essence."

"All right," Dan said. "How do you know all of that stuff, then?"

"Mine are a magical people," the head said. "We grey elves never really die."

*You sure* look *dead,* Dan thought, but figured he'd keep that to himself.

"So long as our people live on, we remain," the head said. "At birth, grey elves inherit the memories of our ancestors. A select few of us also inherit the memories of our *descendants.*"

"Wait," Dan said. He had to call bullshit on that last bit. "How can you inherit memories of things that haven't happened yet?"

"We dream the past and the future," the head explained. "That is how I know you, how I've known you, in fact, for over a century. Now my people are in danger, and only you can save them."

"Me? I'm only a second-level barbarian."

"It has to be you," the head said.

And then Dan understood what was happening.

In *Towers & Trolls*, even the best TMs tended to be pretty ham-fisted when introducing a quest they had prepared.

The trouble was, he didn't want to go off on some side quest. He was having fun with life right now, thank you very much. He would much rather keep having sex with his hot girlfriend than go off to who-knows-where to fight who-knows-what, with no guarantee of even surviving.

"Why does it have to be me?" he asked, prodding a little.

"I saw you in my dreams," the head said. "Only you can save my people."

*Of course,* he thought. Her lines were so predictable that they had to be scripted. He must've missed that appendix in *The TM's Guide*.

"Let me guess," he said. "These dreams, they told you that it has to be me, but otherwise, things were still pretty open-ended, right? Like, it has to be me, but if I agree to help, there are no guarantees. I might succeed or might fail, right?"

"That is correct," the decapitated head admitted.

Dan rolled his eyes. "Sorry. I have a lot going on. I'm going to have to say no. Good luck to your people, though." And he turned away from the head.

"Please," the head called after him. "Listen to me. For my people. For *Holly*."

Dan spun back around. "What? What does Holly have to do with this?"

"In Rothrock Forest, you will find a grove of black walnut trees."

"Is Holly in danger?"

"Caves honeycomb the earth beneath this grove," the head told him. "This subterranean maze is filled with dark energy. The forces of evil congregate here to hold dark rituals and offer unspeakable sacrifices to unnamable gods."

*Yup*, he thought. *It's a quest. A frigging dungeon, with a back story straight out of some T&T module.*

He really didn't have the time for this nonsense, but he had to know if Holly was okay.

"Deep underground," the head continued, "I followed the sounds of combat and came face-to-face with evil incarnate, the necromancer Griselda. The Legion of Light was there, losing a battle against the powerful sorceress."

Dan barely managed not to groan. The Legion of Light? That was a name straight out of Willis's imagination.

"Griselda would have destroyed them all, but I attacked just in time. Back and forth, we battled, momentum shifting one way and then the next. At last, I transcended my strength, fought with the strength of my people, and killed the diabolical necromancer."

"Hey, good for you," Dan said. "So about Holly…"

"Unfortunately," the head said, sounding sad, "at the same moment that I finished Griselda…"

The head moaned.

"She also killed you?" Dan guessed.

"Yes," the head said.

"That really sucks," he said.

He had heard enough. This was definitely an invitation to explore some crazy, high-level dungeon.

All that stuff about him showing up in her dreams was so

much hooey meant to draw him in. Same with mentioning Holly, about whom the head seemed pointedly resistant to providing additional information.

"But maybe you should've known better?" Dan said. "To be fair, caves full of dark magic, a gathering of evil creatures, and some uber-powerful necromancer sound like a pretty tough challenge. Way too tough, I might add, for a second-level barbarian."

"Sometimes," the head continued, "forces of pure evil carry on in death. The necromancer will rise again."

*Of course she will,* Dan thought.

"When she does," the head said, its voice quavering with desperation, "only you can destroy her."

"You seem to have missed the part about me being only second level," Dan said. This head was pushier than a door-to-door salesperson.

"To defeat her, you must—" But just like that, the head went as silent as, well, a decapitated head.

"To defeat her, I must… what?" Dan said.

"Pretty," a voice rasped from behind him, chilling his blood. "Isn't it so pretty?"

Dan spun around and screamed.

He recoiled, bumping into the table hard enough that artifacts clattered to the floor.

"Dr. Lynch," he said, instantly covered in goosebumps. The temperature around him had dropped ten or twenty degrees, maybe more. "You startled me."

"Clumsy boy," Dr. Lynch said.

At least the thing *looked* like Dr. Lynch.

Sort of.

For as ancient and haggard as Dr. Lynch had looked in the old world, that version of her had been a spring chicken compared to the thing standing before Dan now.

Her hair jutted out in all directions, flaring like a white

corona from an emaciated, almost skeletal face caked in makeup. The heavy powder was probably meant to minimize wrinkles, but it made Dr. Lynch look like a mortician had given her a makeover.

She wore an ancient and faded yellow gown that must have been fancy long, long ago but now looked like a funeral shroud draped over her wasted, bony frame. Despite the dimness of the room, Dr. Lynch also wore dark, oversized sunglasses that only served to make her skull-like face look even smaller.

"Sorry," Dan said, and started picking up things that had toppled when he'd knocked into the table with surprise and revulsion.

The room felt even colder now.

The hairs on the back of his neck stood up.

It didn't just feel cold in here. It felt strange. Bad.

"Don't bother, clumsy boy," Dr. Lynch rasped. "Your time is almost at its end."

Dan turned back around and then squeezed back against the table.

Dr. Lynch had inched forward. Her smell hit him then, an overwhelming stench of decay and sickly sweetness, like a rotten chuck roast marinating in cheap perfume.

His gorge rose, but he battled it down, doing his best not to show his utter disgust. "What do you mean?" he asked. "Class just started."

"When I arrived," Dr. Lynch said, "you were speaking with the head."

"I was just talking to myself," Dan lied.

"What did she tell you?"

"I don't know what you—"

"The dead speak in riddles," Dr. Lynch said. "Riddles that would no doubt only confuse a *barbarian*."

Dr. Lynch pronounced the word *barbarian* as if it were a slice of rotting lemon in her mouth.

"However," she continued, "even the most primitive savages can learn lessons from the dead. Lessons concerning their own mortality, for example, and the essential futility of life itself."

"I already told you," Dan insisted. "I wasn't talking with the head."

"Speaking of futility, let us speak of your performance in this course. You are failing," Dr. Lynch said, and the corners of her sunken mouth twisted cruelly upward. "Which comes as no surprise to me. Barbarians don't belong in universities. You lack the requisite intelligence and work ethic to succeed."

Anger leapt up in him. "Are you calling me stupid?"

"Stupid or lazy, take your pick," Dr. Lynch said. She shoved a piece of yellowed parchment into his hands. "Your last chance."

He wanted to shout at her. Who was she to call him stupid and lazy, just because he'd grown up in the forest? But at that moment, her foul breath overwhelmed him, and he started coughing and choking.

He staggered away, hacking and gasping.

When he finally found his breath again, Dr. Lynch was gone.

*What the hell?*

Then he looked down at the crumpled yellow parchment that she'd handed him. Smoothing it out, he beheld a message so jagged and spindly that it might've been written by spiders.

*In one week,* the note informed him, *you will take your midterm examination, which will cover the first thirty chapters of Remedial Treasure Identification: Riddles from the Dead.*

*Fail the test, and you fail this course.*

*No second chances.*

*Should this transpire, I shall have no choice but to inform the scholarship office immediately.*

## MASTER

C overed in sweat and breathing hard, his muscles bulging with exertion, Dan paused and looked down, admiring the view.

Holly was crouched before him, quivering on all fours, her naked body glistening with perspiration.

Holly's perfect ass pressed back into him, engulfing him in her slippery sex. Her waist was so small, he could practically wrap his big hands around it. Her golden hair had come undone and covered most of her lovely back.

He brushed aside the beautiful blond hair, admiring her pale skin and fine lines of her back. He ran his fingers upward, riding the groove of her spine, and flattened his palm against her upper back.

Then he pressed her face and breasts into the bed.

Holly moaned, grinding her ass into him, forcing him deeper into her. "Don't stop," she said, panting with exhaustion and desire. "Don't stop fucking me."

She inched her hips forward and slammed back into him, once, twice, three times, trying to recapture the fierce, slapping rhythm.

But Dan knew her well enough by now to know that she wanted something else even more.

He pushed his hips forward not in a thrust but in a slow, steady motion that flattened her into prone position.

Holly whined, trying and failing to force him to pound her. He held her there with his weight and strength, impaling on his length, his pelvic bone pinning her down so that she could only squirm and whimper, "Fuck me. Please fuck me."

But Dan smiled, playful darkness rising in him. "Please fuck me... who?"

Holly's face turned sideways on the pillow. Her eyelids opened slightly, showing a sliver of purple iris. Her pale cheek glowed rosy red with passion. Her mouth was open, the pink wet tongue glistening inside. Her ragged breathing stirred the strands of blond hair falling across her features.

"Please fuck me," she said, sounding both humiliated and very, very aroused, "master."

"That's more like it," he said and nipped her pointed ear.

He scooped her up, returning them to doggy style, drew back his hips, and thrust into her powerfully.

"Yes," Holly gasped.

Her entire body undulated, pressing back into him rhythmically.

"More," Holly begged. "More, master!"

Turned on by her begging, Dan thrust hard and fast, *slap, slap, slap*, pumping away in perfect time with her undulating body until Holly cried out in her elven tongue, overwhelmed with passion, and they came together in waves of throbbing pleasure.

Afterward, they lay in a panting, sweating tangle of arms and legs, laughing and kissing in the afterglow.

Eventually, Holly rose and padded off to the restroom on bare feet. Dan watched her go, marveling at her perfection and his luck.

He never wanted this to end. He couldn't let that evil bitch Dr. Lynch ruin everything. He needed to get some money, buy the textbook, and study like crazy before the midterm, which Dr. Lynch obviously expected him to fail.

He had to prove her wrong, had to stay in school.

Holly reappeared, and her beauty incinerated all thoughts of Dr. Lynch, academic troubles, or anything else.

"You're gorgeous," he told her. "You know that? Absolutely perfect."

"Thanks," she said, sliding back onto the bed and running her fingertips lightly across his chest. "And you are incredibly handsome, my big, strong barbarian."

"Your big, strong *master*, you mean," he teased, and they wrestled playfully, tickling and nipping at each other.

But after a while, he could see that she was still worried about Campus Quest.

"Relax," he told her. They had already been over it a bunch of times. "Nadia said she had somebody. We're meeting him tomorrow morning."

"Yeah," she said, "right before tryouts. What if he doesn't show? What if he doesn't work out?"

Dan held her head in both hands and kissed her forehead. "You're making yourself crazy with this," he said. "What's the big deal, anyway? Worst case scenario, we don't get to try out for Campus Quest."

Her eyes grew large, filled with something like panic. "Don't even say that."

"I mean it, though," he said. "I hope the guy works out, we get into the games, and win the whole thing, but if not, so what? I mean, what's in it for you?" He grinned. "Other than getting to spend more time with me, of course?"

Holly gave him a playful punch to the shoulder. "Just because I have you wrapped around my little finger doesn't mean that it's mutual, barbarian."

But then Holly grew more serious. "There's the prize money, for starters. I honestly don't need much. If we win, you and Nadia can split the lion's share."

"All right," he said. "Money, then. How much are we talking?"

"Fifty thousand gold pieces."

Dan's jaw dropped, and for a second, he just stared at her.

His share of fifty thousand gold pieces would solve a lot of problems. He wouldn't need the scholarship, for starters. He could tell Dr. Lynch to shove that parchment up her ass. "That much? Really?"

"Really," she said, nodding, her eyes out of focus, her expression distant and troubled.

He caressed her cheek. "It's not about the money for you, is it? Tell me the truth. Why is Campus Quest so important to you?"

She shook her head, looking hesitant. "I'm afraid if I tell you, you won't like me anymore."

He rolled his eyes. "Fat chance! Give it up, woman. Tell me what's going on."

She looked doubtful. "You really want to know?"

"I do," he assured her. "Tell me everything."

## HOLLY'S CONFESSION

olly gazed at him for several seconds, and once again, he was struck by her purple eyes. They shone with sharp intelligence, which he found very sexy, but beneath that glimmer, he sensed so much soul... compassion and emotion and what felt like wisdom, the sort of wisdom gained only by having endured a life of rigorous challenges.

Holly's smile faded, and her eyes went serious. "You know that I'm old, right?"

Dan ran his eyes up and down her perfection. "You sure don't look it."

"We grey elves age far more slowly than you humans," Holly said. She hesitated, seeming to summon courage before continuing. "How old are you, anyway?"

"Nineteen."

Holly laughed, sounding sad. "Nineteen," she said, and shook her head. "Such a bright, fresh flame."

"Are you calling me hot?"

Holly smirked. "How old are your parents?"

"Mom's thirty-nine," he said, then thought for a few

seconds, doing the math. "Dad will be forty-four next month."

Holly bit her lip, looking very much like a troubled twenty-year-old. "My parents are over a thousand years old."

"Whoa," Dan said. "That's one hell of a generation gap."

She laughed again, but he could see that she was still concerned. Then she said, "And Dan... you should know... well..."

"What? Spit it out."

"I'm one hundred and forty-nine years old."

He shrugged. "So?"

"So," she said, "that means that when your father was born, I was already over a hundred years old. Doesn't that freak you out?"

He kissed her inner thigh. The flesh there was soft and supple, the skin smooth and flawless, the muscles beneath relaxed but powerful. "Not at all," he said truthfully. "Should it?"

"No," Holly said, obviously relieved. "But you never know what might freak out you crazy barbarians. You and your primitive superstitions."

"Any superstition that would keep me away from you isn't a superstition worth keeping." He smoothed a hand up her leg. "You're cool and smart and fun, and you're hot as hell. I don't give a damn how old you are."

Holly smiled and kissed him. "I'm glad you're not freaked out. Honestly, I don't feel old at all. As a grey elf, I'm just leaving my 'teen' years."

"Makes sense," he said. "But what does all of this have to do with Campus Quest?"

Holly said, "Until I came here a year ago, I had never left the grove. For over forty years, I was a child. I ran and played, sang and danced, and learned the ways of the forest. I read adventure stories and mythology and the tales of famous elves, some of whom were my relatives.

"But the next century, things got more serious. Grey elves are the keepers of knowledge. That's our job in the world—to endure and keep the knowledge. That's why we stay tucked away in our fortresses in the woods. When my grandmother died, The Great Council gave her seat to my father, making him one of only nine True Druids in the world."

"Wow," Dan said, impressed.

"Yeah," Holly said. "Very wow. My older brother, Briar, cares only for wine and blood. He has a terrible temper and is a great swordsman and protector. Someday, he will become the Lord Protector of the grove, but he will never be a druid. My little sister, Lily, certainly knows the wilderness well enough to become a great druid, but she is too wild for books and studying. My parents expect me to follow my father and carry on the family legacy."

"Sounds like a lot of pressure," Dan said.

"My father is a very serious man," Holly said, "and my mother is a grove scholar. Her life is spent inside books. To both of them, my coming here was absurd. Grey elves don't mingle with other races, and they certainly don't attend college. My parents were dead set against it. They consider college a dangerous distraction."

"How did you get them to let you come here?" he asked.

"I begged them for decades," she said. "I pouted and reasoned and bartered. Finally, I wore them down like steady rain on stone."

"Well," he said, "I'm glad you did."

Holly laughed. "So says the man kissing his way up the inside of my thigh."

"Guilty as charged," Dan said with a grin, and started moving upward from her knee.

She stopped him before he could rise any higher. "Wait," she said. "Hear me out. Then I'll let you ravage me."

He smiled up at her. "That's good to know."

"Coming here, experiencing something outside of the forest, was important to me," she said. "After graduation, I'll return home and spend the next several hundred years protecting the forest and the animals and doing my best to become a great druid. After that, I'll spend my remaining five hundred or a thousand years in the Grove of Knowledge, our great library, reading and adding to the books. This is my last chance to experience life outside the forest."

"Whoa," he said. "Is that what you want?"

She frowned. "I don't know. But I do know one thing. I want to enjoy my time here. Last year was a big adjustment."

"I'll bet."

"But for the next three years, I'm going to have fun and store up exciting experiences. That's why Campus Quest is so important to me." She smiled. "It's so big and bright and loud, so… over the top. It's the opposite of life in the grove.

"I'm not looking to impress anyone by competing. I don't need the money, and I certainly don't want to be famous. I'm not looking to prove anything to my parents. In fact, if we do win, I won't even tell anyone back home.

"Campus Quest is for me. That's it. I really want this experience.

"And yes, I want to win. I think it would be really exciting. I want to experience the rush that you humans feel. Just once, I'd like to stand there, victorious, in front of 80,000 people, burning like a bright, fresh flame."

An embarrassed laugh escaped Holly, and she blushed. "Wow, I guess that all sounds pretty lame, huh?"

"Well," he said, "considering the part about spending another thousand years or so hitting the books, no, it doesn't

sound lame at all. I'll do whatever I can to help you win."
Then he started kissing up her leg again.

Grinning, Holly smacked his head playfully. "Oh, you silly
barbarian. Why am I even telling you all of this?"

"Because you're crazy about me," Dan said and plunged
his mouth between her legs.

Holly purred, slid her hands onto his head, and grabbed
two handfuls of hair. "Yes," she said. "I could go crazy for
you. For a time, anyway. What are you doing for the next
three years?"

Dan lifted his head and smiled up at her. "You're looking
at it."

# THE MAN, THE MYTH, THE MONKEY

D an couldn't quit grinning. He stood there, holding hands with Holly and panning his gaze back and forth across Nadia's dorm room.

He couldn't believe his eyes, couldn't believe the stuffed animals and cheery photo collages, the Penn State paraphernalia, and the posters. Especially the posters! Cutesy posters with little kids hugging, panoramic landscape shots with motivational captions about hope and following dreams, and one poster with a fuzzy little kitten dangling comically from a rope, captioned, *Hang in there!*

"This is hilarious," he said, beaming with amusement.

"What?" Nadia said with a dangerous look on her face. She was dressed in her good-girl attire. Once again, she looked like a cheery, innocent RA, not an experienced thief with heavy connections in the underground.

Dan twisted, spreading his arms. "Everything," he said. "It's all so pink and girly, so *normal!*"

"Yeah, yeah," Nadia said, and slapped her ass. "Bite me."

"Don't tempt him," Holly said. "Why do you think I'm wearing a turtleneck?"

Nadia gave Dan a dismissive wave. "Barbarian boy couldn't handle me."

"Which version?" he asked.

"Either version," Nadia said. "Now look, about this guy we're going to meet, I wanted to tell you a few things."

Holly smiled.

She hadn't slept at all last night. Part of that was Dan's fault, but mostly she had just been too nervous. Dan had awakened a few times throughout the night to find her lying there, staring up at the ceiling.

For as much as Dan hated the idea of working with a magic user, he hoped that this guy would turn out to be the real deal. Anything to help Holly reach her dream.

And to help me win the prize money, he thought. Right now, he couldn't even afford *Riddles from the Past*, the textbook that he was supposed to be studying.

The library's copy was marked as missing, and the university bookstore wanted one hundred and ten gold pieces for a used copy!

He had stood there in the bookstore and flipped through the pages, thinking that he might do a little studying then and there, but the thirty chapters that he was supposed to read took up four hundred pages of tiny print. After thirty seconds of reading, his eyes had glazed over.

*Riddles from the Past* was incredibly dry. And no surprise, considering the author... none other than Dr. G.K. Lynch herself!

Privately, he worried that Dr. Lynch was right. Maybe he really was too stupid and too lazy to even read her book.

*I have to do it*, he thought. *I have to get the book and study it, or my college days are over.*

Unless they won Campus Quest, of course. Then he'd have enough money to carry on without the scholarship.

"His name is Zeke," Nadia said.

"Well, that's promising," Dan said sarcastically.

Holly squeezed his hand, and he reined himself in.

"He's just down the hall," Nadia said. "But before you meet him, keep in mind that it was very difficult to find a wizard on such short notice."

"Understood," Holly said. "You're a miracle worker. We love you for it."

Nadia smiled uncomfortably. "What I'm trying to say is that Zeke is... atypical."

"Atypical?" Holly asked.

"Nontraditional," Nadia said.

"As in a nontraditional student?" Dan said. "So he's old and weird?"

"Nontraditional does not mean old and weird," Nadia said, actually sounding like an RA. "Zeke has just had a different path than a typical student."

Dan laughed. "Last year, when I lived in the freshman dorms, a nontraditional student lived down the hall. He was about thirty, ex-military, and listened to horrible 70s music. Left toenail clippings all over his dorm floor. You walked in there, it sounded like you were walking on crusty snow."

"Ew," the girls chorused.

Dan shrugged. "But the guy bought us booze, so he was okay. Sort of..."

Holly squeezed his hand again. "It's almost eleven," she said nervously. "Campus Quest starts in an hour. Let's go meet this guy."

They headed down the hall.

Nadia stopped outside the last room on the left. Weird, trippy music was coming from inside.

Then Dan recognized it. Pink Floyd, *Dark Side of the Moon*. Which song, he couldn't say.

"One more thing," Nadia said. "Are either of you allergic to monkeys?"

Holly shook her head.

"What?" Dan said. "Monkeys?"

Nadia knocked on the door.

A strange voice called, "Enter at your own risk!"

Stepping into the room, Dan felt a double wave of revulsion.

The first wave was because he was entering a wizard's home. Just the thought of magic made his skin crawl.

The second wave of revulsion was in response to the room itself.

The place was a wreck. Overflowing bags of trash sat on the floor, surrounded by dirty laundry and countless takeout boxes. Fly strips corkscrewed down from the ceiling. The stale air smelled of rotting food, dirty socks, and the unmistakable odor of old people.

Or rather, the odor of one old person.

And a monkey.

They sat across from one another at a chess table. Zeke hunched over the pieces, a tangle of wild, bright white hair hanging down his back.

Across from him, the monkey bounced excitedly up and down.

"Make your move!" the old man demanded, sounding surly.

The monkey took a pull off of a bottle of yellow liquid, wiped his mouth with a furry forearm, and stared at the chessboard with his dark eyes glistening like oil drops. His fur was the color of charcoal, save for a peppering of gray across the muzzle and a little white patch at the top of his skull.

*The only thing he's missing is an organ to grind,* Dan thought.

The monkey's lips peeled back in a fearsome grin, bearing a mouth packed to little white teeth and sharp looking canines. He leaned forward and moved a chess piece. Then he squealed triumphantly, stood up on the chair, and raised his skinny arms overhead, chittering wild monkey laughter and spilling yellow liquid all over the place.

"You drunk son-of-a-bitch!" the old man said, and swung his arm, knocking pieces off the board. "Not again!"

Dan shot Nadia a look. "This is Zeke? This is our wizard?"

Nadia nodded, smiling awkwardly.

Dan tugged Holly's hand. "Come on. Let's go."

"Wait," Holly whispered. "Spellcasters can be eccentric. Let's at least talk to him."

"If you insist," Dan grumbled.

Zeke stood to face them. He was old. Really old. Like eighty or something. His beard was just as white as his hair and even longer and crazier looking. But his bulging blue eyes took the crazy prize.

"Any of you kids a chess master?" Zeke asked. "I need somebody to knock this cocky bastard down a peg or two."

Behind Zeke, the monkey tilted the bottle and chugged long gulps of yellow liquid. The floor beneath him was littered with empty bottles and orange peels.

Zeke stared bitterly at the monkey, shaking his head. "He stays up all night drinking banana beer and eating oranges, but do you think I can beat him? No!"

Dan experienced a fresh wave of trepidation. Because all of a sudden, he recognized Zeke.

Not as a person, but as a type.

Zeke was exactly the sort of magic user that showed up again and again in Willis's adventures. If Dan's suspicions were correct, Zeke would turn out to be one of two types of quirky wizard.

Most likely, he would provide comic relief and a couple of magic missiles, the bare minimum to allow them to join the Campus Quest competition.

Dan shuddered at the only other possibility. Zeke might actually be powerful. *Really* powerful—and completely insane.

Introductions were made. Zeke referred to himself as Zeke of the Planes.

"The Great Plains?" Holly asked.

Zeke looked at her like she was crazy. "Not Plains, *Planes*," he said, and waggled his arms overhead. "Alternate universes and realities, the various planes of existence, high, low, and right here, smack dab in the middle. I've traveled them all, not to mention the Between!"

Zeke burst out laughing as if he'd said something hilarious.

The girls smiled, but Dan glowered at the guy.

Zeke bounced his shaggy white eyebrows up and down at the girls. Then, noticing Dan's sour expression, he narrowed his blue eyes and made a face like somebody had cut the cheese.

The monkey was hitting the bottle and picking up the chess pieces.

Holly went over and crouched down next to him. "And who's this little fella?"

The monkey offered an enthusiastic grin.

"That is my traveling companion, familiar, and room-mate, Zugzwang," Zeke said. "Or, as I call him, Zuggy."

The little monkey took another pull off the bottle and stuck his other paw out to Holly.

Holly tittered and shook the little hand. "Very nice to meet you, Zuggy," she said. "May I pet you?"

"Oh, he would love that," Zeke said. Then, glancing toward Dan, he added, "I wouldn't say the same to your male companion, though. Zuggy hates assholes."

"Hey," Dan said, taking a step forward.

"No offense, sonny," Zeke said, raising his palms defensively. "I'm just an old man, and old men are allowed to say weird shit."

Holly leaned over and scratched Zuggy on his white spot.

"Where did you get him?" Nadia asked.

"I won Zuggy many years ago, throwing dice with the Ebon Corsair, the most feared pirate of the Ivory Coast. The Ebon Corsair had three trademarks. He used his sharpened teeth as weapons in battle, decorated his ship with the decapitated heads of rival captains, and stayed drunk day and night on a highly alcoholic banana mash."

"Yeah," Dan interrupted, "this is all super interesting, buddy, but Campus Quest kicks off in half an hour. Are you really a wizard, or are we just wasting our time here?"

Turning to Nadia, Zeke asked, "I can't understand a word that this guy says. Does he always mumble so much?"

Holly yelped with surprise. Zuggy had jumped into her lap. He threw his long arms around her and nuzzled into her bosom. Holly laughed. "What a little cutie!"

Zeke licked his lips. "That monkey stays drunk all the time. Banana mash is his poison. I tried to dry him out, but he got the DTs so bad. Night terrors and everything. Poor little fella sounded so pitiful, whimpering in the night. Finally, I just gave in. As long as I keep him drunk, he's happy. And he really is one hell of a chess player."

Nadia glanced at her watch. "So, Zeke, you were telling me that you are experienced with magic."

"Oh yeah," Zeke said distractedly, watching as Zuggy chattered at Holly and held the bottle to her lips.

Holly laughed and pushed the bottle away. "None for me, thank you, Mr. Zuggy. It's not even noon yet."

"Either of you have questions for Zeke?" Nadia asked Dan and Holly.

*Yeah*, Dan wanted to say, *which variety of Willis's crazy old wizards are you, Zeke? The comic relief variety, or the holy-shit-*

*why-did-he-just-summon-a-gorgon-while-we're-trying-to-talk-our-way-through-the-city-gates variety?*

Holly stood. "I don't have any questions."

The monkey still clung to her, one arm thrown around her neck. Zuggy leaned away, swinging his bottle back and forth, like a drunken pirate hanging from the mainmast.

Holly beamed. "I have a really good feeling about this. Thank you so much for joining our team, Zeke."

"No problem," Zeke said, and cackled madly. Then he glanced at Dan with seeming confusion. "What are we doing again?"

Dan squeezed his fists and gritted his teeth. They were screwed!

# CAMPUS QUEST

"Wow," Dan said as he and the girls navigated the chaotic celebration that was opening day of Campus Quest.

The day was perfect, warm for October but not too warm, the sky overhead a brilliant, cloudless blue. Music blasted overtop excited cheering, laughter, and a thousand shouted conversations.

The HUB Lawn was packed with event stations, vendor booths, waiting teams, and excited spectators, many of whom wore face paint and carried signs in support of one team or another. A lot of the signs belonged to sororities, fraternities, and campus organizations like ROTC, but Dan saw a lot of ragtag independent teams with names like the Lionesses of Lyons, the Pugh Street Pugilists, and the Beasts from East.

When they reached registration, Dan looked around with a sinking feeling in his stomach. "Where is Zeke?"

Nadia narrowed her eyes, scanning the crowd. "I don't see him."

"Relax, guys," Holly said, beaming. "He said that he'll be here."

Holly had undergone an amazing transformation. Given the buildup to all of this, Dan would've expected her to be a bundle of nerves, but she was relaxed and happy, soaking in the moment.

Meanwhile, his own guts were twisting with anxiety.

He was sick of being broke. Sick of worrying about his scholarship. Sick of people like Dr. Lynch lording their power over him. He needed to win this money.

"Well, Zeke had better hurry," Nadia said. She was back in thief mode, looking super-sexy in high black boots, a skintight black bodysuit, and a little black mask. "Registration closes in fifteen minutes."

Dan paced as time bled away.

"Ten minutes!" someone called from the registration tent. "We close in ten minutes!"

The registration lines dwindled and died away. Every other team apparently had its shit together enough to at least register on time.

"Five minutes!" the official called. Then, spotting Dan and the girls, the official asked if they'd registered yet.

"No," Dan bellowed. "Our son-of-a-"

"Not yet!" Holly interjected cheerily. "We're waiting on our wizard."

Dan paced back and forth, mumbling curses and bloody oaths as the minutes drained away.

"Last call!" the official shouted. "Folks?"

Dan shook his fists at the sky. Why? Why did they have to put their faith in a wizard? Anyone with half a brain knew that you could never trust a sorcerer. Sure, Campus Quest had been a long shot, but at least they'd had a chance, no matter how small. Now…

"He's here!" Holly chimed sweetly, stepping over to registration. "Our wizard is here."

Zeke stepped into view, scratching his beard and looking bored, confused, or both.

"Where have you been?" Nadia asked. Dan didn't miss the edge to her voice. For one reason or another, this competition was obviously important to her, too.

"And what the hell are you wearing?" Dan asked.

Zeke took a second to examine his own clothing - a funny little cowboy hat and a bright poncho fringed with tassels. "Just my normal attire. Why?"

"You're a wizard," Dan said. "Shouldn't you be wearing, oh, I don't know, something wizard-y like a robe?"

"This is my Clint Eastwood look," Zeke said with a crooked smile.

"Which movie?" Dan said. "*The Weird, the Bad, and the Ugly?*"

Holly called them over to registration. "We have to choose a team name," Holly said, as the official looked on impatiently.

Nadia glanced doubtfully at her teammates and said, "How about the Noobs?"

"I love it!" Holly said. "Dan? Zeke? Are you guys cool with that name?"

Dan shrugged. "Sure." He would've preferred a more ominous name, like the Life Stealers or the Death Dealers, but ultimately, he supposed that it didn't really matter.

All that mattered was winning the money.

They each got their assignments, an event station number, and a time. Holly first, then Nadia, and then Zeke. Dan would fight last. And for Dan, it would be a fight.

Today's competition tested the class skills of each team member, so Dan would be fighting. He wished that he could just fight now and get it over with, but he was the last of the team; and because they'd been the last team to register, he was probably the last competitor of the day, period.

Great.

No pressure, Dan.

Moving away from the paths and behind the booths toward the center of the HUB Lawn, they found a grassy patch to stretch out and wait.

On all sides, teams were warming up and spectators were blasting music, catching rays, and tossing frisbees. Nearby, a group of girls in bikinis and shirtless guys poured a bottle of grain alcohol into a gigantic watermelon. Partying hard at noon...

Holly found a space to herself and started praying.

*She's praying to the sun,* Dan thought, but he couldn't be sure.

Nadia started stretching out, twisting at the waist, touching her toes, and drawing the attention of basically every male in the vicinity. Except Zeke, who was shifting around, adjusting his poncho, apparently having some sort of weird wardrobe malfunction.

Turning to Zeke, Dan realized that the white-haired weirdo had actually shown a shred of professionalism. Deciding to give credit where credit was due, he said, "At least you left your drunken sidekick at home."

The monkey's head had popped out of Zeke's poncho with a screech.

"Whoa!" Dan said, staggering backward with surprise.

"Don't go wettin' your pants, sonny," Zeke cackled. "It's just Zuggy."

The monkey crawled free of the poncho, hauling a half-empty bottle of banana beer after it. His fur stuck out in all directions, and his bleary eyes squinted in the bright light of day. The monkey sat down hard in the grass, shook his head, and started drinking again.

"He looks like forty miles of rough road," Dan said.

Zeke stretched out on the grass beside the monkey and pulled his ridiculous cowboy hat over his eyes, siesta style. "Poor little fella's hungover," Zeke said. "That's why he never sleeps. Give him fifteen minutes of shuteye, and he's hungover."

Holly came over, beaming, and kissed Dan. "I'm so happy."

"Happiness looks good on you," he said. "Are you ready?"

"Absolutely," she said, then watched as Nadia did a front walkover and slid smoothly into a full split. "You look hot, Nadia!"

Nadia stuck out her tongue, stood, and did a series of three fast backflips.

"Crom," Dan said. "She's really good."

Holly nodded. "I feel a little guilty, honestly. She's a pretty accomplished thief. She could've signed on with a way more experienced team."

"Speaking of thieves," Dan said, and pointed to where Zeke lay in the grass, already snoring. Zuggy was rooting through the wizard's pockets. The monkey withdrew a fistful of sparkling coins and staggered away into the crowd.

Dan was just about to wish Zuggy good riddance when a voice spoke up behind him.

"Well, well, well," the voice said in an all-too-familiar, taunting whine. "If it isn't Danielle!"

Growling, Dan turned.

Grady and a gang of gnolls leered down at him in *Alpha Alpha Alpha* shirts.

"They'll let anybody into this competition," one of Grady's frat brothers chimed in. The others yipped their horrible hyena laughter.

Then Grady spotted Holly. "Hey, girl, why don't you ditch Danielle and bring that fine body over here."

Dan ripped Wulfgar free of his sheath. The two-handed sword roared a stream of curses.

Grady dropped back a step, and a sliver of curved steel snickered from its scabbard. "Go ahead and try it, Danielle," he sneered. Around him, a dozen frat-boy gnolls drew steel.

Dan set his shoulders.

"Take out the one talking all the shit," Wulfgar advised. "Then drive right through the middle. They'll cut each other trying to get at you."

Dan nodded and stepped forward.

Holly's hand stopped him. "Don't, Dan," she said. "There are too many of them."

Dan shook free. He didn't care how many there were. He was going to water the grass with their blood.

At that moment, a man in chainmail appeared, wagging a finger at Dan and the gnolls. "Save it for the events," the guard said. "Any unauthorized fighting will result in expulsion from Campus Quest."

Grady laughed nastily and sheathed his scimitar. His frat brothers followed suit.

"You losers aren't worth our time," Grady sneered. "Have fun getting eliminated today. If you want to look for us, we'll be the ones winning the whole competition."

Grady and his asshole friends strutted away, cackling mad hyena laughter.

25

READY, SET, GO!

After a while, the monkey came waddling back, straining mightily beneath the weight of a beer ball, complete with a tap on top. He plunked the mini keg down beside the snoring wizard, stretched out on his back, and poured an amber stream into his open mouth.

Dan watched with amazement until Nadia tugged his arm. At last, it was time for Holly to compete.

"Come on, Zeke," Dan called.

Zeke sputtered out of sleep and lifted the brim of his hat just enough to squint up at Dan.

"Wake up," Dan said. "Holly's about to compete."

Zeke waved him off, laid his head back down, and let the hat slide over his eyes again.

"Let me sleep," the old wizard said. "I was dreaming of other planes. At least, I *think* it was just a dream."

*Worthless*, Dan thought, and followed Nadia and Holly across the lawn to a small roped-off area.

Three judges in green robes sat at a table. Before them, a nervous-looking druid with a sprig of mistletoe in each hand was stumbling through an incantation.

Nothing happened.

The judges frowned. One of them, a grim-looking halfling with gray hair, thanked the druid for participating and sent her away.

A few more druids followed. The judges asked each a series of questions, then had him or her demonstrate a spell. Most did better than the first girl, but no one did anything really impressive.

Holly smiled, hands on hips, springing up and down on her toes and twitching her butt back and forth like a sprinter before a big race.

When it was finally Holly's turn, Dan kissed her cheek and whispered, "You got this, babe."

"Woo-hoo!" Nadia cheered, and clapped wildly. "Let's go, Holly! Noob power!"

Holly stepped forward and announced herself to the judges.

All three judges looked up from their clipboards with surprised expressions.

The gnome cleared his throat. "Holly Thorn of Rothrock? Are you the daughter of the Iron Druid?"

Holly nodded, not looking particularly pleased to have been recognized.

The judges stood and bowed to Holly.

Holly smiled uncomfortably, thanked them, and returned the bow.

The gnome asked a series of questions, mostly stuff about the forest and animals and different rituals. Holly answered everything smoothly. Then the gnome asked which spell she was going to demonstrate.

"I will bring an animal under my thrall," Holly said.

"What animal?" the gnome asked.

One of the other judges pointed to a faraway rooftop, where a small black speck sat, looking no larger than a flake of pepper on an elephant. "A small sparrow perches on the eaves of Atherton Hall. Of course, the bird is very far away…"

Dan could tell that the judge was proposing an unusually ambitious challenge, probably testing the guts and power of the Iron Druid's daughter.

Holly nodded. She fluttered a leaf of mistletoe through the air while speaking in Elvish. Then she moved her lips again, emitting not words but birdsong.

Dan couldn't believe it. Holly sounded just like a bird. Unfortunately, there was no way that the little bird would hear her at this distance, not over the pounding music and cheering.

To his surprise, the bird hopped from its perch and took flight, soaring over the crowds, growing larger and more distinct as it came closer and closer, until it fluttered down and landed on Holly's staff.

Holly cheeped and twittered.

The bird hopped along the staff, climbed up Holly's arm, and perched atop her shoulder, singing happily.

Holly responded with birdsong. The little bird tilted its head at her, then twittered a response.

Holly laughed and turned to the judges with a smile. "This little fellow is quite confused," she said. "With all the people milling around, he was sure that the grass was full of worms, but it hasn't rained for days."

The judges laughed.

"Well done," the judge who had challenged Holly said, nodding in approval. "Well done, indeed."

Nadia's event turned out to be an obstacle course. Over a hundred thieves lined up, waiting their turn.

Nadia cracked her knuckles, rolled her head in a wide circle, first one way, then the other, like a fighter getting ready to enter the ring. "Wish me luck," she said.

Holly popped onto her toes and gave Nadia a quick kiss. "Good luck! You're going to do great!"

Nadia turned to Dan, her green eyes shining brightly from within the mask. She gave him a sarcastic smile. "Don't even think about trying to kiss me."

He laughed. "Dream on. Good luck. And hey, if the going gets rough, just pretend you're that little kitten from your poster. Hang in there!"

She flipped him the bird and got into line.

The thieves had to run, jump, tumble, climb a two-story wall without a rope, and pick a lock. The whole thing was timed.

The event moved with surprising efficiency. The course was wide enough for three competitors to run at the same time.

Some were surprisingly unathletic. They ran slowly, couldn't jump far, and tumbled like pieces of dropped luggage.

A few, on the other hand, were fantastically athletic.

Most were in the middle.

At one point, Holly elbowed Dan. "Watch this guy," she said, pointing to a wiry elf at the starting line. "You remember when I told you about the pros, how some of them enroll in college just so they can participate in Campus Quest? Well, you're looking at one."

Wondering how she knew, Dan took a closer look. The guy was older, the elven equivalent of a human in his late twenties. His amber eyes were serious and confident.

An official shouted, starting the race.

The pro was fast. He sprinted out away from the others, leapt over the first obstacle, tumbled under the next barrier, popped up, and sprinted to the ravine, where he leapt into the air, latched onto the rope, swung over the void, and landed softly on the other side.

He hit the wall running. Already way ahead of his competitors, the wiry elf flew up the wall faster than a spider, swung his legs over the top, and dropped two stories to the ground. He sprinted to the next barrier, a freestanding wall with three heavy doors, and set to work on the lock. A second later, the door swung wide open, and he was through in a flash. He crossed the finish line, shattering the standing record by a full minute. The crowd erupted with applause.

Several more waves went. Then it was Nadia's turn.

"Come on, Nadia!" Dan shouted.

Beside him, Holly whispered prayers.

Nadia crouched at the starting line. Then the judge shouted for them to start.

Nadia moved in a black blur. She was way faster than the other thieves, almost as fast as the pro. She rocketed through the initial obstacles, scaled the wall with superhuman speed, dropped to the other side, and sprinted to the locked door. This, too, she conquered with insane speed. She shot through the door and sprinted to the finish line.

Dan and Holly cheered wildly.

Nadia was in second place!

Holly hugged Dan fiercely then stepped back, her purple eyes shining with excitement. "Can you believe this? We're doing great! We have a real shot at making the next round!"

Dan hugged her, feeling simultaneously excited and nervous. The nervousness was a surprise. But then again, his earlier fretting had surprised him, too, showing up uninvited like a long-lost relative that he'd never much liked.

He had thought that he had picked up enough of Wulfgar's belligerent boldness to be done with all that painful half-stepping forever. But here he was, starting to churn again. And once again, it all came down to money.

He really, really wanted to win this competition. Sure, it was a long shot. He had known that all along. But somehow, seeing how well the girls had done, realizing that winning was actually a possibility, made things worse. Suddenly, he realized that their failure or success depended on his performance.

Nadia rejoined them, boiling over with happiness. She gave Holly a big hug and surprised Dan by hugging him, too.

He felt the warmth of her cheek against his face and her firm breasts pressed into his chest.

Something in him stirred.

But then it was all laughter and congratulations, and the trio moved back downhill to wake Zeke, who was up next.

Returning to their patch of grass, they looked around, stunned.

No Zeke, no monkey, no beer keg.

"Where the hell is Zeke?" Nadia asked.

"Wizards," Dan growled.

But Holly kept smiling. "I'm sure he knows what he's doing. He probably woke up and went off to compete."

They pushed through the crowd and made their way to the wizard trials. Dan tensed as they moved through the area, which was split into dozens of roped-off rings. At the center of each ring, a wizard performed spells.

Off to the left, a young wizard in shiny orange robes swept his arms frantically and bugled what sounded like an epic incantation. Unfortunately, his voice broke toward the end. There was a loud crack, a bright flash, and the orange-clad kid flew twenty feet into the air. Squealing with terror, he plummeted back to earth, hit hard, and lay in a pitiful heap.

Onlookers gasped sympathetically. Then one section of spectators exploded in wild, crazy laughter.

"What an asshole!" Grady shouted, pointing at the inca-pacitated wizard. His frat brothers yelped and squealed with cruel laughter.

*Assholes*, Dan thought. *One of these days...*

They reached the end of the wizard rings with no sign of Zeke.

"Where is he?" Dan grumbled. "You guys kicked so much ass. If he messes this up..."

"I'm really sorry," Nadia said. "He was the best I could do on short notice."

"Lighten up, guys," Holly said, still smiling. "There's no reason to think–a ha! There he is."

Zeke seemed to appear out of nowhere.

Zuggy sat on his shoulder. Barely. The monkey was weaving back and forth and holding on to a patch of Zeke's poncho with one paw. Seeing Holly, the monkey squealed with delight and started to bounce up and down. Then he seemed to think the better of it and hunkered back down again, weaving uneasily.

Zeke held the half-empty beer ball in one hand.

Zeke looked sour. "Zuggy's shitfaced," he said. He nodded downhill. "I'm taking him downtown for a cheesesteak before he starts a fight or something."

"What are you talking about?" Dan said. "You can't leave."

Zeke rolled his eyes. "Watch me," he said, and started walking away.

"But it's time for your event," Nadia called after him.

"Stop your fretting, little girl," Zeke called back over his shoulder. "I already went."

"How did you do?" Dan, Holly, Nadia all yelled in unison.

But the mage and his monkey had already disappeared into the crowd.

"I'm sure he did fine," Holly said. She was still smiling, though it looked a bit forced now.

Holly grabbed Dan and Nadia by the arms and started pulling them through the crowd. "Come on. You're up next, Dan!"

# FIGHT!

Five minutes later, they stood before a tall wall of black plywood.

The walled area was massive, taking up a quarter of the HUB Lawn, maybe more. From crowd gossip, they had learned that the inside of the structure was like a maze, with narrow hallways connecting a bunch of slapped-together fighting pits. No one knew who was fighting whom or what the rules of engagement were.

Dan had the world's worst case of butterflies. Like, giant carnivorous butterflies that could only be hit by magical weapons... and only on Tuesdays.

Seeing fighters limping away, nursing grievous injuries, Dan understood that he could lose a hand, a limb, or even his head here, but that wasn't his concern.

He didn't fear combat, dismemberment, or even death.

He feared failure.

If he fought well, the Noobs might move on to compete another day, with a shot at gold and glory.

If he fumbled, however, he wouldn't just flush his future down the toilet. He'd crush the girls' dreams, too.

Holly squeezed him arm and gave him a warm smile. "Lighten up. Nobody can beat my big, strong barbarian!"

Dan forced a smile.

Then Nadia kicked him in the ass and laughed. "Don't mess this up, buttercup!"

An official appeared in the narrow doorway, pointed at Dan, and beckoned for him to follow.

Holly gave Dan a kiss for luck, and he joined the official at the entrance.

"Name and team?" the man asked.

"Dan Marshall," Dan said. Then, feeling stupid, he added, "The Noobs."

The official raised his brows, letting Dan know what he thought of the name, marked his clipboard, and led Dan into a narrow hallway.

On either side, black plywood walls rose twenty feet in the air. Here and there, they passed a door. The walls were too high to see inside the fighting areas, but the thin plywood didn't do much to block the clash and clamor of combat or the telltale smells of blood and piss and shit.

The ground at his feet was spongy, almost swampy. He looked down and realized that it was sodden with blood that had soaked out from beneath the plywood barriers.

To his left, something thudded loudly into a door. The whole wall shivered with impact. A mad scratching started at the door, and a whimpering voice pleaded, "Let me out of here! I don't want to play anymo—"

Another thud, another shiver, an inhuman roar, and the begging fighter's words whipped away in a bloodcurdling scream. Then the scream, too, cut off with a wet crunching sound.

"Ah, here we are," the official said, when they'd reached the next door. "Number nineteen. I'll lock the door behind you. When your opponent enters, it's a fight to the death, anything goes. You will be timed and judged on technique. Understand?"

Dan nodded. His heart was pounding, and his fingers tingled.

"Good luck, Noob," the official said, and opened the door.

Dan stepped through. The door closed and locked behind him, and he was standing in a square, high-walled fighting pit, thirty feet to a side. The ground was covered in well-churned sawdust that had turned pink with blood. The only other feature of note was a door in the opposite wall.

Watching the door, Dan drew his sword.

"Ye-ha-ha!" Wulfgar hollered. "Let's get barbaric!"

Dan wasn't feeling particularly barbaric. In fact, he was feeling a lot like old-world Dan… a bundle of nerves. "Who do you think we'll fight?"

Wulfgar snorted. "Doesn't matter!"

Dan nodded. But it did matter. Big time. "What if it's a pro?"

"Don't be a pussy," Wulfgar said. "Whoever comes through that door, you kill him. Got me?"

"Yeah, yeah," Dan said, staring at the door.

Was it his imagination, or was that door bigger than his?

He squinted, swinging Wulfgar back and forth.

Yeah, the door was bigger, at least a foot or two taller than the one he'd come through. Why would it be so much bigger?

A sound made him jump. An unseen man clearing his throat. Dan spun around but saw no one.

Then the man cleared his throat again, and Dan followed the sound, looking up.

A head was peering over one wall. Then Dan realized that someone was watching from the other side, too. Were those judges? They must have—

*BANG!*

The door flew open, smashing into the wall, and a huge man rushed out.

Dan huffed with surprise and lowered Wulfgar like a lance.

Easily six-and-a-half feet tall with a thickly muscled, green-skinned body armored in filthy rags and what looked like bloodstained splint mail, Dan's opponent had the head of a pig, complete with an upturned snout, short tusks, and wide-set beady eyes that burned with rage.

*An orc,* Dan realized, shock rooting him in place. *A huge orc!*

"Get him!" Wulfgar shouted.

Dan wanted to respond, but he was frozen in place. Not by fear but by shock. Everything was happening so quickly, and everything was so strange!

The orc lifted a bloody war hammer overhead, squealed an inhuman battle cry, and charged.

Wulfgar hollered, but Dan remained frozen, his mind racing as the orc charged. Should he sidestep and swing low? Block the hammer, spin away, and regroup?

But everything happened so fast…

The orc crossed the pit in a flash, while Dan felt like he was stuck in slow motion. This was nothing like gaming, nothing like training, nothing like—

The orc rushed forward, swinging the hammer down like a splitting axe.

And impaled himself on Dan's sword.

Wulfgar's point plunged into the orc's gut just above the beltline. The orc's momentum carried him forward, skewering him through the abdomen. Dan braced himself, not giving an inch.

The orc gave a squeal of pain and surprise. His hammer fell to the sawdust. He snorted, glaring at Dan with his hateful piggy eyes. He shoved himself forward, impaling himself in an effort to reach Dan with his gnarled and bloody hands.

But then the orc shuddered, went rigid with a guttural cry, and dropped to the ground, dead as two hundred and fifty pounds of the world's nastiest bacon.

## THE SKELLER

The bartender clunked four pitchers of beer on the bar. "Six silver," she said.

Dan slapped down an electrum piece. "Keep the change!" he shouted over the crowd noise. He was in a tipping mood. After qualifying for round two of Campus Quest, he was on top of the world!

The officials had allowed him to loot the orc's corpse. He'd come away with a dozen electrum pieces and the hammer, which he'd sold for eleven silver pieces in a shady weapon shop on Calder Way.

The bartender smiled, rang a bell behind the bar, and moved off to help another customer.

Dan carried the pitchers back to the booth. Holly greeted him with a big kiss and slid onto his lap. Across the table, Nadia grinned and rolled her eyes.

Zeke stood at the head of the table, pounding beers and occasionally shouting at Zuggy, who kept climbing on the table and dancing lewdly.

Overall, however, the wizard was clearly overjoyed. He

kept turning to glance gleefully about the crowded bar. "This is exactly why I came to college," Zeke announced.

Dan refilled everyone's mug. Even the monkey's. Screw it.

Holly took a drink, squirmed around in his lap, and leaned close. "Are you trying to get me drunk, barbarian?"

"Absolutely," he said, lowering his voice. He was pretty buzzed already. "Then I'm going to carry you back to my cave and fuck you so good that you're mine forever."

Holly kissed his ear, then nipped at it with her teeth. The warmth and sound of her breath covered him in goosebumps. "I already am," she said.

"Oh yeah?" he said, and realized that despite her playful smile, Holly's eyes were serious.

"Yours and yours alone, my love," she said.

Dan felt a rush of excitement. Maybe she was serious, maybe she wasn't. Back in the old-world, this wouldn't have been possible, but here?

"Works for me, love," he said, and kissed Holly hard on the mouth.

Nadia made fake gagging sounds, as if she was going to puke. "Get a room, you two. You're hurting my eyes."

"You're just jealous!" Holly said.

"Of him, maybe," Nadia said, grinning, "but not of you. I mean, kissing a barbarian?" And she launched into more fake retching.

Dan laughed.

He'd never been in a bar before, but Nadia had gotten them into the Skeller, no trouble.

It was awesome. So much energy, so much excitement.

Word had apparently spread about the Noobs earning a spot in Campus Quest's "Dirty Dozen," because people kept stopping by to congratulate them and hand them free beers.

He enjoyed telling and retelling the story of how he'd

killed the orc, though he left out the parts about freezing up and how the orc had pretty much killed itself.

After a while, Dan left the table to use the bathroom.

He was pretty drunk but not so drunk that he couldn't recognize that this was the longest piss that he or anyone else had ever taken in the history of taking pisses.

Leaving the bathroom, he planned to wrap things up and head home soon. Partying was fun, but he was excited to consummate the victory with Holly.

On his way back to the table, a stranger stopped him.

"My friend," the stranger said.

The guy was older, maybe thirty, with close-cropped black hair and a dark beard split by a terrible scar, which ran in a pale rope up one cheek to a filmy eye as gray and lifeless as a distant moon. The other eye gleamed a brilliant blue. The man was a few inches taller than Dan, with a narrow waist, broad shoulders, and a *lot* of scars.

"Hey," Dan said, offering a tentative smile.

"My congratulations to you," the man said with a strange accent, clapping Dan's shoulder. "Campus Quest!"

"Thanks."

"Very exciting for you, no? But you are strong, I see. A young barbarian, strong and fearless, no?"

Dan shrugged and glanced across the crowded room. He caught a glimpse of Zuggy perched atop Zeke's shoulder, gyrating like a go-go dancer while a semicircle of drunks laughed and chanted. "Anyway, thanks. I gotta get back to my friends."

The man grabbed his shoulder. The grip was incredibly strong, strong as iron.

"But we are talking, my friend," the stranger said. His smile was strained, and the blue eye burned with intensity. "Do not be rude, boy. I only mean to congratulate... and share a warning."

Dan pulled his shoulder free. "What warning?"

"Have your fun tonight," the man said. "Celebrate your victory. But do not be foolish. The competition, it is dangerous. The further it goes, the more dangerous, yes?"

"That's the idea," Dan said.

The man leaned close. "Lies," he hissed.

"Huh?"

"The final stage is a lie, boy. You have done well. Drink your beer. Love your woman. But next round? Maybe do not try so hard. The final stage is not for you. It is a death trap."

"Thanks for the warning, buddy," Dan said, "but I can take care of myself. You have a good night."

*What a weirdo.*

When Dan got back to the table, Holly said, "Fraternizing with the enemy, huh?"

"What do you mean?"

She pointed to where the big guy with the dead eye was now talking to a wiry, familiar-looking elf. It was the thief who'd won Nadia's event, the pro!

"He's on the Sell-Swords," Holly said. "What did he want?"

"Nothing," Dan said, watching the pair disappear into the crowd.

*The final stage is a death trap*, the man's words echoed in Dan's mind.

Had that been a warning... or a threat?

Whatever the case, Dan understood something then. Campus Quest was about to get way more complicated.

# MIDNIGHT STROLL WITH A DEATH TOLL

The streets were packed with people celebrating the Campus Quest kickoff. For as cool as it had been, partying in the Skeller, with waves of strangers swinging by the table to congratulate them and offer free drinks, there was something nice about being anonymous again.

The sidewalks were mobbed with drunks. Long lines waited outside every bar. Loud parties raged on every balcony of every high-rise apartment building. It was cool, floating along with the excited revelers, knowing that none of them recognized him or Holly as Campus Quest competitors.

They crossed the parking lot of Beaver Terrace, slipped past the towering apartment complex, and entered the quieter, more residential corner of town.

Just like that, everything changed.

Every now and then, a shout or peal of laughter would echo in the distance, but these streets were far darker and calmer than downtown. It was a beautiful night, cool but not cold, with patches of starry sky showing through the cloud cover. Here on the backstreets, it was quiet enough to hear the breeze whispering through the trees that arched over the sidewalks.

Dan and Holly walked hand in hand, sometimes talking, sometimes just swinging their arms back and forth, silently soaking in the night, the moment, everything. Dan was very drunk and very, very happy.

Holly surprised him by pulling him behind the hedge of a shadowy yard.

He started to ask her what she was doing, but she raised a finger to his lips and sunk slowly to her knees in the darkness behind the hedge.

Feeling Holly's hands undoing his belt buckle, Dan glanced around nervously. The street was quiet. Here and there, televisions flashed blue and white behind drawn curtains, but most of the houses were dark as tombs. The only sign of life was a black and white cat slinking along the opposite sidewalk.

Holly unsnapped and unzipped his pants.

He grabbed her hands. "We're almost home."

"A hesitant barbarian?" Holly laughed. "The wonders never cease."

Her voice seemed loud on the silent street. Dan looked around nervously. "Let's wait until we get home."

"No," she said, and took his shaft in her hands. "I've been wet for hours." She squeezed him. "I can't wait another second."

And then her mouth closed over him, wet and warm and very willing. Normally, Holly took her time, licking and kissing and teasing. Not tonight.

She gobbled him whole.

Holly took his entire length down her throat. Then she started bobbing her head up and down, slurping and moaning, and fondling his balls with one hand.

Clouds shifted overhead, bathing them in moonlight. Dan glanced down. Holly's blond hair looked silver in the moonlight. She squatted there before him, slurping and moaning. Her free hand plunged into her pants and started working between her legs.

Watching Holly was such a huge turn on. Hearing her muffled moans and the sounds of her wetness as she masturbated was an even bigger turn on. Pressure built quickly with Dan, and before he knew it, he was pushing lightly at her head, warning her, "I'm almost there."

She wouldn't let him push her head away. She sucked harder, pumping her head up and down, kneading his balls, and moaning more urgently as the hand in her pants worked.

Then he couldn't take it anymore. When he climaxed, Holly held half his length in her mouth, working his shaft with her hand and swallowing greedily as he pumped jet after jet of hot seed into her mouth.

He stifled his roar into a growl, trying not to wake the neighborhood, but once he had finished, Holly released him, gasping for air and cried out as she masturbated herself to a powerful orgasm.

Up and down the street, dogs began barking behind closed doors. The porch light of the closest house popped on.

"Oh shit," Dan whispered, and pulled up his pants.

Holly laughed, licking her lips, and rose.

The front door of the house swung open, and someone called into the night.

Dan and Holly ran toward home, laughing like maniacs.

When they turned onto their street, everything got bright and noisy. Across from their apartment house, *Alpha Alpha Alpha* was having a wild party. The frat house's porch was packed, and the front lawn was crowded, with whooping partiers dancing around a bonfire, chanting what Dan assumed was some fraternity victory song.

Unfortunately, Grady and his team of assholes had also made the Dirty Dozen.

*Go figure,* Dan thought.

"Come on," Holly said, tugging him across the darkened lawn behind their apartment house. "Let's go in the back and avoid those jerks altogether."

"To hell with that," he said, his inner barbarian rising up. "I'm not afraid of those assholes, and I'm not going to sneak around, trying to avoid them."

"Please?" Holly said, and bit her lip in a seriously cute way. Then she reached out, grabbed his crotch, and started tugging him toward the back of the apartment. "I want you to take me inside and fuck me."

"Well," he said, "since you asked so nicely…"

They hurried toward the back door but stopped when several figures in midnight blue cloaks stepped from behind trees.

The Acolytes of Eternal Darkness again!

Dan heard a thrumming sound, then a loud slap as something punched into him. He glanced down at the crossbow bolt buried in his shoulder, drew Wulfgar, and stepped in front of Holly, who was reaching into her cloak.

Four acolytes got busy, reloading crossbows.

"Don't just stand there," Wulfgar bellowed. "You're big enough and dumb enough to be a shield, but what's the point? Charge!"

Dan shouted his battle cry and sprinted toward the crossbowmen. Before he could reach them, they loosed another volley.

A line of fire burned across Dan's face. The other quarrels whizzed past.

Then he was on them, leaping and whirling and slashing in a barbaric frenzy.

His first swing sent a hooded head flying in a geyser of blood.

The acolytes dropped their crossbows and pulled the black daggers that they called Slivers of Darkness.

Dan thrust Wulfgar, who was yodeling curses, straight through the chest of another acolyte, then yanked the sword free and let the dead man fall to the ground.

The remaining two acolytes slashed and jabbed with their dark blades, but Dan bobbed and weaved like a boxer, slipping the attacks, and chopped one of the men in half at the beltline.

A dagger plunged into his upper back. Again, he felt only the thump of it, so great was his battle rage.

His attacker was smarter and gutsier than his dead companions had been. He stayed close, pulling the blade free and driving it once more into Dan's back.

The bastard was too close for Dan to use his two-handed sword, so he dropped Wulfgar and bulled backward into his opponent.

The acolyte shouted with fear and surprise and fell to the ground. Dan tripped over him and tumbled backwards onto the dewy grass.

They raced to their feet.

The acolyte was fast, lashing out with his dagger.

Dan batted it away, surged forward, and clipped the guy with an elbow to the jaw. It was a hard shot. The acolyte's head rocked back, and he staggered backward, swinging blindly with the black dagger.

Dan kicked him in the balls. The acolyte groaned and fell to the ground, dropping his blade.

Dan grabbed the acolyte by the ankles, leaned back, pulled with all of his might, and spun, lifting the acolyte into the air. Holding tightly to the acolyte's ankles, Dan whipped his would-be assassin through the air, and drove him head-first into the trunk of a big oak tree. The acolyte's head hit the tree with a hollow *thock,* and Dan felt his opponent's consciousness vanish instantaneously.

Emerging from his battle rage, he became aware of a soft voice speaking.

*Holly!*

He turned and couldn't believe his eyes.

Holly stood over the bodies of two acolytes–where had they come from?–talking slowly and softly to a third acolyte, who nodded slowly.

Dan rushed at the man's back, meaning to crush him, but Holly held up one finger. The meaning was clear: *wait.*

Dan stopped a few feet away, ready to snap the guy in half.

Holly was partially covered in the remainders of a black net. "Now," she said to the blood-soaked acolyte, "what will you tell the other acolytes?"

"I will tell them that you and the barbarian died," the acolyte said.

"That's right," Holly said, and smiled. "Thank you for helping me."

The acolyte looked from his bloody dagger to the dead men and back to Holly. "No problem," he said. "I want to help you."

"Very good," Holly said. "Before you leave, do you have any money or valuable items you could give to me?"

The acolyte nodded, dug around in his pocket, and handed her a small purse. Then he removed a ring and a necklace and handed those to her, too.

"Thank you," Holly said. "One more thing. Why are the acolytes trying to kidnap me?"

"A gift," the acolyte said, his voice suddenly quavering with excitement. "For the Mother of Darkness."

"Why me, though?"

"You're the only grey elf on campus," he said. "In the struggle between darkness and light, you represent neutrality and balance."

"So unfortunate that your friends killed me, right?"

"Yes," the acolyte said. "So unfortunate."

She dismissed him.

The acolyte limped away toward town, leaving a sizeable blood trail.

"What happened?" Dan asked, thoroughly confused.

Holly explained as they looted the corpses. When Dan had charged the four crossbowmen, three other acolytes had rushed Holly. "That must've been their plan," she said. "Kill you and kidnap me."

"That plan didn't work out so well," Dan said.

"No," she said.

Holly's attackers had surprised her with a net. Tangled in its fibers, she couldn't use her staff. Luckily, she had already initiated a spell. When one of the acolytes approached her, she had charmed him. He knifed his brethren before they could join in the fight against Dan.

"And now he'll go tell them that we're dead," she said. "Hopefully they'll leave us alone." She held out her loot, two dozen coins, some jewelry, and the dead men's weapons. "What did you find?"

"Seventeen gold, some silver, some copper, more weapons," he said. "Enough to keep the landlord off my back, anyway. Killing assholes pays a lot better than washing dishes."

Saying that, he realized that he was supposed to have worked tonight. With the excitement of Campus Quest, he'd forgotten all about it.

*Oh well*, he thought. *Let them fire me.*

In T&T, his characters had never gotten part-time jobs. If they needed money, they didn't wash dishes. They fought.

"Not a bad haul," Holly said. "Let's get inside and take a look at those wounds."

"All right," he said, but gave her a wary look. "You wouldn't ever charm me like that, would you?"

"I don't need to," Holly said. "You already give me everything I need." She reached up and touched his face gently, her eyes staring into his. "I was serious back in the bar. But let me say it here, in the open air, for the world to hear. I love you, Dan Marshall of the Free."

In that instant, Dan forgot the throbbing knife wounds in his back and the dead bodies strewn around the yard behind him. "I love you, too, Holly Thorn of Rothrock."

Once again, some small part of him understood that this wouldn't be happening back in his previous life. In that reality, relationships took time, and everyone was afraid to confess love, afraid of getting hurt.

Thank Crom, that world was gone.

He loved this girl. Completely. Whether this love was possible because of the game mechanics or simply because in this world, they were able to do away with all of that old-world bullshit and see everything much more clearly, Dan didn't know and didn't care. All that mattered was that he loved Holly, and she loved him. How and why no longer mattered.

"I'm yours and yours alone," Holly said, "for as long as you'll have me."

"And I'm yours," Dan said. "Forever."

They kissed and hugged.

Holly led Dan to the big oak tree and explained the elvish ceremony, everything to say and do. They placed their hands on the rough bark of the tree and said the scripted vows.

"I, Holly Thorn of Rothrock, promise to love you and serve you, Dan Marshall of the Free, my one and only husband, through sickness and through health, as your faithful wife, until death do us part."

"I, Dan Marshall of the Free, promise to love you and serve you, Holly Thorn of Rothrock, through sickness and through health, as your faithful husband, until death do us part."

They kissed, still touching the tree, and so were married, witnessed by the oak, the night sky, and a handful of corpses that served in some small yet fitting way to color the otherwise Elvish ceremony in barbaric tones.

## 29

# RUN LIKE HELL

"**C**ongratulations and welcome to the quarterfinals of Campus Quest," a silver-haired dwarven woman said.

Dan and the Noobs stood at the edge of a sprawling intramural field, alongside the other eleven teams that had qualified for the Campus Quest quarterfinals. Among the other teams, Dan saw familiar faces: the fighter with the dead eye, his Sell-Sword teammate the wiry Elven thief, and, unfortunately, Grady and the *Alpha Alpha Alpha* team, who had exploded with keening laughter when they'd spotted the Noobs.

Dan clenched and unclenched his fists. One of these days...

He felt strong again. The acolytes had done a number on him—eleven points of damage, according to Wulfgar. Old-world Dan would have needed surgery and a long hospital stay, but Holly had healed his wounds over two sessions, and now he was good as new.

The night was cool and damp beneath the cloudless sky. A heavy mantle of waist-high fog covered the field, glowing in the moonlight. Across the field, a wooden platform floated magically ten stories in the air. A dozen thick ropes hung down from the platform like tentacles. Above the platform, a magical scoreboard shone brightly.

"Out in the world, adventures sometimes go wrong," the dwarven official said with a grin, "and the only thing to do is run like hell."

This drew laughter from the crowd of spectators behind them.

"Your task tonight is simple," the dwarven official said. "Run across the foggy field and climb the ropes. No weapons, no spellcasting. The first six teams to have a member reach the platform will advance to the semifinals."

The official gave them a minute to stretch out.

"Ready, everyone?" Holly asked the Noobs.

"Ready," Dan said.

"Ready," Nadia said, stretching her hamstring.

"I am prepared," Zeke said. Earlier, he had explained that Zuggy couldn't make it. Tuesday evenings, the monkey had chess club.

"On your marks!" The official called.

Dan stepped to the line, ready to run.

Someone shoved his shoulder. "Gonna smoke you, loser," Grady said, shouldering in beside Dan.

"Get set!" the official called.

Dan crouched like a leopard ready to pounce.

"Go!"

Dan sprung out of his crouch and sprinted into the foggy field.

Or rather, he *tried* to sprint. But after just a few steps, he was spilled forward, falling to the ground, surrounded by thick fog.

Grady had tripped him!

Obnoxious laughter whipped away, trailing after the sprinting gnoll.

"Bastard!" Dan shouted and jumped to his feet. He charged, in last place but running fast. Up ahead, he could see his teammates. Nadia out in front, Holly not far behind, and Zeke doddering along, falling farther and farther behind the pack.

Then Zeke yelped and disappeared into the fog.

*Old guy must've tripped,* Dan thought, charging ahead. There wasn't time to help Zeke now.

As Dan zipped past the place where Zeke had fallen, he noticed others tripping and disappearing into the fog.

"Holly!" he shouted, as she, too, fell out of sight.

There was no time to help his beautiful wife. If he thought that she was in danger, he would dive straight into the fog, but whatever was picking off the runners, it was part of the competition.

Those who hadn't fallen still sprinted toward the distant ropes.

Dan ran with incredible speed, eating up the distance. Now he was passing people, entering the pack.

Up ahead, Nadia stumbled but kept running.

That's when Dan heard high-pitched laughter rising out of the fog on all sides. What was in the fog?

His foot tripped over something, and he stumbled forward, barely able to stay up.

Laughter rippled out of the fog around him.

Something grabbed his leg. Then something grabbed his other leg.

Dan roared and kept running, but the laughing creatures held onto his legs, slowing him.

"Get off of me!" Dan shouted and swung his leg in a kick powerful enough to break the grip of whatever had been clinging to him.

"Wee-hee-hee!" A small humanoid flew up out of the fog, laughing as it tumbled through the air. The little man was perhaps two feet tall, with a rust-colored beard. He wore cloggy little shoes with golden buckles and clothes of green: breeches, a coat with tails, and a funny, little top hat with a golden buckle and a four-leaf clover poking from the hat band.

*A leprechaun!* Dan thought. *We're being tripped by fucking leprechauns!*

He shook the other leprechaun free and sprinted forward as fast as he could, stumbling as the little bastards attacked his legs. Somehow, he managed to stay upright and catch up to Nadia, who had fallen but managed to struggle back onto her feet.

"Hey," he said.

"Hey," she said.

Running side by side, they broke from the foggy field and sprinted toward the ropes. A few of the ropes swung back and forth, moving side to side as frontrunners climbed toward the floating platform and victory. The wiry elf was most of the way to the top, far ahead of the others.

On the ground, a few of the teams were trying to start their climbers. The problem was that the ropes were high in the air, perhaps fifteen feet from the ground.

One competitor stood on his teammate's shoulders as a third teammate scaled him like a ladder and managed to reach the rope.

Grady gave a triumphant whoop, leaping from his teammate's shoulders and grabbing the rope. Being seven feet tall had its advantages.

"Stand beneath the rope," Nadia said, and the next thing Dan knew, she was scaling the front of him, her breasts and flat stomach brushing his face as she quickly climbed onto his shoulders. She pressed down into his shoulders then leapt away, jumping for the rope. He watched her fingers swoosh through the air, missing the rope by several inches.

He caught her before she hit the ground.

Grady's teammate exploded with mocking laughter beside them. "You suck, Danielle!"

Dan ignored the asshole, telling Nadia to climb up him again.

"You just like my tits in your face," she joked, scrambling onto his shoulders once more.

"This time, step into my hands," he said. "I'm going to toss you."

He put his hands together, and she stepped into them. He dropped her heels to his chest then pushed up explosively.

Nadia soared up, grabbing for the rope. She was closer this time but still missed it by a couple of inches.

She fell into his arms. No sooner had she hit than she was on standing on the ground again, ready to go. "We need more height. Is there anything to stand on?"

Dan looked around. Nothing. There was nothing.

"Give up, Danielle!" the *AAA* gnoll mocked. "You and your girlfriend are a couple of losers!"

Without a word, Dan caught the asshole with a powerful haymaker to the temple. The gnoll dropped like a two hundred and twenty-five pound bag of shit.

"Focus, barbarian," Nadia said. "This isn't the time to crush your enemies. Eight teams are already climbing."

Overhead, a loud *DING* sounded, and the scoreboard showed *First place: The Sell-Swords*.

The audience cheered loudly.

"I wasn't crushing my enemies," Dan said, stepping onto the chest of the unconscious gnoll. "I was making something to stand on. Every inch counts."

"That's what Holly said," Nadia joked, and climbed up

him again. It was harder to keep his balance, but the unconscious gnoll made a decent pair of platform shoes.

He tossed Nadia hard, and this time, she snatched the rope and started climbing.

High above, the scoreboard gave another *DING!*

Nadia climbed with incredible speed.

DING! A third team had reached the top.

"Go, Nadia, go!" he shouted.

She was flying up the rope faster than he'd ever seen someone climb, but three teams had already reached the top and five other teams were above her, two of them halfway to the platform.

Nadia would need to beat three of the five teams to earn them a spot. It didn't seem possible.

*Please, Crom!* Dan prayed.

Nadia had to be incredibly strong. She continued to zip up the rope, twenty feet, thirty, forty... never slowing her pace.

"Yes!" Dan cried as Nadia passed a flagging climber.

DING! Another team had reached the platform. Dan glanced at the scoreboard and growled, seeing *Alpha Alpha Alpha* appear in fourth place.

"Go, Nadia!" Dan shouted.

*DING!* The fifth spot was taken.

"That's it!" Dan shouted, as Nadia passed another climber. But then he had a sinking feeling.

Nadia was still moving fast, but she still had twenty feet of rope between her and the platform, and the other climber was ten feet above her.

"Go, go, go!" Dan shouted.

Hand over hand, in an impressive display of strength, coordination, and determination, Nadia hoisted herself up the rope, eating the distance between her and her opponent, who was visibly struggling now.

Dan shouted, going out of his mind with excitement as Nadia closed the gap.

Almost there, almost there...

Nadia had caught up, but the other climber was closer, reaching for the platform....

A hand fell on Dan's shoulder. "Hey, asshole," the gnoll said, back on his feet. "What do you—"

"Not now," Dan said, and popped the gnoll with a blistering uppercut that sent him to the ground again.

*DING! DING!* The scoreboard rang twice, the two chimes so close together that they were almost simultaneous.

Had Nadia actually pulled it off?

But then the scoreboard flashed, and the crowd across the field cheered wildly. The quarter finals were over.

In sixth place: ROTC.

Dan groaned, feeling his hopes crumble away.

His team had finished seventh. Campus Quest was over for the Noobs.

## 30

## SAY WHAT?

The spectators clapped and cheered as the platform lowered to the earth like a giant elevator.

For Dan, all that clapping and cheering was just salt in the wound.

So close…

But now it was over. They'd lost, and he was screwed. How could he ever get enough money to buy Dr. Lynch's textbook, let alone study it, before the midterm?

The fog vanished, revealing a dozen competitors hogtied on the ground. There was no sign of the leprechauns, and no surprise there. The little bastards had turned invisible and were no doubt tip-toeing through the crowd, picking pockets.

Speaking of pickpockets, Nadia stepped from the platform and walked to Dan, shaking her head. "Sorry," she said.

He swept her into an embrace and held her. "Sorry?" he laughed. "What are you sorry for? You were amazing!"

To his surprise, she didn't break the hug or crack a joke. She leaned her face into him, letting him comfort her. "I tried so hard," she said. "I just wasn't fast enough."

"I repeat," he said, "you were amazing. I've literally never seen anyone climb that fast." He kissed the top of her head.

"Thanks," she said. "You're sweet. I just feel so bad for Holly. She really wanted to win."

"Yeah," he said, feigning a lightheartedness that he didn't feel, "but at least we made it to the quarterfinals. Top dozen, right?"

They walked back toward the starting line. Dan kept an arm draped over Nadia, who leaned into him.

Holly met them halfway across the field. "Leprechauns!" she said. "I can't believe it." She slid in under Dan's free arm and beamed at them. "You guys were incredible! Nadia, you climbed so fast!"

Then a white-haired madman crashed into them, putting his arms around Holly and Nadia. "Group hug!" Zeke bugled.

Holly and Nadia were clearly disappointed but were doing their best not to show it. Dan felt the same way. Zeke was unfazed.

"Who wants to get drunk?" Nadia said.

"I'm in," Holly chimed.

Dan hesitated. He'd been hoping against hope that they might actually win Campus Quest and score a critical hit on his poverty. But now they had lost, and his precarious scholarship was a big problem. He couldn't study for Dr. Lynch's class, but he could work hard to up his average in other classes. "I should really go home and study," he said.

"No way," Holly said.

"Come out with us, at least for a beer or two," Nadia said.

"Nerd," Zeke said.

Dan was about to tell Zeke where he could shove his wand when Holly said, "Something's going on with the judges."

They were clustered together, talking and pointing and glancing back at the competitors.

A minute later, the silver-haired dwarf announced, "Ladies and gentlemen, if I can have your attention, please. I have an important update."

The crowd hushed. Spectators who'd been drifting toward home paused and turned to listen.

"I regret to inform you that our moderators detected the use of magic during this competition. It appears that the West Halls Warriors used a levitation spell during the climbing portion, thereby violating the rules for this event."

Confused murmurs burbled through the onlookers and competitors, save for the West Halls Warriors, who frowned at their feet, grumbling.

"The West Halls Warriors are hereby disqualified from the competition," the official said. "This moves ROTC into fifth place and the Noobs into sixth place."

"Yes!" Holly pumped a fist in the air, her purple eyes gleaming. "We're in the semifinals!"

The Noobs shouted for joy and crushed together in an embrace. This time, Dan was so happy that he didn't even mind Zeke joining in.

Holly kissed Dan.

Nadia asked him, "You still going home to study, crybaby?" She gave him a playful smile and slapped his ass.

Grabbing her wrist, Dan smiled back at her and said, "No, I'm not—and put my wallet back."

## 31

## MISCHIEVOUS ELF

H olly sighed and let her head loll back. "Now, that's what I call a victory celebration," she said.

The Skeller afterparty had been a blast, everyone cheering for the Noobs and handing them free drinks, but Dan and Holly had left early to celebrate in her apartment instead.

*Best idea ever*, Dan thought, lying beneath her, staring up at round undersides of her beautiful breasts.

But then Holly climbed off of him and padded into the kitchen. Watching her perfect ass twitch back and forth as she walked, he felt himself growing hard again. "Hey," he called. "Get back here. I'm not done with you."

"Oh, yes you are," she called from the kitchen. "For tonight anyway."

"What are you talking about?" he asked. "We're just getting started." He got to his feet and headed for the kitchen.

Holly met him halfway, clutching her druidic spells book to her chest and grinning up at him mischievously. "I have to study," she said.

"Yeah, right," he said. "Your grin gives you away. You're up to something."

Holly giggled–again, mischievously–but she pointed to his clothes, which he'd shed haphazardly, as they'd crossed the floor, stripping naked and kissing, hungry for each other. "Out with you, barbarian," she said. "Don't make me use my charm spell."

"You wouldn't."

"Try me."

"Wait," he said. "You're serious? You want me to leave?"

"I'm serious," she said, and even though she was still wrestling with a smile, he could see that she meant it.

"All right," he said, and started picking up his clothes. "You want to cuddle for a few minutes first?"

"No," she laughed. "What kind of barbarian asks to cuddle, anyway?"

"The kind who's in love."

She gave him a kiss. "I love you, too. Now get out and let me study." She flopped down, still naked, and popped open her book.

Pulling on his pants, Dan said, "You're doing that on purpose?"

"What?" she said, feigning innocence.

"Sitting there, all hot and naked, knowing that I'm going to go crazy over in my apartment, picturing you studying like that."

Holly laughed. "You and your dirty barbarian mind. Now go. If you don't make me ask again, I'll give you a little surprise later."

They kissed goodbye, and he left, grumbling.

What was Holly up to? She was probably telling the truth about having to study, but he could tell that there was more to it than that. Her purple eyes were shining like she was a kid dying to share a fun secret.

He shrugged and went into his apartment. Oh well. Maybe he'd bang his head against his Battlefield Strategy and Tactics textbook for a while.

But as soon as he walked into the apartment, Willis and Dan's gaming friends poured out of the living room, hooting congratulations.

"Dan the man!" Willis squeaked.

"You did it, you magnificent bastard!" Rick shouted.

"Uh oh, hide the prostitutes!" Jerry said predictably.

They mobbed him, slapping high fives and clapping him on the back, out of their minds happy for him.

Dan grinned like a madman. Between Campus Quest and spending time with Holly, he'd barely seen his friends for days. It felt good that they were so excited for him.

They shared their pizza, asking him all about the competition, which they'd watched on TV. Dan had fun, telling what it had been like, dropping the gnoll.

"Oh yeah," he said. "And I got married, too."

"*What?*" they shouted collectively.

For as crazy as it had been for them to see their friend on TV, kicking ass in Campus Quest, it was even harder for Dan's friends to believe that he had a girlfriend, let alone a wife.

When he told them that it was Holly, they refused to believe it.

Dan shrugged. He wasn't going to waste any time trying to convince them.

"Want to play Dullards & Drudgery?" Willis asked. He grinned, scrunching his glasses up his nose. "Jerry's working overtime to pay his HOA fees."

Rick laughed, pointing at Jerry, who was scowling now. "The dumbass was so excited about the new condo, he didn't even check the monthly fees!"

"Thanks, guys," Dan said, snagging another piece of pizza, "but I need to study and hit the rack."

Heading for his room, he grinned, wondering if Holly's mischievous surprise involved coming over for a visit later. Willis would probably have a heart attack.

Dan went into his room and flicked the switch, but the overhead light didn't turn on. The only light was a shaft of blue-white moonlight shining through the window.

"What the hell?" he said.

Had the light burned out? How did electricity even work in this world? Was it a type of magic, or—

He tensed, feeling a breeze.

He hadn't left the window open.

Glancing in that direction, he saw that the window was indeed open, and the screen was out... as if someone had broken into his apartment!

The acolytes?

Something rustled softly in the shadows.

## THE INTRUDER

Dan fell into a defensive stance, one hand on Wulfgar's pommel, ready to draw.

A cloaked figure stepped into the moonlight.

"Hold it right there," Dan said. "Who are you? Tell me now, or I'll split you in half."

Rich laughter filled the room. Familiar laughter. Female laughter.

"Nadia?" he asked.

"Split me in half, huh?" Nadia said. "You promise?"

"What are you doing here?"

"I came to see you," Nadia said. "And to let you see me." She unclasped her cloak and let it fall to the floor in a dark pool at her ankles. Not that Dan was paying any attention to the cloak.

Nadia's naked body shone like marble in the moonlight. For as great as she always looked in her leather bodysuits, she looked far better in nothing at all. Nadia was longer and lither than Holly, with comparatively smaller breasts that were still large and round and looked incredibly firm. Her lovely, sinuous body moved slowly toward him, flowing as smoothly as water in the moonlight.

Her beauty froze him in place. He could only stare and grow hard as she approached.

Nadia reached up, laid a hand on his chest, and smiled impishly. "What's the matter, barbarian? Cat got your tongue?"

His fingertips brushed her side, just above the hip, the skin there smooth and soft and warm.

"Holly was right," Nadia said, sounding surprised. "You can be gentle."

"I can't do this," he said, letting his hand fall away. "Don't get me wrong. I like you a lot. You're cool and funny and mysterious and strong and *insanely* hot, but I'm married now. Holly—"

Nadia laughed. "Oh, you silly savage. Who do you think sent me?"

He didn't understand for a second. "Holly told you to do this?"

"Well, I wouldn't say that she *told* me to do it," Nadia said, and bit her lip. "She knew that I wanted you, and she thought that you wanted me."

He had a troubling thought. "She didn't mind the thought of you, of us…"

"Don't worry," she said, smoothing her hands over his big shoulders. "Grey elves are different than humans. They live 1500 or 2000 years, and males outnumber females three-to-one. Polyamory and polygamy are the norm. Sharing you with me doesn't mean that anything's wrong. She's still head over heels in love with you."

Dan thought for a second. Holly had talked a little about this stuff, pointing out how their vows were different, but he'd mostly ignored the conversation, wrapped up in her and her alone.

Nadia said, "Did she happen to mention having a little surprise for you tonight?"

Dan nodded. "You're the surprise?"

"Yup," Nadia said. She stepped back and did a little pirouette in the moonlight, three hundred and sixty degrees of mouthwatering perfection. "Do you like your surprise?"

The prudish expectations of Dan's former existence crumbled away. Old world or new, he would never go behind Holly's back. But if Holly wanted this, and Nadia wanted this…

He reached out, pulled Nadia to him, buried a hand in her thick chestnut locks, and twisted her face to him.

She gasped and smiled, her green eyes shining brightly.

"Holly wants this?" he asked.

She nodded, her lips parting.

"And you want this?" he asked.

She gave him a wolfish grin and took his hand in hers. "Why don't you feel for yourself and tell me whether or not I want it."

Nadia guided his hand between her legs and shuddered at his touch. Her soft, silky sex was soaked and swollen.

He kissed her hard on the mouth and worked his fingers back and forth across her wet mound, not penetrating her but using his whole hand to cup and massage her, up and down, up and down.

Nadia kissed him urgently, passionately, and unsnapped his jeans. When she had him in her hands, she broke the kiss, stepped back, and stared down in wonder.

"Oh my gosh," she said with a laugh of nervous disbelief. "You really are a barbarian."

Dan brushed her hands away, dropped to his knees, and lifted one of Nadia's muscular legs over his shoulder. He breathed in her wonderful scent. Then he reached around, grabbed her perfect ass, tilted her pelvis upward, and plunged his mouth between her legs, licking and kissing her, tasting her juices and making her squirm.

Nadia grabbed the back of his head and pressed his mouth into her, moaning with pleasure. Her whole body quivered. Seconds later, she surprised him, crying out and bucking against his mouth, and soaking him in her essence as a powerful orgasm wracked her.

"No more," Nadia gasped, and pushed his head away. She lifted her leg off his shoulder and stood there, bent in a quivering half crouch, gripping her sex and still convulsing with aftershocks of pleasure.

"Well," he said, "that was fast."

She laughed. "I've wanted you for so long."

Dan stood. Now it was his turn to laugh. "So long? I've only known you for what, a week?"

"When you want someone as much as I've been wanting you," Nadia said, "a week can feel like an eternity."

She reached out, grabbed his erection, and tugged, leading him toward the bed like a dog on a leash. "Now let's see what you can do with this big two-handed sword of yours."

She stopped at the edge of the bed and took his face in her hands and kissed him, slowly and passionately. Then she broke the kiss and rubbed a thumb along his jaw like a woman checking the edge of a blade.

"Your whiskers are rough," she said, and helped him out of his clothes. "But do you think you could be gentle with this, too? At least to start? I'm out of practice, to say the least."

She was serious. Nadia was strong, capable, and fearless, always confident, always snarky, never weak. Her unexpected vulnerability only stoked his desires, making him feel like being anything but gentle.

But he nodded and kissed her and lowered her to the bed.

She stared up at him, green eyes glowing, and pulled him on top of her. His throbbing manhood didn't need a guiding hand. The head found her opening. He pushed gently forward a single inch, letting her feel its girth.

Nadia gasped, a look of concern coming onto her face.

Dan's heart was pounding now, and he wanted nothing more than to plunge into her, but he reached up and brushed a dark lock of hair from her worried eyes. "Relax," he said with an easy smile. "We'll take our time, okay? You just tell me how you're feeling."

She nodded, a slight smile coming onto her beautiful face. They locked eyes. Nadia bit her lower lip and gave a little nod.

He eased into her—an inch, two, three, his girth stretching her—until she breathed in sharply. Then he paused, rocking his hips subtly, until she nodded again.

In this way, they synced their bodies and minds and emotions, until nod by nod, inch by inch, he filled her.

Nadia's chestnut bangs had fallen again, covering one eye. The other eye fluttered in ecstasy, and her full lips parted. Her hands wrapped around his powerful triceps.

"I've never... so huge," she said, and gasped when he pulled halfway out and buried his length again. "That's it," she said, moving against him. "More, more."

33

## WE'LL SEE...

Afterward, they cuddled and talked.

For Dan, pillow-talk Nadia was a surprise. He'd seen two other sides of her–streetwise thief and shiny, happy RA–but now she was relaxed and happy and sweet. This felt like the real Nadia. And if it was, he liked the real Nadia very, very much.

When he told her this, Nadia shook her head, looking genuinely troubled. "Don't be fooled," she said. "Let's just say that I have a wild side. If you knew the real me, you'd kick me out of here."

"So dark and mysterious," Dan joked, but he pushed her to tell him about her life.

They talked for a long time.

Nadia was an orphan, who'd grown up in foster care in Philadelphia and the suburbs. Life had been tough, and she'd bounced around a lot, so she was always the new kid.

Early on, she understood that teachers, who knew that she was a foster kid, treated her differently. Some teachers paid her little attention, probably assuming that she wasn't worth their time, since she'd likely move away soon; other teachers treated her with suspicion, as if she might steal their chalk or possibly infect the other students with lice; and the worst teachers of all patted her head and made every day a pity party.

Meanwhile, Nadia knew that she was smart and capable, so she became very competitive at an early age. Whenever she stayed in a school district for a few months or longer, she rose through the academic and athletic ranks.

No matter how well she performed, however, Nadia always learned the same, bitter lesson; a lesson learned every year by countless kids in schools across the nation. You can fight your way up the ladder, but skill and hard work won't get you to that final rung. In too many towns, you can't earn head cheerleader, quarterback, or king or queen of the prom unless you come from the right family.

Nadia still tried. She craved success back then, she explained, seeming embarrassed and sad and perhaps a little angry. As a kid, she had wanted so badly to impress everyone and had worked hard to be the best at everything, hungry for some accomplishment that would prove that she had risen above her circumstances.

"It was bullshit," she said, shaking her head. "All bullshit."

Meanwhile, outside of school, life in the chaotic, often brutal foster system taught her stealth and struggle. By six, she had learned to steal food for her foster siblings and herself. By seven, she'd learned to steal without getting caught. Soon after, she learned how to read people, fight, and escape any placement.

After fleeing several abusive foster placements, she spent most of middle school in juvenile detention and group homes, where she met dozens of streetwise kids, from whom she learned pickpocketing, burglary, and the secrets of both the underground and the knife culture.

Through it all, however, she maintained her dual realities.

Whether she was stealing food to feed her foster siblings or learning the correct angle at which to plunge a blade into a victim's kidney, she maintained perfect behavior and grades at school.

"And that's where Nadia the RA was born?" Dan said.

"Not born, exactly," Nadia said, tracing a scar on Dan's shoulder. "Nadia the RA. is as much a part of me as Nadia the thief. But yeah, that's how I learned to separate my worlds. For the record, though, neither of those personas is the 'real' me, if there even is such a thing. People think they have a real self. I'm not so sure."

Dan thought about that for a second. Who was he, really? Was he old-world Dan, playing a role here in this new world? Or was his inner barbarian the real him, a core self that he never could have become in the old world?

*I'm both and neither,* he thought. *I'm some kind of weird hybrid, changing more and more each day.*

"Even if we do have a true self," he said, "maybe we have a different true self day to day, you know what I mean?"

Nadia smiled sadly. "That would be nice. But some of us will never escape our inner truth. I would do anything to be Nadia the thief or Nadia the RA either one, and nothing else."

Dan caressed her neck and kissed her forehead. "Well, whoever you are tonight? I really like this version of you."

Before Nadia could respond, the bedroom door swung open.

Dan shot out of bed, ready to fight.

"It's okay," Holly said, closing the door behind her. "It's just me."

Old-world Dan would've panicked, but he crossed the floor and kissed Holly. "Nadia tells me that you set this up."

Holly shrugged and smiled. "Are you complaining?"

"Not at all."

Holly trailed her fingertips over his bare chest. "I didn't

think so. Nadia was crushing hard on you, so I told her to go ahead."

"Um," Nadia said, "I'm right here, you know."

Holly grinned at her friend. "And you're even prettier when you blush like that, hon. But don't forget. I warned you what would come of all this. He is a barbarian, after all."

"What do you mean?" Dan said. "I was gentle with her."

"I'm sure that you were," Holly said. "But you're a barbarian, all the same. Harems are part of your culture."

"And yours, Nadia tells me," Dan interjected.

Holly gave him a little nod. "True, so that makes me a perfect first wife for you. As a powerful barbarian, you'll gather wives, and with each wife, you'll gain power. I warned Nadia that if she went through with this, you'd make her your second wife."

Dan looked back and forth between the women. This conversation was crazy. Old-world Dan would've been freaking out, but he just grinned, feeling amused and intrigued and something else...

Proud?

Strong?

He wasn't sure, exactly, what this other feeling was, but he liked it and realized that he'd felt it before.

Then he understood. This thing he was feeling, it was his inner barbarian surging, increasing its power over him, just as it had after he'd first had sex with Holly.

"Whoa," Nadia said, still blushing. "I am nobody's wife. You elves and barbarians are crazy. This was just sex to me."

Holly laughed.

"What?" Nadia said.

"We'll see," Holly said, smiling mischievously.

Nadia fake-scowled at her. "I hate it when you do that."

"Hate it when I do what?"

"The whole 'we'll see' thing," Nadia said.

177

Holly laughed again. "That's because you know that I only say it when I'm right!"

Nadia rolled her eyes. "You just want me to do that thing you talked about."

Now it was Holly's turn to blush.

"What thing is that?" Dan asked, suddenly very interested.

"Don't worry about it, barbarian," Holly said. "Whatever my deluded friend is talking about, it's not happening tonight. I have to study. Besides, tonight is for you two."

Holly threw her arms around his shoulders and kissed him deeply and hungrily. Then she twiddled her fingers at Nadia, who lay, completely uncovered and incredibly gorgeous on the bed, smiling at them. "Bye-bye, second wife."

Nadia laughed and pointed at the door. "Be gone with you, troublemaking elf."

## A SOFTER, MORE SENSITIVE TWO-HANDED SWORD

fter Holly left, Dan and Nadia made love again.

"You're sweet," Nadia murmured as she was falling asleep. "Would never marry you. Wouldn't do that to you. Couldn't risk…"

Then she fell asleep in his arms.

Dan lay there, wondering about Nadia's big secret. For one reason or another, she wanted him to think that she was secretly a monster.

At one point, she'd told him, "You don't know me, Dan. You can't. And someday, after you really know me and can't love me anymore, you'll understand my reluctance. Please remember then that I still love you and always will, no matter how hard that might be to believe."

Maybe this was just her way to fend off Holly's aggressive suggestions that Nadia marry some guy she'd only known for a week.

Dan listened to the soft susurration of Nadia's breathing and thinking about everything that Holly had said.

Finally, he disentangled himself from Nadia, scooped up Wulfgar, and carried the sword into the bathroom to talk.

Wulfgar was, after all, supposed to be more than just a weapon. He was supposed to be Dan's mentor, too.

"Listen, dumbass," Wulfgar said, wasting no time once Dan had unsheathed him. "Holly is right. Make your move. Make Nadia your woman."

"But—"

"Shut up and listen," Wulfgar said. "This isn't about sex. This is about living the life you want—and the life that they want. Do you love her?"

"Who, Nadia?" Dan said, his heart jumping a little at the notion. "How could I possibly know after such a short time?"

"For a college boy, you're pretty fucking stupid, you know that? You don't need a slide rule to measure how you feel about a woman, genius. And love doesn't give a shit how long you've known Nadia. How does she make you feel?"

"I like her," Dan said, feeling another thrill. "I like her a lot, but—"

"Do you want to take care of her? Protect her?"

"Definitely."

"Do want her in your bed?"

Dan laughed. "Of course."

"Do you give a shit about her? Deeply, I mean. Do you want to know all about her? Do you care about what she wants, what she needs, even when it has nothing to do with your sorry ass?"

"Yeah," Dan said, meaning it, "but why do you have to insult me all the time?"

"Because you're dumber than a glass hammer. Do you want Nadia to bear your children?"

Dan leaned back. "Children?"

Internally, old-world Dan squawked, *You're way too young to think about any of this, especially children.*

Outwardly, however, Dan only nodded.

Blocking out old-world Dan, he thought over Wulfgar's questions. And suddenly it was all so simple.

"Yes," he said. "I want to have kids with her. I want all of this stuff."

He shrugged, suddenly calm and certain of everything in a way that his former self, who tended to overthink everything except for gameplay, never could have been. "I do love Nadia. I love them both and want them both to be my women, my wives."

Wulfgar chuckled. "Maybe there's hope for you yet, shit-for-brains. Let's talk experience points."

Dan nodded. He'd been wondering but hadn't bothered to ask. After all, he'd recently leveled up, and to move from second to third level, he would need to earn another six thousand experience points.

So far, he'd only killed an orc and a few acolytes, and his total loot haul was around twenty gold pieces.

"For the orc, acolytes, and gold, you gained one hundred and twenty experience points," Wulfgar said. "In the quarter-finals, you fought your way through the leprechaun trap, knocked out the gnoll, used him as a stepping stool, and helped your team make the semifinals—all while acting like a barbarian. That earned you another two hundred experience points."

"Wow," Dan said, surprised—and wary. Since this world was clearly based on the gamemaster style of Willis, and Willis was super stingy with experience points unless the characters needed to advance in order to survive upcoming challenges, receiving points for performance and staying in character made Dan wonder what horrors were headed his way.

"For having sex with Nadia, you earn another five hundred experience points," Wulfgar said, "and for handling it like a man and coming to your senses about love and marriage, you get an additional five hundred."

"So I'm getting way more points for having sex and falling in love than I am for combat?"

"For now, you are," Wulfgar said. "Right now, this is all about you ditching Dan the Dweeb and becoming Dan the Barbarian. Building a harem is the barbarian way, and having a harem isn't just about banging a bunch of girls. It's about getting to know them, recognizing their strengths and weaknesses, their desires and fears. It's about protecting and nurturing them and being man enough to know that he can count on them to protect and nurture him, too."

Dan laughed. It all made a lot of sense, and the worldview that Wulfgar was painting appealed to him deeply, but the sword had left himself open for a counterpunch, and Dan couldn't just let that opportunity slip away. "You know," he said, "for a supposedly barbaric two-handed sword, you're a pretty sensitive guy."

"Fuck you, buddy," Wulfgar said. "I wouldn't have to play Dr. Phil if you weren't trying to micromanage experience points like a little bitch!"

Dan roared with laughter.

After a few colorful curses and death threats, Wulfgar joined in.

Which was pretty hilarious, until a soft rapping sounded on the bathroom door, and Nadia asked him why he was locked in the bathroom, laughing like a madman.

Dan opened the door, kissed Nadia, and held her by the shoulders. "I'm laughing because my life is so crazy," he said, "and because I just realized that Holly is right. I love you, Nadia. No shit. I love you, and I want you to be my woman."

"What?" Nadia said, leaning away from him. She tried to look skeptical but couldn't hide her red cheeks or the way she was trying and failing to hide a very happy smile. "You and elf-girl are crazy, do you know that? This is just sex, okay? I don't need a man, and I'm certainly not looking to become somebody's woman—or wife!"

Dan laughed. "We'll see."

Nadia rolled her eyes. "Don't you start saying that, too." Then she took his hand and leading him toward the bed, said, "You woke me up with your laughter. Now you have to pay the consequences."

"Oh yeah? What consequences?"

Nadia crawled onto the bed. Up on all fours, she pointed her A+ ass in his direction and smiled at him over one shoulder. "You can start by fucking me until I forget just how crazy you and Holly are."

## THE TOWER OF TERROR

Dan and the Noobs stood once more upon the intramural fields. Before them, they could see only empty fields and hear only the breeze and the honking of geese flying south in the bright blue sky of what was yet another spectacular October day.

Campus Quest wizards had used their sorcery to conceal the actual event from the six teams who had made it to the semifinals.

Earlier, all six teams had stood here at the edge of the field. One by one, however, each of the other teams had been called, and one by one, they had entered a magical door that had appeared out of thin air. The door was a spherical black portal with nothing visible beyond. Once through the magical door, the team disappeared completely.

Five of the six teams had disappeared through the door. Only the Noobs remained, and they had no idea what awaited them beyond the portal.

"Could be anything," Zeke said, seeming more curious than concerned. "It's right in front of us," he said, pointing at the seemingly empty field. "We just can't see or hear it."

The breeze shifted, and Nadia sniffed the air like a dog. "The wizards didn't disguise everything. I smell blood and shit and decay."

Dan and the others couldn't smell anything.

"You have an amazing sense of smell," Holly said, bouncing on the balls of her feet, doing her sprinter-before-a-race routine, either to warm up or to burn off nervous energy. And today, she actually was nervous. They all were.

Things had gotten very real.

During the chaos of the first day, the idea of actually making the finals had been a dream, nothing more.

Then, at the quarterfinals, the challenge hadn't seemed all that daunting, and moving forward had still been such a long shot that the pressure wasn't too bad.

Today, however, they were one step away from making the finals, and they had no idea what lay in store for them.

So yeah, they were nervous.

"I don't like that you can smell decay," Holly said. "Could mean undead, and we're the only team without a cleric."

Holly didn't have to explain. Clerics could turn the undead. But the Noobs had a druid instead of a cleric.

"Screw it," Nadia said, in between impressive stretches.

Dan was happy to see that she'd worn studded leather armor today. He'd miss the view afforded by her usual attire but knowing that armor would make her safer more than made up for it.

"Maybe it's a giant rabbit with bad breath," Nadia joked. "If so, you can work your mumbo-jumbo on it, and those clerics—"

The portal popped into existence fifty feet away, looking to Dan like the business end of a shotgun.

"Here we go," Holly said.

An unsmiling official in wizard's robes stepped into view and beckoned them forward.

Dan gave both of his girls a quick kiss, then exchanged nods with Zeke. The monkey stared at the portal and screeched anxiously.

They went through the portal and found themselves in a different world.

"Crom," Dan said, his breath frosting the air.

They stood upon a gray and lifeless plain. Stretching away in all directions as far as the eye could see were ancient tombstones, most canted badly to one side or sinking into the loamy soil, which was covered in pale moss and clusters of gray mushrooms which rose like misshapen hands from the unholy graves.

Gone was the warm, bright day. In this magical space, all was cold and gloomy, the air redolent with the smells of death, both fresh and far gone.

Before them rose two structures.

A glowing scoreboard showed the current team rankings and each team's final time.

Unsurprisingly, the Sell-Swords were in first place. Unfortunately, second place belonged to *Alpha Alpha Alpha*. ROTC was currently in third.

Fourth and fifth place didn't matter.

ROTC was the team to beat.

Yes, but beat how?

The second structure dominated the landscape, rising up from the cemetery like a giant rot-spotted forearm with a massive fist at the apex.

But this was no arm.

It was a tower.

A bone white tower, fifty feet tall, with an iron door at its base.

And at its apex, that was no fist.

It was a skull.

A bulbous stone skull, easily ten feet tall, with a sinister grin and empty eye-socket windows staring blankly out at the macabre landscape.

Dan unsheathed Wulfgar.

"What kind of fucked up sorcery is this?" the sword bellowed, voicing Dan's loathing.

Dan couldn't respond, of course, not unless he wanted his teammates, who couldn't hear the sword, to think that he was a few bolts shy of a full quiver.

"Nice place," Nadia growled sarcastically, and filled her hands with glowing daggers.

"Bad energy here," Holly said, and gave her glowing staff a slow spin as her purple eyes panned back and forth, scanning for danger.

"Reminiscent of the Plane of Dusk," Zeke mused, seemingly unperturbed.

Zuggy scrunched low on his shoulder, chittering like a frightened monkey.

Then the voice of the official, who had disappeared once they entered the portal, spoke out of thin air. "Behold the Tower of Terror."

A chorus of chilling, high-pitched laughter tittered from the direction of the ominous tower.

Dan set his shoulders and tightened his grip on Wulfgar like a batter at the plate.

"Directly before you," the disembodied voice continued, "is the grave of the dread necromancer Ballok Shazar."

"What an asshole that guy was," Zeke said offhandedly.

"Behold the tombstone," the voice of the official said, and the large tombstone directly before them glowed with an eerie green aura. *Here lie the remains of Ballok Shazar*, the chiseled inscription read, *whose shade now stalks the dark planes beyond death!*

Beneath these words, at the center of the stone, a keyhole appeared, glowing as red as the fires of hell.

"This monument is more than a grave marker," the voice of the official said. "It is a door between our plane of existence and The Plane of Sorrow. To complete your challenge, unlock the grave door. To earn a spot in the final stage of Campus Quest, unlock the door more quickly than at least three of the opposing teams. Farewell."

A click sounded high above, and beside their team name on the scoreboard, numbers appeared, ticking upward with every passing second.

# THE QUEST FOR THE KEY

"Here goes nothing," Nadia said, and putting away her daggers, pulled out various picks, bars, and levers.

"Watch out for traps," Holly said, leaning forward to inspect the tombstone.

"You can't pick the tombstone lock," Dan said. "Trust me."

"Don't be so sure," Nadia said. "I kick ass at picking locks."

"It won't work," Dan repeated. Once again, his mind reached back to countless hours he'd spent gaming with Willis. If Willis's design sensibilities infused this game, Dan was 100% positive that they wouldn't be able to simply pick the tombstone lock.

"How can you be so sure?" Nadia asked.

*Because Willis would've put too damned much work into the challenge for them to beat it with an ordinary set of thieves' picks and tools*, Dan thought.

But he said, "The organizers would never create all of this, call it the Tower of Terror, and let us beat the challenge without us having to go inside that thing."

He hooked a thumb toward the tower, and at that exact moment, another barrage of creepy, high-pitched laughter trilled from the tower windows.

"The boy is very stupid," Zeke said matter-of-factly, nodding at Dan, "but this time, he has a point. There will be a key inside."

Holly nodded. "Not just inside," she said, and her gaze scaled the tower. "The key will be up there, inside the skull."

"Yup," Dan said. They would have to go all the way up there to get the stupid key. The Willis-ness controlling this world wouldn't want the Noobs to miss any of the creepy-ass monsters that it had cooked up for them, after all.

*Knowing Willis,* Dan thought, *the key will be made of something weird, like glowing gemstone.*

One other thing bothered him, though.

He looked over his shoulder, scanning the gloomy boneyard with wary eyes.

"What is it?" Holly asked.

"All these graves," he said. "Where are the zombies? They should be digging their way out of the graves, coming for our brains."

Another mad cackle sounded above.

"Let's go," Wulfgar said. "Stop flapping your lips and kick in that door!"

Dan nodded. The sword was right. Too much thinking, not enough action.

"Where are you going?" Nadia said, as Dan marched away.

"I'm going through the door," he said, "and then I'm going to fight my way up the tower and get the key."

The door was made of heavy timber reinforced with iron. Dan tested it with a push and was surprised when the unlocked door swung open.

He peered warily inside.

The smell hit him like a sledgehammer.

It smelled like the whole world had died. And not just the people, plants, and animals. The inside of the Tower of Terror smelled like the world itself had turned to flesh, then died, and was now rotting on the shoulder of some intergalactic highway.

As he reeled from this horrible smell, his eyes and ears registered something like a vast ocean, dead and gray and hungry, rolling toward him, moaning and hissing.

"Crom!"

Dan grabbed the door handle and yanked hard.

The gray wave hit the door just as Dan slammed it shut. On the other side, muffled by the thick wood of the door, came a light pattering, like the sound of a soft rain.

Dan just stood there for a second, trying to breathe. What he'd just smelled, heard, and seen would haunt him for the rest of his life.

"What is that?" Holly said, pointing to a tubular gray something lying on the ground. "It fell out when you slammed the door."

*That's because I cut it off when I slammed the door*, Dan thought. But he was still so stunned that his mouth didn't seem to be working.

"Is that a finger?" Nadia said, sounding disgusted. "I think that's a finger."

Dan faced his teammates. "Um... this door isn't going to work."

"Why not?"

"I found the zombies."

"All right," Holly said. "Zombies look frightening, but they're actually a fairly easy monster. How many?"

"Too many," he said.

"How many?" Nadia asked.

"All of them," he said. "Millions." And he told them what he'd seen.

Beyond the door, the Tower of Terror was truly terrifying —and absolutely impossible. From the outside, the tower had a circumference of perhaps forty feet, but when he'd opened the door, he hadn't seen what looked like the inside of a tower, let alone a tower of those dimensions.

Through some black sorcery, the tower door opened onto a nightmare landscape that stretched away for miles and miles in a flat and gloomy plain. Beneath a leaden, other-worldly sky, zombies covered every inch of this sprawling doomscape, packed shoulder to shoulder, chest to back, in a writhing, rotting mass of wagging arms, dead eyes, and gaping mouths filled with rotten teeth.

Dan's teammates stared at him for several silent seconds.

Then Nadia clapped her hands sharply together and said, "Well, looks like I'd better climb this wall, then."

Nadia walked the wall, inspecting its surface. Then she clamped a dagger between her teeth like a pirate and started climbing.

Dan could only stand there and watch, wishing that he could be more than a spectator, though he did have a great view of Nadia's A+ ass.

Nadia ascended the wall with remarkable speed, scaling ten feet, twenty, higher...

Then a leering blue-gray face with insane, bulging eyes leaned out of a window above her.

*A ghoul,* Dan thought, and saw the monster wrestle something onto the window ledge.

"Look out!" Dan shouted.

The ghoul cackled madly and dropped a large chunk of stone.

"Oh shit!" Nadia shouted.

The stone smashed into her head.

An icy spike of terror skewered Dan's heart as Nadia's head jerked to one side.

Nadia's limp body sloughed away from the wall and plummeted without so much as a whimper.

## 37

## DESPERATE MEASURES

**D**an moved quickly, shuffling his feet back and forth, and caught Nadia before she could hit the ground.

Nadia's limp body slammed into him. Dan stayed under her, but the impact smashed him to the ground. It hurt like hell and knocked the wind out of him, but at least he had broken her fall.

Nadia was unconscious and badly hurt, bleeding from a deep gash in her head. Panicking, Dan tried to rouse her, touching her face and calling her name, but it was no good.

Inches away, another stone slammed into the ground with a startling *whump*.

Then *whump... whump... whump...*

Ghouls leaned from windows up and down the tower, defenestrating stones.

Dan scooped Nadia into his arms, retreated to safety, and laid her gently on the ground. Holly crouched beside her, inspecting her injuries.

Boiling with rage, Dan glared at the tower. Ghouls leaned

from all of the windows, jabbering and cackling and sticking out their inhumanly long tongues.

*Whump.*

Another stone hit the ground.

That's when Dan recognized the stones then for what they were. The ghouls weren't just dropping stones. They were dropping tombstones.

Of course they were.

This place was just some sick theme park.

Suddenly, he wanted to kill not only the ghouls but also whoever had designed this twisted place.

Dan turned back to his fallen friend. "Nadia," he pleaded, "can you hear me?"

But then Holly took him by the face, her purple eyes boring into him.

"Leave us be," Holly said, and her voice was steel. "I have this. Go get that key."

She pulled mistletoe from her cloak and started to cast what Dan now recognized as a healing spell.

"Right," he said, and pushed Nadia's injuries out of his mind. He had to trust Holly to handle that, while he focused on the key.

He sprinted back to the tower, where Zeke stood studying one of the tombstones that had punched into the ground.

The wizard turned to Dan with an incredulous smile and pointed at the tombstone. "I think I knew that guy."

"Can't you do something?" Dan shouted.

Zeke scratched his beard, seeming to think it over. "I guess I could cast a levitation spell."

Dan couldn't believe it. "Levitation? Why didn't you–" but he cut himself off.

This wasn't the time to berate the crazy old wizard. Minutes were bleeding away, Nadia was seriously hurt, and this was their only chance at making the finals of Campus Quest. They had to get up there and get that key.

"All right," Dan said, changing the tone of his voice. "That's great. Float on up there and get the key."

Zeke pointed at himself, looking badly startled. "Me? I can't go up there."

"Why not?"

Zeke nodded toward Zuggy. "This monkey is terrified of heights."

Dan glanced at the scoreboard and ground his teeth with frustration. Time was slipping away. If they didn't beat the third-place team, they would lose.

In that moment, old-world Dan spoke up.

*Maybe losing would be okay. If the semifinals are this danger-ous, the finals will be much harder, teams will be able to attack other teams, too. Really,* old-world Dan reasoned, *it would prob-ably be better to just bow out now.*

*Fuck you,* Dan told his former self.

No more half-stepping. No more fretting. No more settling for mediocrity. This was his chance at gold, girls, and glory!

"Levitate me, then," he told Zeke. "Lift me up to that skull."

The wizard got busy. A pinch of this, a dash of that, a twiddle of the fingers, and a stream of mumbled gibberish. Then, explaining that vertical levitation was much simpler than horizontal, he had Dan stand twenty feet out from the wall, beyond the range of the ghouls' projectiles but still in line with the skull's face.

Seconds later, Dan lifted off the ground.

An inch, a foot, a yard, up and up he rose, higher and higher. It wasn't like flying. He just lifted weightlessly up and up toward the great, grinning skull high above.

A spasm of primal fear shuddered through him. Not at

the skull or the ghouls or even the thought of falling. What chilled his marrow was the realization that magic had him in its grasp.

A twisted cackle sounded overhead. High above him, a ghoul leaned into view, hauling a tombstone onto the window's ledge. With a squeal of delight, the ghoul launched the stone into the air.

Dan was twenty feet out from the tower. He had thought that he would be safe. But the ghoul was leaning out of one of the highest windows and had thrown the stone hard. Now the gray slab was tumbling straight toward Dan.

He couldn't change directions or jump to one side. As the stone hurtled toward him, Dan braced himself and swung his cursing two-handed sword as hard as he could.

*Clang!*

Steel met stone. The force of impact jolted out of the sword, through Dan's hands, and up his arms. But he had swung accurately and hit the stone hard enough to send it spinning away.

"Is that the best you've got, you rotten assholes?" Wulfgar shouted.

Ghouls filled the windows, sneering and jabbering and making obscene gestures toward Dan, who rose past them, up and up and out of their range.

Wulfgar ranted, saying terrible things about their mothers.

Dan glanced over his shoulder at the scoreboard.

He had a little over eight minutes left.

He had no idea what he would face inside, but the Noobs still had a shot.

A dark cloud burst from an upper window and raced toward him in a rush of eager flapping and high-pitched squeaking.

*Bats!*

The gruesome flock attacked him like a swarm of giant mosquitoes.

Dan screamed and swung his arms as the bats crashed into him, clinging to his clothes, scratching his flesh, and chomping down wherever they could sink their teeth.

A plump bat thudded into his forearm, grabbed hold with sharp claws, and sunk its teeth into the meat of Dan's arm just below the elbow.

That's when Dan, roaring with pain and revulsion, realized that these were not bats.

No, not bats.

Rats.

Winged rats.

Huge, New-York-City-subway-sized rats with leathery bat wings, glowing red eyes, and curved incisors that flashed like miniature scimitars.

Rats covered him, squeaking and biting and scratching, tearing his clothes and flesh. They were tangled in his hair and crawling inside his shirt. So many clung to his cloak that their weight pulled the cloak against his throat, choking him.

Dan squeezed his eyes shut and screamed.

Leathery wings flapped against his face. Sharp claws ripped at his flesh. Screeching, scrabbling, slashing rats covered every inch of him. Scimitar teeth sunk into his arms, his nose, the back of his neck.

Holding Wulfgar in one hand, Dan bellowed with rage and plucked rats as quickly as he could. They were huge, as big as rabbits, but he was strong and wild with fear and revulsion and desperation, and he snapped their bones like twigs in his crushing grasp.

Grab, crush, toss away.

Grab, crush, toss away.

Again and again.

But every time that he peeled away one rat, two more

replaced it, scrabbling and screeching and fighting for the space that Dan cleared.

He would never crush them all. There were too many of them, and they were too vicious. They would tear him to ribbons before he could kill them all.

Then, as suddenly as the rats had burst from the window, they were gone. With a collective squeak, they detached as one, darted away like a flock of sparrows, and plunged into a lower window and out of sight.

Dan roared after them and swung Wulfgar back and forth, half-mad with pain and panic. His clothes were tattered. Every inch of exposed flesh was sliced and torn. His arms and face oozed blood from hundreds of stinging wounds that were likely teeming with infection.

*To Hades with infection!*

He couldn't float here, fretting like an old woman. He just needed to make it to the end of the event. Campus Quest healers would be waiting, and they could fix pretty much anything this side of death.

Dead was dead.

*So don't die, asshole,* he told himself, and realized that he was sounding more and more like his ill-tempered two-handed sword.

Dan wiped blood from his eyes and noticed that his upward movement had stopped. He now hovered fifty feet above the ground, face-to-face with the gigantic skull.

Perhaps that's why the rats had left. Perhaps, like monsters he had faced in T&T, the rats were magically contained to a specific portion of the challenge.

The skull's eyes were indeed wide-open windows. No glass, no bars, no ghouls.

*All right,* he thought. *Here we go.*

He looked down at Zeke and motioned toward the skull.

Dan started floating slowly forward. He held Wulfgar out before him. The sword raged, thirsty for blood.

So far, with millions of zombies, ghouls, and flying rats, the Tower of Terror had definitely lived up to its name. What was waiting inside the skull?

For as certain as he was that the key would be somewhere inside the skull, he was equally certain that its guardian wouldn't be some weak-ass monster like a skeleton. In T&T, Tower Masters didn't design challenges like that.

On the flipside, however, the final guardian wouldn't be something impossible, like a vampire. After all, most of the Campus Quest competitors were fairly low level.

As he neared the window, he glanced again at the scoreboard and he saw that he only had six minutes left.

Time was running out fast.

Then his boots touched down, and he was standing on the stone window ledge.

He felt the levitation spell leave him.

Dan was on his own.

## 38

## INTO THE GIANT SKULL

"Crom," Dan breathed as he stood on the eye-socket window sill and surveyed the interior of the great skull.

More sorcery.

He saw no torches or candles or electric lights, and yet the interior of the skull was filled with light—that same eerie green illumination that had surrounded the tombstone of the evil necromancer, Ballok Shazar.

How he loathed sorcery!

At the center of the room, the key floated in midair. Seeing it, Dan chuckled grimly. Just as he had expected, the key was made of sparkling red gemstone, as if it had been crafted from an enchanted ruby in the mind of Willis.

A strange fog covered the floor and ceiling. Otherwise, he saw only the sparkling key floating in the weird green light. Nothing else. No monsters, no resurrected necromancer, not even an obvious hiding place for some creepy final guardian.

Was it possible that he had already *earned* the key?

After all, he had found a way to the top of the tower,

avoided an army of zombies, battled psychotic ghouls, and survived an onslaught of flying rats.

Perhaps that was enough. Perhaps all that he had to do now was grab the key, secure his rope, and slide back down. He certainly hoped so. Because he didn't have time now to do much more.

But his barbarian's sixth sense prickled, telling him that the situation couldn't be that simple.

He narrowed his eyes at the misty floor and remembered the fog from the second challenge. Were more leprechauns waiting in this fog? In the Tower of Terror, they wouldn't be normal leprechauns, of course; they would be frigging zombie leprechauns, moaning in brogue, with their flesh rotting green, not gray.

He banished these thoughts. This mist was too low to conceal leprechauns, zombified or otherwise. It was only inches high, not feet high.

*Besides,* he thought, *you're running out of time. Quit thinking and get moving!*

He jumped down, hit the floor running, and stumbled. The fog stuck at his boots then ripped away, slowing him. In three lurching strides, he reached the center of the skull.

The crystalline key floated in the air, winking red.

There was no time to worry about tricks or traps. He snatched the key from the air and shoved it into his pocket with a triumphant yawp.

No electric shock fried his hand. No trap door opened beneath his feet. No poisoned arrow plunged into his chest. At last, he'd gotten a lucky break!

Now he had around five minutes to tie off the rope, slide down with the key, and unlock the tombstone.

Piece of cake!

But as he turned to leave, he almost toppled to the floor. The fog had enveloped his boots, rooting him in place. Looking down, he was instantly covered in goosebumps.

That wasn't fog locking him in place.

It was spiderwebs.

Which meant that the smoky substance overhead was actually spiderwebs, too.

Giant spiderwebs.

And giant spiderwebs meant…

The webs overhead vibrated. And with a soft rustling, a giant spider crept into view.

The monster waddled with unnerving silence, the size of an unshorn sheep, its furry body borne upon eight chitinous legs, the needle tips of which tiptoed along the smoky strands with an uncanny delicacy.

It moved closer in short bursts. Move, stop. Move, stop.

A profusion of small, black eyes gleamed like so many blood blisters upon the spider's blunt head, staring hungrily at Dan from above a set of impossibly huge fangs dripping a fluorescent yellow ooze.

Poison!

Straining frantically, Dan yanked a foot free–*thank you, 18/92 strength!*–but then Wulfgar was yelling, "Come and get it, you eight-legged son-of-a-whore!" and Dan saw that the spider was trundling straight at him.

No more herky-jerky stop-and-go creeping. The giant spider was coming for him now!

"I really don't have time for you now!" Dan yelled. As the spider pounced, he swung Wulfgar in a short and calculated chop. The massive arachnid retreated. A few of its bony legs dropped to the carpet of spiderwebs.

Dan grunted, pulled his foot free again, and stepped closer to the window.

The spider rushed forward, snapping at him with its oozing fangs.

Dan leaned away from the attack and drove Wulfgar forward. Bellowing curses, the sword plunged into the monstrous spider, skewering the fuzzy carapace and punching out the other side with a crunch.

The spider screeched horrifically as its exoskeleton split wide and burst like a piñata, raining down not candy but a dark and stinking jelly of gelatinous spider guts.

The spider uttered a dying squeal, waggled its remaining legs, and went still.

Dan swung his sword, dislodging the corpse and tossing it aside.

*All right,* he thought. *Now pull free of these webs, rappel to the ground, and unlock that tombstone.*

He yanked his leg as hard as he could, ripping free of the clutching webs. Then he swung his hips, turned toward the window, and roared with surprise.

He hadn't heard the second spider, which now dangled inches away from him. Before Dan could even react, the spider's head whipped forward and chomped down on his arm.

Dan screamed as gigantic fangs plunged into the meat of his forearm. Instantly, he could feel poison burning inside his flesh, spreading away from the pain of the wound as the spider shook its blunt head back and forth like a pit bull.

Wulfgar slipped from his grasp and fell, cursing, to the floor.

Dan grabbed the spider with his free hand and wrenched it from his arm, screaming again as the fangs tore free.

The huge spider went wild, chittering and snapping its fangs, which now dripped with both venom and blood. Its rash of blood-blister eyes glared at Dan with savage malice.

Dan tightened his grip, bellowed wordless rage, and thrust his arm forward as hard as he could, smashing the spider into the wall beside the window.

The spider shrieked and hissed, digging its pointed legs into Dan's arms like so many needles.

Dan ignored the pain and piston-punched the spider into the wall again and again, *bam, bam, bam!*

Then something cracked, and the spider shifted across its middle, losing shape as it came apart in Dan's hand, breaking into a furry mess of cracked exoskeleton and stinking jelly. Its legs pulled free of Dan's flesh and retracted into its ruined and lifeless body.

Cursing like Wulfgar, Dan tossed the dead monster aside and ripped his sword from the cobwebs.

Poison burned like fire in his veins.

His muscles twitched and jerked. His heart pounded alarmingly in his chest. War drums of pain drummed in his skull.

Dan's breathing was rapid and shallow, making him feel like he was suffocating. His extremities tingled with intensifying numbness, and the room around him was growing wavy and indistinct. The venom was coursing through him, shutting down his systems, trying to finish him.

The room spun around him. His body sagged, threatening to collapse.

Dan shook his head.

"No!" he yelled at himself. "Finish this… the key… have to win."

With all his might, he pulled once more, yanking his feet free of the clutching floor and losing a boot in the process. He hauled himself up onto the window sill and cursed when he nearly tumbled into the open air.

For a few seconds, he wobbled there, steadying himself with one hand and regaining his balance.

It was a long way down.

Staring out into the void with blurry vision, he groaned at the scoreboard.

49 seconds.

That's all the time he had.

He tried to pull the rope off his shoulder and over his head, but his body was clumsy and slow.

*Have to get it,* he thought fumbling with the rope. *Have to tie it off and...*

His body spasmed painfully, cramping with poison, and the pain cleared his thinking momentarily.

There wasn't time to secure the rope and climb down. Besides, the poison was moving fast. Soon he wouldn't be able to grip the rope.

He glanced again at the scoreboard.

32 seconds.

31.

Then he looked down to where his three teammates stood, far below, shouting up at him. Yes, three. He grinned with grim satisfaction. Holly had saved Nadia.

An absolutely insane idea occurred to him.

"Wulfgar! How many hit points do I have left?"

"21, you crazy barbarian!" the sword yelled.

21 hit points…

Fifty feet…

1-10 points of damage for every ten feet.

Which meant…?

His cloudy brain struggled with the calculation, then tossed it aside like a dead spider.

"To hell with math," Dan said, and gripping Wulfgar in one hand and the key in the other, he stepped off the window ledge and dropped like a tombstone.

## 39

# WHERE AM I?

**D**an awoke.
Sort of.
All was darkness.

He could see nothing, smell nothing, hear nothing, feel nothing.

Not even his own body.

He just *was*.

Dan was a formless consciousness, alone in an endless void.

He remembered falling. Remembered the girls screaming up at him. Remembered pounding through a cloud of screeching rats, whipping past a discordant chorus of ghoulish laughter. Remembered giving one final barbaric battle cry and slamming into the ground with a crunching explosion of pain and…

Nothing.

He could remember nothing else.

Now he was here, alone in this strange non-space.

*Holy shit,* he thought. *Am I dead?*

Was this the afterlife? Would he spend an eternity alone, feeling nothing, only thinking, thinking, thinking?

Then a familiar voice bellowed, "Wake up, asshole!"

*Wulfgar?* Dan asked–or rather, *thought*, as he didn't seem to have a mouth at the moment.

Wulfgar must have heard him, however, because the sword's voice said, "The one and only."

*Am I... dead?*

"Not yet," Wulfgar said. "But hey, if you see a bright light soon, you might want to sit tight and not go rushing to it like some kind of moth, all right? Because you're at -8 hit points. If you drop two more points..."

Dan would have nodded with understanding if he'd had a head. *So I'm... what? Unconscious?*

"Flesh-and-blood Dan is out like a wet torch," Wulfgar said. "You, though? You're just sort of in-between."

*Wait... if I'm not flesh-and-blood Dan, who am I?*

"We're still trying to sort that out, aren't we?" Wulfgar said. "Look, I figured I would bring you up to speed on some stats, while we, you know, wait and see if you're going to die."

*Great,* Dan thought, hoping that his sarcastic tone would somehow resonate despite his lack of vocal cords.

"Let's talk experience points. You were sitting at 7343. You get 152 more for killing a bunch of flying rats, 200 for getting the key, and 810 for killing the spiders. That puts you at 8505 experience points."

That was good, Dan thought, but he still needed around 3500 points to reach third level. And the semifinals had made it abundantly clear that if he survived and the Noobs made the finals, he would really need to reach third level to have any chance of surviving the challenge.

"Finally," Wulfgar said, "in light of your original mission statement to make your sorry-ass life more like my kick-ass life in T&T, you get an additional 500 experience points for being a crazy bastard and jumping off that tower. You might've looked before you leaped, but you sure didn't think. That's the most Wulfgar-ish thing you've ever done, so you're up to 9005 points now, tough guy."

*Thanks, I guess.*

"You were a complete madman! I mean, old-world Dan used to do stuff like that with a made-up character, but you jumped yourself. Talk about barbaric!" The sword's laughter filled the void.

*Yeah,* Dan thought-spoke, *and about my crazy jump... how many hit points does flesh-and-blood me have now?*

"You're at -9," Wulfar said. "But don't go embarrassing us both with some sappy farewell. Your girlfriends unlocked the tombstone, and the healer just arrived…"

# THANK YOU

"**I** love you, Dan," Holly said, gazing into his eyes.

They stood in the living room of Nadia's apartment in the center of town. Dan was feeling pretty good for a guy who'd almost died only a few hours earlier. He felt good as new, in fact, thanks to the healers.

He and the girls had gotten cleaned up, changed, eaten, and were heading to the Skeller when Holly and Nadia had changed direction, leading Dan to Nadia's apartment, which he hadn't seen until now.

The place was spacious and clean and really nice in an understated way, looking nothing like a thieves' den or the dorm of a cheery RA. This was the tastefully simple retreat of a private woman who knew what she wanted.

"I love you, too, Holly," Dan said with a smile. Then he turned and slid his hand under Nadia's chin. "And I love you, Nadia."

Nadia's face turned bright red, and she laughed, sounding both embarrassed and happy. "I love you, too," Nadia said. She reached out and took Holly's hand. "I love both of you."

The girls hugged. Then they shared a knowing look and turned back toward Dan.

Holly said, "We want to thank you."

"Yes," Nadia said. "Thank you for being there for me, for catching me when I fell, for saving my life." She lifted her mouth to his and gave him a slow, soulful kiss.

When they broke the kiss, Holly was staring at Dan with a glimmer in her purple eyes. "I want to thank you for saving her, too, and for all that you did today. Because of your bravery, we made the finals, something I've dreamed of doing for a long time."

Holly lifted onto her tiptoes. As usual, her kiss was passionate and lively, her tongue probing playfully.

"You're both welcome," Dan said, feeling a little embarrassed.

The girls were treating him like he was some kind of hero. In actuality, he had just done his part.

Besides, as Zeke had pointed out shortly after Dan had awakened, Dan should have spared them all the drama and just *dropped* the key. In Dan's defense, he had been out of his mind with pain, poison, and panic... but still, he didn't think anybody should be patting him on the back right now.

"Really," he said, "you guys don't have to thank me."

"Oh," Holly said mischievously, "we're going to thank you. Right, Nadia?"

Nadia smiled, and her face burned bright red again. But her eyes gleamed with mischief, just like Holly's. Mischief and excitement. "Yes, we are," Nadia said. "We are going to thank you *properly*."

Each of them took one of his hands, and without saying a word, they led him through the apartment and into a bedroom.

Dan didn't know exactly what they were up to, but you don't need an intelligence score of 18 to know that if two loving, beautiful women lead you into a bedroom, you should probably just go with the flow and see what happens.

Like the main living space, the bedroom was bright and clean and understated. A comfortable looking, queen-sized bed with a downy white comforter and several colorful pillows dominated the room.

Holly stood before him.

Nadia stood behind him.

The girls moved in, hugging him from both sides. It felt great. He loved them both.

He draped his left arm around Holly's shoulders and held her close. Meanwhile, he reached back with his right hand and rubbed Nadia's hip affectionately.

Both girls stepped back a few inches.

Holly reached up and unclasped Dan's cloak. He felt Nadia catch the garment and toss it aside. Then Nadia's hands grabbed the bottom edge of his T-shirt.

Holly licked her lips as Nadia peeled Dan's shirt up over his head.

The girls rubbed their hands over his bare upper body, massaging his muscles, tracing the lines of his abdomen, and tickling up his spine. Then they began kissing his chest and back, his neck and stomach, feathering his upper torso with light kisses.

Dan was hard as a rock. He reached for Holly, but she grabbed his wrist, pressed it to his side, and shook her head.

"We're thanking you," she said, playfully stern. "Just stand there and receive our gratitude."

The girls crouched down and lifted his legs one at a time, removing his boots, then stood again. Holly stepped close, draped her slender arms over his shoulders, and lay her blond head against his chest, nuzzling into him.

Behind him, Nadia snaked her muscular arms around his

waist. She pressed her body into his back and rubbed her face against his shoulders, like a cat showing affection.

Holly unbuckled his belt and unsnapped his jeans. As soon as the button popped free, Nadia's hands hooked into his waistline and pulled his pants to the floor.

Suddenly, he was standing there, stark naked and fiercely erect.

Holly stepped back. She looked him up and down, as if studying every inch of him, and smiled wickedly. "You just stand right there, mister," she said. "Don't make a move."

Nadia moved into view and stood beside Holly. Simultaneously, they began to slowly undress, taking their time, teasing him, both of them staring into his eyes.

And then they stood naked before him.

Both women were achingly beautiful and yet very different. The contrast between their beauties only served to make each of them more beautiful.

Holly was short and blond, fine-boned and exquisitely curvy, with intelligent purple eyes and exotically pointed ears, his utterly lovely slice of summer, his grey elf princess.

Nadia was brunette and taller, halfway between Holly's height and his own, with a slender yet powerful acrobat's physique and bright green eyes that shone with hope and hurt, his tough yet vulnerable orphan, both beautiful and beautifully complicated.

He smiled. "My two women," he said, feeling a surge of love. "My two, incredible, gorgeous women."

"Your two wives," Holly said.

Nadia laughed nervously. "Two *women* is fine, thank you very much."

Holly laughed. "Still in denial, huh?"

Dan reached out and caressed each of their faces. "I don't care what you call yourselves. I'm yours, you're mine, and you are both beautiful."

Holly smirked. "That's a very generous thing for our husband to say, but he has forgotten the rules of this game." She removed his hands and returned them to his sides.

Dan shrugged. "What can I say? We barbarians don't play by the—"

Nadia cut him off with a kiss, pressing her lovely breasts against his bare chest.

"Fuck the rules," Dan said, and cupped her A+ ass in his hands.

"Oh no you don't," Nadia scolded, and peeled away his hands. "Put them behind your back if you can't control yourself."

Dan did as he was told. Sure, he was a rule breaker, but some games were more fun than others, rules or no rules, and he very much wanted to play this game.

Nadia moved to his side and turned his head toward hers and resumed their kiss. He could feel her desire in the kiss but even more so, he could feel her love, and yes, her gratitude, not so much for catching her when she had fallen, he suspected, but for binding his life with hers and lifting her out of loneliness.

For a girl who showed the world so many different faces, Nadia was incredibly transparent during this intimate moment. He could tell what she was feeling, could feel it in her kiss, hear it in her breath, and sense it in the energy coming off of her quivering body.

Dan understood that Nadia was opening herself to him, allowing herself to be vulnerable, trusting him to protect her true self, and this only made him love her more fiercely. It was all he could do not to crush her in a loving embrace.

What Holly did next, however, certainly helped to distract him.

Her soft lips kissed the tip of his throbbing member one time, gently.

He couldn't see Holly. She was down below, and he was busy making out with Nadia. But he could nonetheless picture Holly in his mind. He had watched her kiss and lick and tease him many times.

Tonight, Holly didn't bother with licking and kissing and teasing. Her warm, wet mouth closed over him, and she plunged her head forward, taking every inch of him down her throat. She kept him like that, buried to the hilt, for several seconds.

Her hand cupped his balls, squeezing gently. She made soft suckling sounds as her tongue moved side to side, massaging the base of his shaft.

Nadia broke the kiss, took his face in her hands, and fixed him with a smoldering look that burned with both love and lust. Then she leaned in to kiss his neck. Her kisses moved up to his ear, where she kissed and nipped, her breath hot and ragged with desire.

"Are you ready?" Nadia breathed.

"Yes," Dan said, his voice thick with passion.

With Nadia's lips pressed to his ear, he felt her smile. "Are you sure?" she asked.

He nodded.

Without another word, Nadia dropped to her knees beside Holly.

The grey elf pulled her head back, letting his entire length flop free of her mouth. She gasped for air and smiled playfully up at him, her lips shining with saliva. Then she shimmied over a few inches, making room for Nadia.

Dan looked down, amazed at the sight of his two women, crouching side by side before him, pressed up against one another, each with an arm around the other's waist.

Their heads moved forward in unison to kiss and lick him. While one mouth attended to his balls, the other licked up and down his shaft. Then the mouths switched places.

Back and forth, they teased him like this for several minutes.

Dan had never been so aroused. Hot, urgent pressure built in him.

Holly and Nadia stopped swapping roles and both focused on his member, working up and down both sides of the shaft with quick licks and soft kisses.

Dan felt like he was going to explode. But he played their game, rules and all, and stood there, aching, with his hands pressed together behind his back like a soldier standing at parade rest.

The girls grew more eager. Their kisses came faster and harder and louder. Humming with pleasure, they licked both sides of his shaft, pressing their tongues firmly into him and lapping his whole length, both of them at the same time.

Then Nadia took his root in one hand and started pumping up and down as the girls' mouths moved upward from the shaft to its head. As Nadia's hand squeezed him tightly, working up and down, up and down, both girls sucked and kissed the head, slurping and moaning.

Their cheeks pressed together, as if their mouths were jockeying for position. Meanwhile, each girl rubbed the other's back. This show of affection was sweet and feminine and curiously arousing.

Holly took him into her mouth and sucked hard, her cheeks going hollow. Then Nadia pushed Holly's head playfully aside and took her turn, mouthing only his swollen tip, sucking hard.

Back and forth they went, one girl watching as the other sucked, back and forth. Sometimes, as they swapped places, their lips brushed in fleeting kisses, and this only made the urgent pressure swelling in Dan rise more savagely.

"Can't... last... much longer," he groaned.

Instantly, the girls ceased their ministrations.

"Well," Holly said, and popped to her feet, making her gorgeous breasts bounce in a *very* interesting way. "We can't have that. Not yet, anyway. First, we have to change positions."

Holly reached around behind Dan's back, took one of his wrists, and led him to the bed, where she told him to lie down on his back with his hands behind his head. She positioned him so that his ass was at the edge of the bed, his legs were bent, and his feet still touched the floor.

The mischievous grey elf grinned, clearly enjoying her temporary control over him. She crawled onto the bed, slid around behind him, and crouched down, pressing her knees into his bent arms, pinning them in place, giving him a lovely view of her flat stomach and the impressive swell of her breasts.

Then Holly's small hands covered his eyes like a blindfold, and she said, "All right, Nadia. Now show our husband how thankful you are."

Dan groaned, aching for release and driven out of his mind by these two, hot women.

His knees were pushed roughly apart, and Nadia's sleek, smooth body slid in between his legs. Her hand took his shaft, her mouth closed over the head, and she went to work on him.

Mercilessly this time.

Nadia couldn't deep-throat him the way that Holly could, but that didn't matter. Her mouth slid up and down, exerting just the right amount of suction, while one hand fondled his balls and the other pumped the lower shaft in time with her bobbing head. She stuck to this rhythm, pleasuring every inch of him, sucking and pumping, sucking and pumping, moaning with hunger.

Above him, Holly was moaning, too, all but panting, and

though he couldn't see her, he could feel her hips gyrating in the open air, mad with lust.

Hearing his two women, picturing them, feeling them, Dan could take no more. He growled and tensed.

"Finish him, Nadia," Holly commanded. "Show your husband how grateful you are. Swallow every drop."

Dan roared and exploded in Nadia's mouth, bucking with the most intense orgasm of his life.

Nadia did as she was commanded, sucking and slurping and moaning more loudly than ever, pumping away with her hand, milking him as he filled her mouth with his seed.

Holly released him and scampered off the bed.

"Holy Hades," Dan groaned, looking up at the ceiling. "That was amazing!"

He felt Holly push in between his legs beside Nadia, who laughed happily. Then he heard wet kissing sounds, propped up on his elbows, and looked down to see the girls kneeling between his legs, locked in embrace, sharing a greedy kiss, swirling their tongues together, mixing their saliva and the remnants of his seed.

He sat up and put a hand on each of their heads, caressing them gently.

Holly pushed his hand away and turned to him, shaking her head. "Oh no you don't, mister," she said in a mock scolding tone. "You lie back down. We're not done thanking you yet."

"Screw that," Dan said, and stood. "You're right that we're not done. Far from it, in fact. But I'm through with your rules. Now I'm going to thank both of you for being brave, beautiful women, for winning today, for saving my life, and for being mine."

Holly's mouth dropped open in mock shock.

Still hard as granite, Dan gave Holly a cocky grin, then turned pointedly away from her. He grabbed a fistful of

Nadia's gorgeous chestnut locks, guided her onto the bed, and pushed her flat, face down. Her legs hung over the edge, her thighs pressed up against the side of the mattress, and her perfect ass lay before him, switching back and forth, betraying her arousal.

"Spread your legs," he ordered.

Nadia obeyed, and her glistening slit came into view. She turned her head, blindfolded by her dark hair and panting with anticipation.

"Lift that sweet ass up in the air," Dan told her.

Then he glanced over his shoulder at Holly, who watched, trembling and transfixed, her hand making wet sounds as it worked furiously between her quivering legs.

"You," he said, and shook his head. "No touching. Put your hands behind your back and watch me thank Nadia. Then she will watch as I thank you. *Properly*."

## 41

## MOTHER WOLF

Later, after properly expressing their gratitude, Dan and the girls left Nadia's apartment and headed toward the Skeller.

"It's them," someone called from across the street, pointing excitedly. "It's the Noobs!"

An excited female voice cried out, "Is that Dan the Barbarian?"

Dan ignored them and swaggered on, a beautiful woman under each arm.

"Oh, boy," Nadia said. "You're really loving this, aren't you?"

"Hades yeah," Dan said. "We're rock stars!"

They were all over the news. Campus Quest was a big deal, and Dan's leap from the tower had stolen the show. On TV, analysts were arguing whether he was brave, stupid, or an attention whore. After all, they agreed, he could've simply tossed the key down to his team.

Holly and Nadia had teased him as they flipped through the channels, all of which seemed to be replaying Dan's crazy jump.

Dan laughed it off. He'd survived, thank Crom. That's all that mattered. This was his fifteen minutes of glory, and he wasn't going to let a bunch of chickenshit analysts ruin it for him.

If he'd learned one lesson in the semifinals, it wasn't look before you leap; it was the same lesson that Wulfgar had been hammering into him since day one in this new world.

Less thinking, more action.

In the finals, he was going to have to be bolder than ever.

They turned down a dark, empty street. Halfway down the block, Holly stopped them, her pointed ears twitching. "Wait," she said.

Four small, cloaked figures stepped from the alleyway. Halflings?

Dan took a step forward, one hand on Wulfgar. "Leave us be if you wish to live," he growled.

One of the figures stepped forward and spoke in a girl's voice. "Mother Wolf."

Nadia smiled. "Goldfinch," she said warmly, and opened her arms to the girl, who rushed into her embrace.

The others stepped forward, hugging Nadia in turn.

*Not halflings,* Dan realized. *Children.* Probably the same street urchins that he had seen in the Diner, when he'd first met Nadia.

Two girls, two boys. Nadia hugged each, calling them by name.

Goldfinch was a pretty slip of a girl in her early teens, half-elven and strawberry blond. She stared at Nadia with obvious admiration.

The other girl was a short and heavyset half-orc around the same age as Goldfinch. She had wide-set eyes, a squashed nose, and a long mouth that lifted into a charming smile when Nadia caught the girl trying to pick her pocket. "Nice try, Toad," Nadia said, mussing the grinning girl's hair.

The youngest and tallest of the crew was Stork, a stick-thin boy with a big nose, who couldn't seem to stop moving. He shifted anxiously from foot to foot and constantly glanced about, checking his surroundings.

*A perfect lookout,* Dan thought.

The shortest member of the group actually was a halfling —and a child, though an older child than the rest, Dan could see by his features. The boy was around three feet tall but rugged, with a wrestler's build, a square jaw, and dark, brooding eyes.

The boy turned to Dan with a slack face and a challenge gleaming in his dark eyes. "Who's this?"

"Badger, this is my friend Dan," Nadia said. "And you all know Holly."

Dan offered his hand.

Badger gave a little nod but wouldn't shake.

Dan had to suppress a grin. What a little hard-ass this kid was. It wouldn't do to go grinning at him, though. The kid probably had a temper, and though Dan could snap him in half, Nadia–or "Mother Wolf," as the urchins called her–clearly cared about the boy. Besides, Dan had to admire the little bastard's toughness.

"What do you have for me?" Nadia said.

The kids were silent for a few seconds. Stork shifted nervously back and forth, scanning the street.

"It's okay," Nadia assured them. "Holly and Dan are family."

"These," Toad said, and withdrew an oilcloth sack bound in filthy twine. She unparcelled it, revealing a tarnished brooch set with a milky gray stone, a brass letter opener, a simple copper ring, a jade comb, and a thimble.

Nadia examined each item, pocketed the lot, and handed back the sack and twine, along with several silver pieces and a stack of coppers.

"Thank you, Mother Wolf," Toad said, and handed the tall boy a silver. "Stork stood watch."

"Very good," Nadia said, and tossed Stork an additional silver piece. "We all have our function. Speaking of which, I trust you've been keeping everyone safe, Badger?"

The halfling hard-ass nodded. "Kicked the shit out of some asshole who tried to steal Toad's loot," he said, "and I hamstrung a slaver who tried to steal Goldfinch last night."

Goldfinch nodded, her pretty eyes huge.

"Thank you, Badger," Nadia said, handing the boy a gold piece. "We would be lost without you."

The fierce boy had a hard time hiding his smile. Nadia's praise clearly pleased him even more than the gold piece, but he was just as clearly struggling not to reveal that.

"Now," Nadia said, turning to the tiny blond waif, "sing for me, Goldfinch."

For the next several minutes, the little girl rattled off an incredible amount of information with impressive detail. Transactions, betrayals, plots, exchanges; people, places, times; impending deliveries, probable ambushes, and recent incarcerations.

"Very good," Nadia said, digging out payment.

"There's more, Mother Wolf," Goldfinch said. "Men in dark blue cloaks have been looking for you," she said, and glanced at Dan and Holly, "and for them."

Dan tightened his fists. Holly had thrown the Acolytes of Eternal Darkness off track by charming one into falsely reporting that she and Dan had died, but apparently the assholes had seen them, alive and well, on a Campus Quest TV broadcast.

"Also," Goldfinch said, seeming nervous, "Gruss wants to see you, Mother Wolf."

"Why?" Nadia said, and although her voice was calm, Dan could see concern in her emerald eyes.

Goldfinch said that she didn't know what Gruss wanted, but his people had been spreading the word that he wanted to see Nadia. Immediately.

Nadia paid the girl, then sent the street urchins on their way, wishing them well.

"Mother Wolf, huh?" Dan said, as they started walking toward the Skeller.

Holly smiled and kissed Nadia's cheek. "More like Saint Nadia, Patron of Lost Children."

"Ha ha," Nadia said, clearly uncomfortable. "I might be a lot of things, but believe me, a saint isn't one of them."

Ignoring her, Holly said, "All the street kids you see around town? Nadia takes care of them."

"I pay them for information," Nadia said.

"And teach them."

"Yeah," Nadia said, and laughed. "I teach them to pick pockets and locks. Then I fence their stuff for profit."

"Miniscule profit," Holly said. "And you keep them from having to go to other fences, who would gouge them at best, or sell them into slavery at worst."

Nadia's face twisted with anger then. "Well, that doesn't make me a saint, okay? The whole world is full of assholes, looking to hurt and exploit kids. If I was a saint, I'd kill all of them."

"Let me know when you're ready to earn your sainthood," Dan said. "I'll give you a hand."

Nadia smiled at that. "And I'm stupid for helping these kids. I guarantee that's why Gruss is looking for me. I help kids, he takes offense. They're on the streets, hustling, so they belong to him. That's how Gruss sees it. I say they belong to themselves. Not that I'll ever share that with him. I'd rather keep my head than speak my mind, if you know what I mean."

"Wait," Dan said, anger rising in him. "Is this Gruss guy threatening you?"

"Forget it," Nadia said.

"Fuck that," Dan said. "I'll chop his head off."

"No," Nadia said, dead serious, "you won't. I appreciate the sentiment, but you have no idea what you're talking about... or, more to the point, *who* you're talking about. Nobody fucks with Gruss."

"Who is he," Holly said, "head of the Thieves' Guild?"

Nadia shook her head. "If Gruss tells the Thieves' Guild to jump, they pay him 10% *then* ask him how high. Gruss was an enforcer for the Philly Syndicate. Rose through the ranks. Now he runs the center of the state."

Nadia frowned. "And he's fucking crazy. I mean brutal. He's into sending messages, which usually means cutting off a body part or two."

Dan wouldn't think about that. "If he touches you, I'll—"

"No, Dan," Nadia said. "Seriously. If you even look at Gruss the wrong way, he'll cut your eyes out. I'll avoid him for now. Then, after Campus Quest, I'll take him a gift, try to smooth things over."

"We'll go with you," Holly said, and Dan could see that she was feeling just as protective as he was.

"Actually, you won't," Nadia said. "I don't want either one of you stepping foot in that world. If–oh joy... look. It's our friendly neighborhood death cultists."

Half a dozen figures in dark blue cloaks appeared at the far end of the street. They didn't seem to have recognized the Noobs yet.

"Great," Holly said. "It was nice when they thought we were dead. Sorry to have pulled you in, too, Nadia."

"I was already in," Nadia said. "The acolytes just didn't know it yet. If someone threatens either of you, they threaten me, too."

"Um," Dan said, "hypocritical much?"

Then Holly steered them into an alley.

"Wait," Dan said, tugging like a kid who doesn't want to leave a playground. "I was going to kill those guys."

"Forget them," Holly said, traveling deeper into the alley. "We just made the finals of frigging Campus Quest, remember? Tonight, we celebrate. I'd rather drink and sing than kill and bleed."

"I'm with Holly," Nadia said. "Tonight, we party. We have the rest of our lives to kill assholes."

## 42

## PARTY!

The Skeller was crazy.

As soon as Dan and the girls approached the long line of people waiting to get inside, everyone started pointing and calling out to them. Doormen whisked them to the front of the line, and the packed bar went insane, a mob of strangers congratulating them and handing them free beers.

Eventually, they fought their way to the back room, where a live band was blasting a pumped up blend of heavy metal, hip hop, and, strangely enough, Reggae.

People jammed the room, swaying to the music, waving their arms overhead, and chanting, "Seek! Seek! Seek!"

*Seek what?* Dan wondered, hoping they stumbled into another weird cult.

"Look!" Holly shouted. She grinned and pointed toward the center of the crowd, where a man was bodysurfing across the crowd, kicking his arms and legs like a delighted baby.

Of course, babies didn't have long, white beards.

"Zeke! Zeke! Zeke!" the crowd chanted.

The music cut off mid-song, and the singer, a huge guy in

shades, grinned and pointed at Dan and the girls. "Ladies and gentlemen, it's the Noobs!"

The adoring crowd crushed into them, shaking their hands and screaming congratulations and asking questions that Dan couldn't hear.

The music started up again. Looking ecstatic, Zeke fought his way over, hugged the girls, and slapped Dan on the arm.

Leaning close to Dan, the old wizard said, "This is the greatest day of my life! This is exactly why I came to college!"

Dan couldn't help but laugh. He patted Zeke on the back.

Sure, he hated sorcery, but Zeke wasn't all bad. Dan forgave the wizard for his weird ways and inconsistent Campus Quest performance. After all, they never would have gotten the key without his levitation spell.

Turning back to the crowd, Zeke shouted, "You're awesome! You're awesome! You're all totally awesome!"

Everyone roared and hauled him back into the air. Then Zeke scooted away on their hands, waving his limbs and cackling like a madman.

People handed the Noobs free beers and cleared out a corner table for them.

Zuggy sat in a pretty girl's lap at the next table, pounding beer and playing chess against a smart-looking kid in glasses and a pointy wizard's hat. The kid scratched his high forehead and stared with apparent frustration at the board. Despite the kid's intelligent face, pocket protector, and the implications of the book at his elbow–*Advanced Game Theory: Magical Applications for Really Smart Students*–the drunken monkey was clearly whipping his ass.

Dan laughed but had to wonder what such a pointyheaded genius was doing here in the Skeller. And where had they gotten a chessboard?

Then Dan laughed even harder, remembering that this

world was far from logical. This sort of thing always happened in Willis's adventures.

Increasingly, Dan was forgetting that this world was merely a construct. Day by day, moment by moment, this existence felt more and more real to him, as if this world were his true home and the old world, along with old-world Dan, had been nothing but fiction.

To Hades with it. He was happy.

A kid with a red, beefy face leaned in, pointing at Zuggy. "The monkey's drinking!"

"Yeah," Dan said.

The red-faced kid turned to his friends. "The monkey is drinking!"

They roared with laughter.

"Hey, monkey," the red-faced kid shouted, reaching across the table with a shot glass filled with amber liquid. "Do a shot, monkey!"

Zuggy looked up from the game with glowing eyes and reached for the shot, but Dan blocked him. That looked like whiskey, and Dan hadn't forgotten Zeke's warning.

*Zuggy's allergic to whiskey,* Zeke had told them. *It makes his knuckles bleed.*

Dan settled into the booth between Holly and Nadia, who looked beautiful and happy and both kept touching him, putting their arms over his shoulders, squeezing his arms and legs, resting their hands in his. It was an awesome night, and the free beer kept flowing.

Eventually, he pounded a beer and stood, feeling buzzed. "Gotta go see a man about a unicorn," he told the girls.

"One with a long, thick horn?" Holly teased.

"I'll let you see for yourself later," he said.

She swatted his ass. "Hurry back."

He fought his way through the crowd, shaking hands and giving high fives.

The bathroom was mercifully muffled. He took care of business, enjoying the brief respite from the noise and attention, and then headed back out into the madness.

Just outside the door, he was stopped by a big man with a black beard and a dead eye.

"We have met before, you and I," the man said, smiling. "Here. In this very place. You remember, yes?"

"I remember," Dan said. "You told me that the final stage was a death trap."

"Yes, I tried to warn you," the man said. "But here we are, yes? You make me very sad."

"Yeah, well, I gotta go."

"My friend," the man said, "do not be hasty. I am called Broadus, yes? I fight for the Sell-Swords." He extended his hand.

For half a second, Dan considered pulling a Badger and snubbing the guy, but then he shook hands and discovered that Broadus's grip was every bit as strong as his own.

"You are in over your head," Broadus said. "Be careful not to lose it." He made a slicing motion across his scarred neck.

"Right," Dan said. "Good luck keeping your head attached, too." He didn't know if Broadus was trying to be friendly or trying to psych him out. He just knew that he was done talking to the guy. "See you in the stadium."

Dan turned to leave but bumped into another member of the Sell-Sword team: the wiry elf.

The elf clapped Dan on the back. "You should listen to my friend. Sometimes, youth and strength aren't enough."

The elf handed him something… a pouch, Dan realized, with what felt like a good number of coins inside.

*Hey*, he thought. *This is* my *pouch.*

"You must have dropped it," the elf said.

"Bullshit," Dan said. "You picked my pocket."

The elf grinned. "Relax, boy. Your coins are safe. Count them later, you'll see. You might even find something extra."

"A little something," Broadus said. "A tip, yes? A clue. Our compliments, for sure. No problem. Maybe this clue, it wakes you up. Helps you understand the lie. Maybe you come to your senses and stay far away from the stadium."

"Don't count on it," Dan said, and turned away from them.

They were trying to scare him off, he realized now, trying to eliminate some competition. Heading back through the bar to his reunite with his friends, he had to shake his head. Did the Sell-Swords really think that their line of crap was going to make him forfeit?

He was a barbarian, not a Barbie doll!

Reaching the back room, he heard a loud ruckus and pushed his way to the corner table.

The kid with the red, beefy face was sprawled out unconscious on the table with a bloody nose. Zuggy crouched on his chest, pounding the kid's bloody face with looping haymakers.

"Break it up!" Dan shouted. He grabbed the monkey, hauled him off the unconscious idiot, caught the girls' attention, and nodded toward the exit.

## PIZZA SHOP SHOCKER

Out on the street, the night was refreshingly cool and quiet.

"Fools never should've given him whiskey," Zeke said, following along after them with Zuggy in his arms. The monkey still struggled, gnashing his teeth and beating the air with his bloodied knuckles.

"He decked that guy with one punch," Nadia marveled.

Zeke nodded. "He only weighs twenty pounds, but he can really crack." Then the old wizard pointed to a glowing sign outside a pizza shop. "Let's get him a couple of slices to soak up the whiskey."

Standing inside beneath the buzzing fluorescent lights, smelling the pizza, Dan realized that he was starving.

"What do you girls want?" he asked. "My treat."

The three of them decided to split two pizzas and a two-liter soda at home.

Waiting to order, Dan opened his money pouch, thinking, *That elf better not have stolen any of my money.*

Then, looking inside, he recoiled.

Mixed in with his coins was a little clay head, roughly the size of a ping pong ball.

*Not just any head, though,* he realized with a chill.

It was a replica of the head he had talked to back in Dr. Lynch's classroom. The grey elf who'd tried to sucker Dan into some wilderness side quest. It was definitely her, stitched eyes and all.

The thief must've put it in there when he'd lifted Dan's purse.

"What the hell is that?" Nadia asked.

Holly leaned in, looking horrified.

Dan told them about the Sell-Sword thief and raced through some of what had happened in Dr. Lynch's room, when the head had spoken to him.

"I'm so confused," he said. "Why would the Sell-Swords put this in there? What message are they trying to send? They said it was a clue, but how would they even know about the head? And how did they know that I knew about the head?"

"Divination," Zeke said darkly.

"So, they've been spying on me?" Dan said. "With magic?" The idea made him feel like he was covered in ticks.

Before Zeke could respond, Holly spoke up, clearly distressed. "Back up," she said. "What did the head say?"

Dan gave her the gist.

Holly was incredulous. "Why didn't you tell me about this?"

*Because I just thought the great gamemaster in the sky was trying to lure me into some stupid adventure,* Dan thought, but what he said was, "I don't know. It was all just weird. It wasn't a big deal."

"Wasn't a big deal?" Holly said, her pale cheeks flushing with anger. "A spirit from beyond death–a *grey elf* spirit–tells you that the forces of evil are rallying, and you didn't think that was a big deal?"

"Hey, sorry," he said. "I didn't know if it was real, you know? And then my teacher showed up, and she's the world's biggest bitch, and—"

"Yeah," Holly said, frowning. "You did tell me all about your mean teacher. So that was important enough to share, I guess."

"I didn't want to worry you over nothing," he said.

"Well, this isn't nothing," Holly said. She shook her head. "As soon as Campus Quest is over, I have to head home and tell my family. And you're coming with me, husband."

*Great,* Dan thought. *Just frigging great.*

The final round of Campus Quest was tomorrow.

A couple of hours ago, he was riding high, and his only concern was whether or not they would win.

Now, win or lose, one of the women he loved was going to report to a mob boss with a reputation for mutilating people. Meanwhile, his new wife was going to drag him into the forest and probably lead him into what sounded like a high-level meat grinder dungeon.

Oh yeah, and he'd also get to meet her parents, his *in-laws*, who just happened to be grey elves, the most xenophobic of all races.

*Unless I get lucky and die in the finals tomorrow,* he thought. *Then I won't have to worry about either problem.*

He'd meant it sarcastically, but strangely, the thought sent an icy chill tiptoeing up his spine.

44

---

## THE FINAL ROUND

W hen Dan and his teammates marched onto the field, the entire stadium, with over 80,000 spectators in attendance, cheered wildly.

Officials had already briefed the Noobs. This final event would take place beneath the stadium in a dungeon filled with challenges and obstacles, including numerous monsters. Their goal: to capture the final treasure, the Chest of Champions, which contained four golden crowns and a check for 50,000 gold pieces.

*Give me strength, Crom,* Dan prayed. *Let us win.*

Nadia was deeply competitive but more importantly wanted to prove something to herself. Holly wanted to experience victory for victory's sake and once in her life bask in the glory of public adoration.

For Dan, things were much simpler. He hadn't studied for Lynch's midterm and was definitely going to fail his independent study, which meant that he would soon be losing his scholarship. If he was going to stay in college, he needed to win this prize money.

The three teams would enter the dungeon simultaneously

but at different locations, none of which would afford advantage in time or level of difficulty. Eventually, the passageways would join the main system of caverns, and past that point, Campus Quest allowed no-holds-barred team-versus-team combat.

The Noobs continued their long walk across the football field.

Dan smiled grimly and raised his hand toward each quadrant of the massive stadium. Beside him, Holly beamed, waving one slender arm enthusiastically overhead. On his other side strode Nadia, all in black, her dark cloak fluttering behind her, a satisfied smirk showing beneath her black mask.

Dressed in his colorful poncho and ridiculous cowboy hat, Zeke waved to the crowd with a staff, which he had apparently added to look more wizard-like. On Zeke's shoulders, Zuggy grinned, bouncing up and down, pumping his gangly arms overhead.

Since they were currently in third place, the Noobs were the first to take the field. As instructed, they walked straight to the 50-yard line, climbed onto the wooden stage erected there, and waved at the roaring crowd.

*So many people,* Dan thought.

Willis and his gaming friends were out there somewhere. So were former coworkers from the dishwashing job Dan had quit, classmates and teachers, past and present, and countless people whom he had known casually since coming to Penn State. He felt a wave of gratitude, knowing that all of these people were cheering for him.

This morning, Dan had received a letter from his mother saying that the whole clan had been invited to a viewing party at Dan's old elementary school. It was clear that his mother didn't really understand much about Campus Quest, but that didn't matter to Dan. He desperately wanted to make his family and the Free proud.

Of course, not everyone would be rooting for the Noobs. He imagined Dr. Lynch in her dark sunglasses, scowling and shaking her head, offended that the university had allowed a barbarian onto campus in the first place.

The entire *Alpha Alpha Alpha* fraternity and most of the Greek organizations would be out there in the bleachers, hoping for Dan's death.

And, of course, the Acolytes of Eternal Darkness would be watching, on television if not in attendance, biding their time, waiting to strike again.

*Good,* Dan thought. *Let them watch. Let them see my strength, and when we meet again, I will use their fear against them.*

"Next up," the announcer said, "the team from *Alpha Alpha Alpha!*"

Dan watched through narrowed eyes as the gnolls charged onto the field, resplendent in the best magical armor that money could buy.

Over the last two days, several big chain armorers had approached Noobs, too, offering sponsorship. The armorers would loan the Noobs magical weapons and armor so long as they agreed to wear cloaks emblazoned with the armorer's logo.

Dan had taken one look at the glowing equipment and declined. He wanted nothing to do with bulky armor, which didn't match his barbaric fighting style at all, or with magical items, which made his skin crawl.

Grady and the AAA team fell in beside the Noobs. Grady waved at the crowd, a cocky smile on his hyena face.

*He isn't even surprised to be here,* Dan thought. *The prick probably assumes that he'll win, probably feels entitled to winning.*

As the announcer introduced the Sell-Swords, Grady

leaned slightly forward and called to Dan from the corner of his sneering mouth. "I'll be looking for you down in the dungeon, Danielle."

"I won't be hiding," Dan said.

Since middle school, Grady had made Dan's life a living hell, but Dan had changed.

Grady had changed, too, of course. Now, instead of just being a fantastically athletic bully with a silver spoon shoved up his ass, he was a fantastically athletic seven-foot-tall gnoll wearing enchanted armor and bristling with magical weapons. Growing up in this world, Grady had probably trained under the finest weapons instructors as well.

But life wasn't all about how much damage you could deal. Eventually, it also came down to how much damage you could take.

It came down to toughness.

It came down to heart.

And while Grady had lived a childhood of privilege in the white fortress alongside the Susquehanna, Dan had scraped and scavenged to survive in the wilderness across the river.

If the Noobs and *Alpha Alpha Alpha* clashed in the dungeon, Dan vowed to find a way through that magical armor, to wipe the sneer from Grady's muzzle, and finally, after all these years, to do what he should have done long, long ago and test the heart of his lifelong antagonist.

The Sell-Swords took their time crossing the field. All business, they didn't even bother to wave.

Broadus towered at the center of the team. Like the gnolls, he wore glowing plate mail, but his equipment was far from new. From his well-worn boots to his dented great helm, every scrap of Broadus's equipment bespoke deep experience.

With him were the wiry Elven thief, a heavily armored dwarven cleric gripping a glowing war hammer, and the team's spellcaster, a fierce-looking black-haired woman in blood-red robes.

The Sell-Swords had won every event so far and were heavily favored in the betting world to win it all.

While Dan would welcome a fight with Grady down below the surface, he very much wanted to avoid clashing with the Sell-Swords.

Their riddles continued to haunt him. He still didn't know how to take Broadus's warning that the finals were a lie and a death trap, and he hadn't managed to make any sense of the gruesome clue that the wiry elf had left in his pouch.

The rest of the Noobs insisted that the Sell-Swords were just trying to psych them out, which made a lot of sense. After all, none of the Sell-Swords were "real" students. They were mercenaries who had enrolled just to be eligible for Campus Quest. To them, this was an investment. They were, as the saying goes, in it to win it.

"To the thousands in attendance and the millions watching around the world," the announcer boomed, "welcome to the final round of this year's Campus Quest!"

After the excited cheering settled down, the announcer breezed over the historical importance of the competition, gave thanks to sponsors and everyone who had worked so hard behind the scenes in order to make this competition possible, and welcomed spectators of note, including the Dukes of Philadelphia, Pittsburgh, and Harrisburg.

The dukes' introductions set the crowd to buzzing.

Over recent months, tensions had been rising between the Dukes of eastern and western Pennsylvania, and both were reportedly courting the Duke of Harrisburg, no doubt trying to strike an alliance that would tip the scales in their favor when war inevitably broke out between Pittsburgh and Philadelphia.

As a barbarian from the wilds of northern Pennsylvania currently living in the rural center of the state, Dan cared little about these power struggles. He just wanted to get on with the competition.

The announcer handed the mic to the chairwoman of Campus Quest, who droned on for a while before asking everyone to stand for the national anthem.

After that, the Penn State cheerleaders charged onto the field and whipped the crowd into a frenzy.

Then, at long last, the three teams were asked to leave the stage and spread out across the field. Reporting to their assigned locations, each team stood within a glowing circle.

Dan felt Holly's hand slide to his.

"Ready?" she asked, her purple eyes shining with excitement.

"Ready," he told her, and took Nadia's hand.

Nadia smiled and reached out to grab Zeke's hand, too.

Then the circle of grass upon which they stood lowered into the ground, carrying them down a dark shaft. As they descended slowly, sinking deeper and deeper into the earth, a barrier slid into place overhead, blocking out the sun and sky and cheering of the crowd.

This was it.

45

# THE DUNGEON

The platform lowered them into a cavern roughly the size of Dan's apartment. The stone floor was more or less level, and flickering torches hung in grommets along the rough-hewn walls.

Grabbing a torch, Dan realized that he'd made a mistake preparing for this event.

How was he supposed to use Wulfgar while holding a torch? And what if they had to fight in a tight passageway? He couldn't even draw the sword, let alone swing it.

A second later, he held a torch in one hand and a knife in the other, feeling ridiculous.

"Very intimidating, barbarian," Nadia joked.

"Yeah, yeah," Dan said. "You know what they always say. It isn't the size of a barbarian's knife, it's—"

"Goblins!" Holly shouted.

Dan spun around just as Holly jabbed the end of her staff into a goblin's throat, dropping him. Then she jerked to one side, dodging the blade of another attacker.

Shouting in their ugly, guttural language, a large gang of

goblins was pressing forward out of a narrow passageway, trying to flood into the chamber.

Dan rushed forward, counting–four, six, ten… and lost track, seeing the clamoring mob of goblins still in the passageway, pushing toward the fight. There had to be twenty-five or thirty goblins, maybe more!

Dan stopped counting and drove his knife into the chest of the closest goblin, reducing their number by one.

Two goblins continued to attack Holly. Three turned on Dan.

With their burly shoulders, stubby necks, and brindle hides striped in shades of mud and moss, the goblins reminded Dan of pit bulls. They were short, between four and five feet tall, and very aggressive, with big eyes, pug noses, and wide mouths tangled with crooked teeth.

Dan blocked and parried, ducked and dodged, stabbed and slashed. He wanted to bowl them over with his superior size and strength, but bull rushing them would be stupid. The goblins would break around his charge, then slide in behind him and cut him to ribbons.

Dan cursed as a sword grazed his thigh, slicing through the new jeans he'd bought for the event. The cut burned, draining blood.

Dan counterattacked, punching his knife through the bulging eye of the goblin who'd cut him.

Another goblin surged at Dan, growling as it swung a crude hand axe.

Dan sidestepped the sloppy attack, mesmerized by the goblin's enraged face. Inked in blocky black letters across the brindled forehead, a tattoo read, *GREETINGS*.

*Weird*, Dan thought, and jammed his knife into the goblin's eye.

Weirder still, he soon realized that the other goblins also had tattooed foreheads.

He killed *KEEP* with a disemboweling rake across the gut, then stomp-kicked *WHEN* in the face, driving the little bastard backward and impaling him on the spear of GOING, whom Dan finished seconds later, drilling him with a one-two combination, stunning him with a hard jab to the forehead and driving the knife hilt-deep through the goblin's upturned nose.

Then Dan realized his mistake. He should have put his back to Holly's, forming a hard center with three-hundred-and-sixty-degree coverage.

Everything had happened so quickly, though, and the wily goblins had forced Dan and Holly slowly apart, further opening the passageway. More of them flooded through the gap.

Nadia charged into the fray, spinning through the goblin ranks, her glowing blades flashing. To either side of the whirling thief, goblins dropped, clutching vainly at gaping wounds she'd slashed across their throats.

But there were still so many goblins. As they surged forward, threatening to overwhelm Nadia, Dan switched tactics.

He retreated into the center of the cavern. This opened a hole in the Noob's defensive wall. The goblins howled with bloodthirsty glee and rushed at Dan in a muddy river bristling with swords and spears.

But Dan hadn't just redirected the flow of attackers. He had also given himself space.

"Come on!" he roared, and ripped Wulfgar from his sheath.

Then Dan went completely apeshit, hacking and slashing, kicking and stomping, breaking bones and spilling guts in a mad frenzy.

The single-minded goblins came on, climbing over fallen comrades and slipping in the wet mess of steaming entrails.

Dan slaughtered wave after wave of attackers, his battle cries inseparable from the roared curses of his blood-soaked two-handed sword.

Then it was over.

Dan stood upon a stinking carpet of dead goblins, panting for breath and covered in hot blood.

Having moved to that red place beyond pain, he now forced himself to survey his wounds. The goblins had slashed and stabbed and bitten him. Minor wounds covered him.

He turned to his women, who stood together, examining corpses and talking. "Everyone okay?"

They nodded. Holly's bracers and Nadia's speed and dexterity had kept them safe.

"Well done," Zeke said, emerging from the shadowy rear of the room with a tentative look on his face. Zuggy's head popped out of his poncho, looking just as wary.

"Nice of you to lend a hand, Zeke," Dan said sarcastically, and bent down to pry a battered short sword from the hand of a dead goblin. Even a third-rate short sword would be better than his little knife in cramped quarters.

Zeke joined the girls, who were talking excitedly.

"Come on," Dan said. "We don't have time to loot corpses."

"We're not," Holly said. "They have words on their foreheads."

"Yeah," he said. "Goblins are weird. Let's go."

"This one says NOOBS," Nadia said, pointing to a female goblin missing an arm.

"It's some kind of message," Holly said.

"Eat at Joe's," Dan joked, but then he glanced at one of the dead goblins at his feet and noticed another, smaller tattoo on its eyelid.

"Hey," Dan called. "SKY here has a number tattooed on his eyelid. 21."

The Noobs soon realized that all twenty-nine of the goblins had tattooed foreheads and eyelids.

"Put them in order," Holly said. "Where's number one?"

Dan groaned. "We don't have time for this. The other teams aren't fiddling around with corpse puzzles. They're racing toward the treasure."

But his teammates ignored him.

"Here's number one," Nadia said. "GREETINGS."

Holly smiled. "NOOBS is number two. Find number three."

That's when Dan realized that his teammates might be onto something and pitched in.

The Noobs hurried, untangling corpses, pulling down eyelids, and lugging dead goblins into the main chamber, where they assembled the world's most morbid puzzle, which turned out to be some kind of poem.

> *Greetings, Noobs.*
> *Good luck to you.*
> *Here's a riddle,*
> *To help you through:*
> *Keep going down,*
> *Till you reach the sky.*
> *You'll reach the chest,*
> *When both knights die.*

"SOUNDS LIKE WE HAVE TO KILL SOME KNIGHTS," DAN SAID. Truth be told, he hated riddles, preferring to hack and slash his way to glory. "Maybe they're guarding the final treasure?"

"How do we reach the sky by going down?" Holly mused.

"Only one way to find out," Nadia said. "Keep moving downward."

## 46

# GRUESOME FRUIT

**D**an led the way, torch in one hand, crappy little sword in the other.

They hurried along the passageway, which sloped gently downward into the earth. When the corridor T-ed into another rough-hewn hallway, they chose the side that sloped downward and hustled forward until they arrived at a large wooden door.

"Hold on," Nadia said, examining the door for traps. She inspected the edges slowly, tracing them with the tip of her dagger. Dan could see her jaw muscles clenching and unclenching.

"It's fine," he said, and reached for the door handle. "We don't have time to keep slowing down."

But Nadia held up one hand. "Wait."

Leaning forward, she squinted at the door handle. Then she turned, stared into the darkness behind them, and told everyone to press up against the walls.

Once the Noobs had flattened themselves against the corridor walls, Nadia lay upon the floor, reached up, jabbed at the door handle with her dagger, and jerked her arm back to her body.

*Whap-whap-whap!*

Three arrows vibrated, now jutting from the center of the wooden door.

"Good call," Dan admitted.

"You can't rush everything in life," Nadia said, and they opened the door.

That's when things got strange.

Not that a riddle tattooed across the foreheads of dead goblins wasn't odd, but the space beyond the door was *remarkably* bizarre.

Stepping into the room was like stepping onto the peak of some flat-topped mountain.

The room was cold and dark and windy. Powerful gales howled through the darkness, extinguishing their torches and making them squint. The freezing wind roared over them, making their cloaks crack like flags in a storm.

Without their torches, they could see nothing.

At least *Dan* could see nothing.

"I see no heat," Holly reported. The wind was so loud that she had to shout it twice for them to hear her.

*Ah yes,* Dan thought. *Holly's an elf. She has dark vision.*

As he understood it, dark vision allowed elves to see heat signatures but not much else, so it wouldn't be much good to them right now.

No one bothered to relight the torches. There would be no shielding them from this wind.

Nadia pulled out her magical daggers, which gave off a weak glow. Crouching down, she examined the floor.

"Careful," Nadia said, pointing past Dan's feet. "Drop off. Big one."

Dan looked at the floor where Nadia was pointing, and his heart did a backflip.

There was no floor behind him.

The Noobs stood upon a stone rectangle, the top landing of a set of stone steps that descended into the unknown. To either side, a dark void gaped, screaming icy wind.

"We have to keep going down," Dan shouted against the roaring wind.

"Wait," Holly said. "I'm going to try something."

Holly lifted one hand and spoke, her words lost in the raging wind.

Then *pop-pop, pop-pop-pop…*

Softball-sized bundles of blue-white flame whooshed from her outstretched palm, arching out into the darkness like Roman candle pyrotechnics.

Dan's jaw dropped.

Holly swiveled side to side, launching balls of flame up, down, out, and away, partially illuminating the vast space around them. The fiery projectiles were magical, so the wind didn't affect them. They simply soared through the darkness, then tumbled away and sputtered out.

The Noobs were standing atop a wide set of stone stairs that descended into a massive cavern. Just how massive, they couldn't say. The flames trailed light across a wide-open space, then petered out without any sign of a ceiling or walls or a floor. Only a set of stairs descending into a yawning darkness howling with freezing wind.

Then the spell died, and they were in darkness again.

Everyone hesitated for a moment. This was clearly the way down, if they wanted to follow the riddle, but the steps were pitch black again, and one wrong step or a stronger blast of icy wind could send one or all of them plummeting into the void.

"I'll go first," Dan said, moving past them.

He started down the stairs, testing each new step, sliding

his boot back and forth, doing his best to make sure that he wasn't angling off one side or another.

The wind battered him, forcing him to hunker into a crouch.

Dan had inched his way down perhaps a dozen steps when Zeke said, "Oh screw it," and a globe of bright light sixty feet across encircled them. The gigantic cavern remained in shadow, but noon-bright light revealed the stairs and landing behind them and a long stretch of stairs before them.

"Keep going," Zeke told Dan. "The light will move with us."

Not for the first time, Dan felt like strangling the old man. "You can cast a light spell?"

"I congratulate you on your firm grasp of the obvious," Zeke said.

Dan frowned. "Why didn't you cast it before?"

The wizard shrugged. "I like to play it cool," he explained as they descended. "Let you kids have your fun. But darkness creeps me out. Reminds me of the Plane of Ever-Shade."

The weird old wizard launched into a series of weird recollections about his extensive travels through parallel dimensions, making Dan wish that the wind would blow hard enough to drown out the old man's non-stop rambling.

Dan didn't know exactly how long they descended those stairs. He only knew that it felt like forever.

They had traveled at least a mile when they reached the tips of the highest spikes. Continuing their descent, they realized that to either side of the stairs rose a forest of spikes, some of which bore gruesome fruit: suits of armor impaled with drooping skeletons still inside.

*Guess they didn't have a wizard with a light spell to guide their way,* Dan thought, and he shouted to Zeke, "How much longer will this spell work?"

"Oh, a while," Zeke said, matter-of-factly.

*We'd better make it to the bottom before it gives out,* Dan thought.

He couldn't imagine going back at this point. But crawling down another mile or two of dark steps with ice cold winds blasting them didn't sound great, either.

The cold was intense. As a barbarian from the Endless Mountains, he was no stranger to winter, but he hoped that the others were holding up all right.

Fifteen minutes later, they finally reached the bottom of the massive cavern. The Noobs cheered and embraced.

The ground beneath their feet was soil, soft with loam. The wind wasn't so intense down here, but a loud creaking filled the air. The sound was many-noted and rhythmic, like a thousand boats, moored and rocking in an unsteady sea.

It was the spikes.

And Dan saw then that the spikes were trees. A tightly packed forest of tall, straight, limbless trees sharpened to points.

"Man," Dan said, "whoever made this place is fucking weird."

They followed a winding path into the forest. Dan took point, Wulfgar in hand, and the sword launched into a curse-laden rant about just how much he hated this creepy-ass place.

"Shh," Dan said, hushing the sword.

He had heard something, faintly, in the wind. Though the sound had been too faint for his conscious mind to identify, it had sparked a bone deep, primal fear that made the hair on his arm and the back of his neck stand up.

What was coming for them out of the darkness?

"I heard it, too," Holly said, sounding worried. "It sounded like... there!" She pointed into the darkness. "Three heat signatures. Four… no, five. They're big, coming fast, running on all fours. They're giving off a lot of heat!"

47

# KILL THAT ONE FIRST!

**D**an squinted into the darkness, wishing for night vision. Around him, everyone prepared for battle. Holly laid her staff at her feet, strung her bow, and nocked an arrow.

Nadia filled her fists with glowing daggers.

Then Dan spotted five sets of glowing red eyes racing through the darkness, coming this way.

A thunderous bark shook the darkness. Then another. Then the charging beasts were all barking and growling.

One by one, the eyes disappeared as huffing flames billowed out, giving the rough impression of huge, dark shapes moving very quickly. Then the flames died away, and the red eyes returned, having drawn much closer.

"Hellhounds," Zeke said, sounding pleasantly surprised. "Terribly interesting creatures."

"Great," Dan said. "Do you know a spell that will kill them?"

"I suppose so…"

"All right. Use that spell, then."

A jet-black dog the size of a pony burst into the light and

paused, glaring at them with bright red eyes. The beast panted, tiny jets of flame cycling from its nostrils.

The hellhound uttered a low growl. A fiery froth leaked from its terrible, snarling muzzle. A line of sizzling drool snapped off and hit the ground with a hiss.

*It's drooling lava,* Dan thought.

Four more hellhounds trotted into view and stood growling just behind the first dog.

"Everyone! Attack that one!" Nadia shouted, pointing at the biggest hound. "Kill the alpha first!"

Dan wanted to argue.

Nadia's suggestion flew in the face of everything he'd learned playing T&T. It was a mistake to pile up damage on the strongest monster. Even if you killed it, that would leave all those other fiery jaws to do damage. Better to kill as many attackers as quickly as possible, then pile up on the head honcho.

But Nadia delivered her command with such confidence that he and the rest of the Noobs followed her order.

The huge hellhound roared like a lion, filling the air with a burst of flames.

Dan heard a twang, and one of Holly's arrows sunk into the beast's chest.

The hound charged.

Dan raced toward the beast, drawing back with Wulfgar, ready to swing.

The hellhound's fiery gaze locked onto him. The red eyes glowed even more brightly, and the monster's smoldering jaws pulled back in a diabolical grin.

A glowing dagger plunged into its neck. A second arrow sunk to the fletchings in the muscular black chest.

Unfazed, the hellhound launched growling into the air, pouncing straight at Dan.

Dan braced himself and swung his cursing sword with all

his might, swinging downward in a powerful axman's chop, aiming for the space between the glowing eyes.

Wulfgar slammed into the gigantic dog's skull. Then the whole world exploded in flames.

Everything was heat and blinding brightness.

The gigantic dog hit Dan like a charging bull, knocking him off his feet. Wulfgar ripped out of his hands.

Dan hit the ground hard, still blinded and hurting from the flames. He grunted as the dog, hurtling over him, pounded down on his chest with its massive rear paws and kicked away, shredding his new shirt and carving lines of fire in his flesh.

Dan rolled onto all fours with barbaric speed, his face screaming with burn damage, his nostrils filled with the smell of singed hair.

But his vision had returned. He scanned the ground for Wulfgar but couldn't see his sword anywhere.

"Over here, asshole!" Wulfgar shouted, and Dan followed the voice to where the hellhound was wheeling to charge again. Wulfgar was lodged in the dog's forehead like an axe in a stump.

Apparently, the hellhound didn't care. It paused just long enough to give Dan another demonic grin and charged back in for the kill.

Dan got to his feet, tugged the crappy goblin sword from his belt, and roared defiantly.

The beast was too strong, he realized, too strong to kill with this glorified frog sticker, but maybe he would get lucky and score enough damage that the others could finish the monster. Though by the sound of things, the Noobs were now busy fighting the other hounds.

The demon dog coughed flame and hurtled toward Dan, Wulfgar shaking back and forth along with its roaring head.

Dan bellowed, ready to thrust the puny sword as hard as he could.

The hound raced toward him, flying through the air, opening its jaws to roast him with another blast of infernal flames–and then yelped and spun away, skewered through the center by a crackling yellow arrow the size of a javelin.

The hound thumped loudly into the ground and lay in a steaming heap. The arrow sizzled and dissipated.

"Crom!" Dan uttered. He ran to the corpse, pressed one boot into the dead dog's muzzle, and yanked Wulfgar free.

Then he turned to see two more hounds, dead on the ground, and the remaining pair bounding away through the forest of spikes in full retreat.

Sizzling yellow arrows jutting from the dead hellhounds wavered and extinguished.

Dan ran to his friends.

Nadia's face was torn and bleeding, and one arm was burned.

Holly had been bowled over and stunned. Raking claws had torn off one of her sleeves and ripped bloody lines down her arm.

Dan helped Holly to her feet, and she blinked, looking around and clearing her head.

A second later, Holly was back to herself. Surveying the damage, she prepared to heal Nadia, whose wounds were the worst.

Nadia shook her head. "Wait. The burn hurts like hell, but I'm fine. These wounds won't slow me down or hurt my performance. Hold onto your healing spell in case someone gets hurt worse."

Holly nodded. "Good thinking."

"Also good thinking to suggest killing the alpha first," Zeke said. "Had we concentrated on the others, we'd still be fighting, but with the alpha dead, the last two lost their nerve.

"Which is good," he added with a crazy grin, "because I'm all out of enchanted missiles."

*Enchanted missiles?* Dan thought. *Those were enchanted missiles?*

As a barbarian, he loathed magic, but as a former T&T player, he understood that *enchanted missile* was a pretty weak spell, unless it was cast by a high-level wizard.

Zuggy screeched anxiously, bouncing up and down on the wizard's shoulders and pointing down the path.

Zeke started walking in that direction, saying, "My simian companion is clearly ready to make like a shepherd and blow this hotdog stand."

The Noobs followed after the bizarre wizard and his anxious monkey, Dan wondering just what level Zeke would need to be to cast enchanted missiles that powerful.

## TEAM VS. TEAM

A t last, they reached the end of the forest, which terminated at the base of a sheer cliff of black stone that rose up and up and out of sight. The path led to a metal door set in the cliff wall.

Finding no traps, they opened the door and found themselves staring into a large circular room, perhaps one hundred feet across and lit with torches. Along the circular walls, spaced evenly, were three other doors, identical in every way to the one they now held open.

Low stalagmites covered the most of the floor, looking more like melted wax than stone. Overhead, their mirror image, a forest of pointed stalactites, covered the ceiling.

"What do you make of the numbers?" Holly said, pointing to the numbered placards hanging over the doors.

"We're looking out of Door Three," Nadia said. "Door three for team three?"

"Could be," Holly said. "Maybe this is the junction point, where all three teams enter the main dungeon."

"If so," Dan said, pointing straight across the room at

Door One, which stood slightly ajar, "the Sell-Swords already came through here."

"They must've gone that way," Nadia said, pointing to Door Four, which also stood partially open.

"Makes sense," Holly said. "If teams one, two, and three all enter the junction through numbered doors, that leaves only number four."

"Like a cattle chute," Nadia said.

Dan nodded. Things were about to get a lot more dangerous.

Could the Sell-Swords be waiting right behind that door to ambush them?

Of course they could.

But would they do that? Or would they race ahead, running toward the treasure?

Hopefully the latter, and hopefully the Sell-Swords carved a path all the way to the Chest of Champions, killed one of the knights mentioned in the goblin forehead tattoo poem, and softened up the other knight before getting wiped out.

Was this a likely scenario?

No, but a barbarian could dream.

"Let's go," he said, stepping into the circular room. "Maybe we can get ahead of *Alpha Alpha Alpha*."

For as much as he would enjoy ambushing Grady and his asshat pals, Dan would enjoy winning 50,000 gold pieces a lot more.

Zeke tapped Dan's shoulder and pointed to the smooth ground near the wall. "I would suggest that we all stay close to the wall on our brief and hopefully uneventful sojourn to Door Number Four."

Dan shrugged. The old guy was insane but also clearly more experienced than Dan had assumed. So he stuck to the wall, reached Door Four, and cracked it open to peer inside.

He relaxed. "The hallway is clear. And it slopes downward!"

Then something banged behind him, the room filled with shouting, and his shoulder jerked hard as if punched. Looking down, he saw the business end of an arrow sticking six inches out of the front of his shoulder, the head dripping blood.

*His* blood.

He'd been shot.

He could feel the shaft in his shoulder.

Then everything was screaming and chaos.

Arrows zoomed past, shattering against the wall. Misfires clatter-chattered, ricocheting off stalagmites.

*Alpha Alpha Alpha* roared insults, unloading on them with long bows.

Holly returned fire, nailing Grady center mass, but the arrow shattered on his magical breastplate.

Grady yipped his maddening hyena laughter and pointed at Holly. "You'll pay for that, blondie!" Then, shifting his yellow eyes to Dan, he grinned. "Here we come, Danielle!"

Dan flipped him the bird and held the door for his teammates.

Nadia zipped under Dan's arm and into the hallway.

An arrow grazed Dan, slicing a line of fire across one ass cheek.

The gnolls advanced, crouching low and using the stalagmites as cover. All of them yipped their crazy, keening laughter as they hustled forward.

Holly dipped under Dan's arm and followed after Nadia.

"Come on, Zeke!" Dan called, waving toward the door. But that's when he realized that the old man, whom he had assumed was just standing there being weird, had been deflecting spells.

As Dan watched, the AAA wizard popped up and

launched a bolt of energy straight at him.

Dan froze in terror, watching the crackling projectile streak toward him.

At the last second, the deadly energy angled sharply and bounced away, as if it had hit an invisible shield.

"Better luck next time, sonny!" Zeke cackled and scooted past Dan, Zuggy shrieking from inside his poncho. "Have fun with the drop rocks!"

Dan lunged through the door, turned to pull it shut, and saw a stalactite detach from the ceiling and drop.

The heavy stone slammed into a gnoll. The point punched into the hyena-man's neck between the back of his helmet and the top of his armor, skewering him through the middle.

Dan slammed the door shut.

Nadia slid in beside him and hammered iron spikes into the edges of the door, jamming it. "That ought to buy us some time."

Dan nodded toward the arrow still sticking through his shoulder. Feeling the shaft parting the flesh within his muscle was as unnerving as it was painful.

"Snap this, would you?" he asked Nadia. He couldn't pull the barbed head back through the wound, and he sure as Hades didn't want to drag the feathers through there, either.

"All right," Nadia said, grabbing the shaft. "This is going to hurt."

He nodded. "Do it."

Nadia held the shaft close to his shoulder and snapped it with her other hand.

She was right. It did hurt.

Dan growled as he pulled the arrow out the front.

Then they hurried after Holly and Zeke, who were just disappearing around a bend in the passageway, heading ever down, down, down.

# 49

## WAY, WAY DOWN

S omeone–presumably the Sell-Swords–had obviously come this way before them.

Even in the funhouse illumination provided by torches held in jogging hands, Dan detected the signs of the mercenaries' passage: boot prints in the grit, an already triggered trap, which left a pendulum scythe dangling in the middle of the corridor, and commencing after that, a blood trail.

The blood looked fresh.

Yes, the Sell-Swords were in the lead, but the Noobs were close on their heels.

Behind them, a loud boom echoed through the twisting passage.

*Alpha Alpha Alpha* had breached the door.

*That's okay,* Dan thought. *We have at least a quarter of a mile on them.*

But the gnolls were tall and athletic, and their magical armor wouldn't weigh them down. With every leaping stride, the hyena-men would eat up the distance, gaining on the Noobs.

Seeing a wide-open door ahead, the Noobs paused.

"Why leave it open?" Nadia asked. "Why not close and jam it to slow us down?"

"Maybe it's a trap," Dan said, remembering Broadus's warning. "An ambush."

"Or maybe they're just hurrying," Holly said, "making the most of their lead."

Behind them, the yipping laughter of the gnolls grew closer.

"I'm going in," Dan said, and charged into the room.

Passing through the open door, he gritted his teeth, expecting an attack, but none came.

The room was small, with three exits. An open passage carried on straight ahead. Another led to a set of stairs that went up. The final exit yawned at the center of the room. Within, a ladder disappeared into a dark shaft.

"Keep going down," Holly said.

Dan nodded. "Nadia," he said, "spike that door shut. We don't want the frat boys dropping flasks of burning oil down on us."

Zeke's light spell had expired, and everyone needed both hands to climb, so the descent would be made in complete darkness.

Dan dropped his torch into the shaft. The flaming torch fluttered, banging back and forth off the tight walls of the shaft, falling thirty feet before it extinguished. After that, Dan could hear the thing clattering far below, still falling.

Dan lowered himself down the ladder, one rung after another, his sweaty hands slippery on the metal rungs.

The shaft narrowed around him. His backpack scuffed along, dragging against the stone. From time to time, his elbows banged into the side of the shaft.

If the space grew any tighter, he'd be jammed in place and would have to cut loose his gear.

His barbarian soul yearned for open air, snowy mountain peaks, raging rivers flanked in ferns, open fields rich with game, and great forests of old timber tumbled with mossy stones.

This was not natural. He could feel the stone pressing in around him, growing narrower with each passing moment, tightening around him like a squeezing fist, threatening to squeeze him to a stop here in the heart of the earth, a mile from air and light and life.

Then his pack dragged, catching, and both shoulders knocked into the walls of the shaft.

"Wait," he cried, but it was too late.

Pain exploded in his fingers as Holly's boot crushed down on that hand.

She lurched to a stop above him, then cried out, and for several seconds, the shaft echoed with thumps, cries of pain, shouted curses, and the screeching of an agitated capuchin monkey.

Dan strained and twisted and managed to dislodge himself without having to cut loose the pack. Then he was moving down the ladder again, rung after rung.

He hated this. Hated the feeling of the walls pressing around him. Hated the feeling of so much soil and stone overhead, sealing him away from the living world like a mile-thick coffin lid.

But most of all, he hated feeling so helpless.

Any second now, the gnolls could reach the shaft and start dropping rocks, knives, or flaming oil down on them.

Likewise, the Sell-Swords could be waiting down below, poised to kill the Noobs as soon as they reached the bottom of the ladder. It would be a perfect pinch point murder hole.

But then the shaft opened up and the ladder ended, and Dan dropped to the floor of a large room lit with flickering candlelight. The candles burned upon a heavy wooden table that stood against one wall.

Candlelight glittered over the piles and piles of shining treasure.

Tearing his eyes from this fortune, he helped the other Noobs drop from the ladder.

Stretched on the floor beside the table was further proof of the Sell-Swords' passage: the remains of what had been a very, very large man stitched in zippers of blue scar tissue. No amount of stitches would put the giant back together now, however. His massive head lay several feet from the rest of him, smashed like a rotten pumpkin.

"Well," Holly said, pointing at the dead hulk after Dan had helped her down from the ladder, "I guess that following the Sell-Swords does have some advantages."

"Flesh golem," Zeke said, examining the corpse.

"I hear the gnolls," Nadia said, looking up at the dark shaft. "What do we do? Hurry after the Sell-Swords or kill these bastards as they come out of the shaft?"

Dan was tired of running, tired of worrying about *Alpha Alpha Alpha*, tired of Grady. "Let's waste the gnolls."

"I say we keep moving," Holly disagreed. "I want to win this thing, and we have to hurry if we're going to catch the Sell-Swords."

"This flesh golem was very nicely crafted," Zeke said, oblivious to the debate.

"Good point, Holly," Nadia said. "Let's win this thing."

"All right," Dan said, disappointed, and stepped to the table, reaching for a beautiful golden necklace. There was such a thing as hurrying too fast. The Sell-Swords hadn't even bothered to scoop the loot. "In case we don't win," he said, "I'm going to snag a few months' rent before we split."

"No!" Nadia shouted. "Watch out for traps!"

But even as she shouted her warning, Dan's hand closed around the golden necklace.

Then it was too late.

Dan held the necklace, but the table rushed up and away, taking the walls and ceiling with it.

What the Hades? How could the table, the whole room be flying up and away?

Around him, the Noobs screamed.

Dan realized that the room wasn't rocketing up and away. The floor had disappeared. Now he and the Noobs were falling, dropping into the earth!

He slammed into something but kept moving, sliding on his back along what felt like a steep ramp. His teammates hollered in the darkness around him as they slid faster and faster, tunneling through the earth, whipping along what felt like one of those colossal water park slides.

But Dan feared that if they were hurtling toward water, it would be filled with piranhas or crocodiles.

They whipped around a corner, dropped down an even sharper incline, rushed over a hump that pitched them into the air for several seconds, making Dan's stomach lurch before they crashed down again. They slid into a wide turn that went on and on, tightening, looping the Noobs in a sickening corkscrew as they spiraled deeper and deeper into the dark heart of the world.

Then the ramp disappeared, and an explosion of white light blinded them as they tumbled into open air, screaming as they fell.

## 50

# HIGH IN THE SKY

They landed without so much as a grunt upon a soft cushion of billowing white vapor, which stretched away in a bright and swirling plain. Overhead and to all sides, the plain was surrounded by the bright blue of a perfect October sky.

Looking around, Dan realized that the surrounding blue didn't just look like the sky.

It *was* the sky.

Through some cursed sorcery, the ramp had dumped them out of a magical hole onto a cloud high in the sky.

Crawling to the edge of the cloud, he looked down and felt a rush of vertigo. Miles below them sprawled what, from this height, looked like a miniature replica of State College. His eyes went to the corner of the town and focused on the tiny oval that he realized was Beaver Stadium.

The Noobs stood, uninjured, and launched into rapid-fire questions.

How had they gotten here?

How were they able to walk on the cloud?

Why wasn't it cold and windy?

How could they breathe up here? Wasn't oxygen sparse at this height?

Finally, Zeke answered all of their questions with one word: "Magic."

"Meanwhile, the dungeon is down there, a mile below the surface," Dan said. "We're screwed!"

"Not necessarily," Holly said. "Keep going down till you reach the sky. That's what the riddle said, and we've done it. We've reached the sky."

Dan nodded. "What now?"

"Look," Nadia said, pointing across the cloud. "Some kind of structure."

In the distance, vapor stirred, revealing a mound at the center of the cloud. Atop the mound stood a huge white pavilion straight out of ancient Greece. Dan saw broad steps, tall columns, and a triangular mantle, all of which looked to be carved from white marble.

"Let's go," he said, and started marching in that direction.

Beneath their feet, the cloudstuff bent but held. It was like crossing a massive white trampoline.

Reaching the structure, they climbed the steps, which were indeed carved of stone.

They stepped onto an open patio tiled in marble and hedged in a rectangle of huge columns. At the center of the pavilion, the biggest man Dan had ever seen sat behind a massive table covered in huge chess pieces.

The man stood.

*He's twenty feet tall,* Dan thought, completely awestruck.

The giant's skin was robin's egg blue. He had a full head of silvery white hair and a long silver beard. His flowing white toga exposed his muscular shoulders and arms as thick as tree trunks.

*We don't stand a chance,* Dan thought. *We could never beat him.*

The giant's sky blue eyes sparkled down at them, and a bright smile split his silvery beard.

"Greetings, Noobs," the giant thundered. "I am Nimbus."

Nimbus returned to his seat and gestured across the table at a tall chair against which leaned a human-sized ladder. "A friendly game of chess?"

Nadia grimaced. "There is no such thing as a friendly game of chess."

"What are the stakes?" Dan asked.

"If you win," Nimbus said, "I return you immediately to the dungeon… along with a detailed map that includes every chamber, challenge, trap, and shortcut. There are a *lot* of shortcuts."

The Noobs exchanged excited glances. That sort of map would almost guarantee victory.

"What if we lose?" Holly asked.

"If you lose," Nimbus said, "I grind your bones to make my bread." He snickered. "No… I'm serious. I make a *killer* banana bone bread. It was my grandmother's recipe, but if I may be so bold, I think I've taken it a step further. Trust me. It's to *die* for."

Dan scowled at their massive host. Wasn't threatening to kill, mutilate, and devour them enough? Did the giant really have to throw in painfully lame puns like some third-rate fantasy writer?

"What if we refuse to play?" Nadia asked.

"Good question," the giant said. "If you refuse to play, I also return you to the dungeon. No map, though, I'm afraid. You will reappear where you left off, in the treasure room at the middle of the dungeon. And yes, there would be a floor under your feet again."

Dan, Holly, and Nadia huddled up.

"Let's head back," Nadia said. "This isn't worth the risk."

"But if we head back now," Dan said, "the other teams will both be in front of us."

Holly shouted up at the giant, "How good are you at chess?"

Nimbus shrugged. "I used to be all right, but I haven't played in a while."

"Shit," Nadia said. "Did you hear him? That's code for he's really fucking good."

"All right, all right," Holly said. "Let's not panic."

"Fuck it!" Wulfgar roared. "Let's play!" Then the impulsive sword lowered his voice as if the others could actually hear him, and asked Dan, "What's chess? Is that the one where you hop over the guy and he kings you?"

"We'll play," Zeke crowed.

A menacing smile spread across the giant's silver-bearded face.

"No, we won't!" Nadia shouted. She grabbed Zeke's arm. "What are you, crazy? Did you miss the part about him grinding our bones to make good ol' Granny's banana bread?"

"Yeah," Holly said, suddenly having second thoughts. "Having a map would be great, but it's probably not worth the risk. Besides, shortcuts always end up biting you in the ass."

*Not always,* Dan thought, remembering Willis's T&T adventures.

Willis loved tempting his players with high-stakes gambles. If you were bold enough to risk everything and lucky enough to win, the rewards could be staggering. Of course, if you lost, the shortcut didn't just bite you in the ass. It rose up beneath you like a great white shark and bit off your ass and took your legs with it.

"We play," Zeke said again, stroking the white patch on

Zuggy's head. "Look, guys, I know that Zuggy might be a hopeless alcoholic."

The Noobs nodded in agreement.

"And he might get a little violent on whiskey," Zeke added.

"A little violent?" Dan said. "He almost killed the kid in the bar."

Zeke nodded and said, "And he might even be in the habit of spitting in Dan's beer when he isn't looking…"

"Wait," Dan said. "What?"

Zeke glanced at the monkey with a tight smile, his voice thick with emotion. "But this little bastard can play chess. I've spent my life traveling all over this world and visiting the other planes of existence, high and low alike, and I have never encountered a chess player who could beat my little buddy, Zuggy."

The monkey grinned.

He and the wizard exchanged a fist bump.

"You want us to risk our lives on the chess play of a monkey?" Nadia said. "No. Fucking. Way."

Then, turning to the giant, Nadia said, "Hey, Mr. Nimbus, if these guys want to play, and I want to just head back right now, is that cool?"

The giant shook his silvery head. "Sorry. This is one of those group decision situations. One for all, all for one, that sort of thing?"

"Shit," Nadia said. "Holly?"

Holly bit her lip. "The monkey is a good chess player. He beat Zeke."

"Zeke's crazy," Nadia said, then laid a hand on Zeke's arm. "No offense."

Zeke fluttered a hand. "None taken."

"Zuggy also destroyed that kid in the bar," Holly said. "Not the one who gave him a shot of whiskey. The smart looking one in the pointy hat. I'm torn. What do you think, Dan?"

Dan's mind had been racing during the debate.

If they went forward with this game, they could all die.

If they went back to the dungeon, they would almost certainly lose, but they would likely survive.

Nadia said no.

Zeke said yes.

Holly wavered in the center, waiting for Dan's vote.

Ultimately, however, none of them convinced Dan.

Willis convinced him.

If Willis had designed this adventure, there would be no safe choice. They could live or die, succeed or fail. Willis never slaughtered or lifted up his characters. Their success was always based on their decisions, their actions, and, of course, their luck.

But Willis would never have included an NPC like Zuggy and put all that time into developing the monkey as a chess player if Zuggy wasn't a great player.

This setup would be Willis's way of testing the Noobs' nerves and having a good laugh if the monkey actually saved their asses.

"Let's do it," Dan said. "Kick this giant's ass, monkey!"

## 51

# THIRTY-SIX CHAMBERS OF DEATH

The Noobs scaled the ladder and stood together atop the great chair. The edge of the massive chessboard was level with Dan's beltline.

Nimbus was positively giddy, so much so that he offered Zuggy the white pieces and the first move.

"Shall we begin?" Nimbus said, playing it all droll. "Or should I preheat my oven?"

Zuggy grinned at the Noobs and gave each teammate a fist bump. Then the monkey clambered onto the table and dragged the pawn in front of his queen out two spaces.

"Pre-dict-able," Nimbus said in a singsong voice, and pushed his own queen's pawn.

"We're doomed," Nadia groaned.

"No, we're not," Zeke said. "You want to put a little wager on it?"

Nadia rolled her eyes. "Nice try, grandpa. That way, if we survive, I owe you, but how am I supposed to collect if we die?"

"Good point," the wizard conceded, then he clapped, grinning at the board. "Nice move, Zuggy."

The game quickly developed into a positional lockdown, with each player building complicated pawn structures and marshalling his forces as best he could, given the locked center and heavily contested spaces.

Zeke hadn't been wrong about Zuggy. The monkey was obviously one Hades of a player.

Unfortunately, the giant was just as good… and really, really annoying.

Nimbus talked trash constantly, mocking Zuggy's moves, rolling his eyes, and sighing. He also insisted on snacking throughout the game. He kept reaching into his toga for crackers and biscuits, crunching them loudly, smacking his lips, and then dusting his hands, covering the board in giant crumbs.

The game was slow, neither player rushing to capture material, both of them seeking instead to dominate positionally.

Honestly, it would've been pretty boring if it hadn't been for the whole life-and-death thing.

Then the game got bloody.

An exchange of knights led to a break in the pawn structure. The giant rushed the breach, trading pieces until he peeled open the center.

Zuggy bounced up and down, chittering anxiously, and moved his remaining knight to safety, avoiding the threat and pitching ahead into enemy territory.

Dan held hands with Holly and Nadia. He didn't know much about chess, but he knew it was bad when the giant lined up both rooks in a menacing battery on an open file. Next, Nimbus would slide his queen in behind his rooks.

Nimbus had ripped center wide open, and now he was looking to force a back-rank mate.

The monkey had to think defensively, had to push a pawn to buy space for his castled king.

Instead, Zuggy attacked recklessly, zipping a bishop across the board to snatch a pawn and throw a meaningless check.

Nimbus rolled his eyes and chuckled with contempt. "Charge," he mocked, and stretched out a giant hand to capture the bishop.

Then he paused, his huge face twisting with confusion and concern.

Zeke cackled like a maladjusted rooster. "In yo face, Nimbus! You see it now? You were so focused on your rooks that you forgot all about Zuggy's knight."

"Wait," Nimbus said, studying the board with a look of desperation. "This can't be right."

Hope surged in Dan. Could this really be happening?

Zeke cackled again. "You take the bishop, and Zuggy moves his knight. Mate in one!"

"Wait," Nimbus said, still looking for a way out.

Dan studied the board. Okay—there it was. But Zuggy had to be careful.

Nimbus's king was trapped. Zuggy's knight could deliver check by hopping to the right or the left. If he went to the right, it would be checkmate. If he got excited, however, and moved to the left, Nimbus would be able to capture the knight and roll him up in short order.

"Be careful," Dan said, and explained the situation.

"Stop your fretting, sonny," Zeke said. "The Zug-Master has this."

The monkey leaned on his knight, yawning theatrically.

Beaming, Dan squeezed the girls' hands. Nadia smiled back, finally believing that something good could happen. Holly, on the other hand, was studying the board, a look of panicked revelation dawning on her features.

"You must address check," Zeke crowed. "Make your move, El Gigante!"

Growling with frustration, Nimbus captured the bishop.

The monkey grinned, picked up the knight, and waddled forward to make his move. To Dan's relief, he was going toward the safe square and checkmate. Against all odds, they were seconds away from earning that map.

As Zuggy was about to make the winning move, however, Holly slapped the table and shouted, "Stop!"

The monkey hesitated.

Everyone turned in her direction.

"Don't do it," she said. "Go to the left."

The monkey gave her a confused look.

"Why in the world would he do that?" Zeke said. "That would be check, not checkmate, and then Nimbus would just take his knight."

"Exactly," Holly said, a bright smile coming onto her face. "Nimbus couldn't block the check and has no place to run. He would *have* to take the knight."

Zeke arched one wintry eyebrow. "Um… you do understand that checkmate is the objective here, right?"

Holly laughed. "In chess, maybe. But this is more than chess. Remember the riddle? *'Keep going down, Till you reach the sky. You'll reach the chest, When both knights die.'* Nimbus, what happens if Zuggy throws check from the left?"

The giant made a face. "I take his stupid knight. Duh."

"You know what I mean," Holly said, her smile growing sly. "What happens to us?"

Nimbus sighed and rolled his gigantic eyes. "All right, all right. I'm forced to capture the checking piece, both knights die, and I deliver your team directly to the dungeon's final chamber."

The Noobs cheered as Zuggy changed directions and threw suicidal check.

Nimbus struggled to repress a grin. "Very clever, little elf."

Then he captured the knight, and the Noobs were again blinded by a flash of bright light.

## 5 2

## THE CHEST OF CHAMPIONS

Zipping straight to the final chamber ended up being a mixed bag, in Dan's opinion.

Sure, there were some really cool aspects.

For starters, they skipped half of the dungeon, along with a ton of tricks, traps, and monsters. The Noobs simply materialized together at the center of a large, ornate hall.

The room itself was even a plus. After crawling through dirty passageways of rough stone, it was pleasant to stand on tiles of polished marble beneath a high-vaulted fresco ceiling supported by massive golden columns. The fountains were a nice touch, too, as were the beautiful tapestries hanging along the walls.

Then there was the treasure. At the far end of the room, sitting atop a sparkling carpet of gems and gold pieces, waited the glowing trunk that could only be the Chest of Champions.

It was a breathtaking sight.

As was the final pleasant surprise, that being the dead hydra spread in many pieces across the shiny tiles, its eight decapitated heads orbiting the big corpse like sour moons.

Dan felt a rush of excitement, seeing the intact treasure and the far-from-intact guardian, lying very dead on the floor at their feet.

There was really only one downside to their arrival. Though, in all fairness, that was a pretty big downside.

Sword points slid against their throats as they appeared.

Dan stood on his tiptoes as the blade pressed into his flesh, threatening to open his throat wide.

"You did not heed to my warning," Broadus said, holding the blade to Dan's throat. "This you should have done."

A quick glance told Dan that all of the Noobs had blades to their throats. The Sell-Swords had gotten here first, killed the hydra, and waited for the Noobs to arrive.

"I understand that now," Dan said with a nervous smile. "But I don't get it. You won. You beat the dungeon, killed the hydra, and earned the treasure. Why wait here for us? Why not grab the Chest of Champions, head up to the surface, and claim your victory?"

Broadus shook his head. "If only things were that simple. We release you now, yes? But on your honor, you do not attack us?"

The Noobs happily agreed to those terms, and the blades came away from their necks.

Broadus spread his arms and turned. "All a lie," he said. "A death trap."

Dan shrugged. "But we made it. We all made it."

Broadus shook his head solemnly. "The true fight, the thing that brought us here, is behind that wall." He pointed his sword toward an ornate tapestry.

"But the treasure is right there," Nadia said, pointing at the glowing chest. "Is there some kind of trick or trap? Why not just carry the treasure up those stairs?"

"We did not come here to win," Broadus said.

"Works for me," Nadia said. "Mind if we, um, you know…"

Broadus waved his hand dismissively. "The treasure is nothing. We do not care about money."

"Don't care about money?" Dan said. "You're mercenaries."

The Sell-Swords laughed hard at that.

The wiry thief reached into his tunic and withdrew a chain, upon which a circular pendant glowed like a miniature sun. "We're not mercs, kid. We're Legionnaires."

"Legionnaires?" Dan asked, totally confused.

"You're members of the Legion of Light," Holly chimed in, sounding excited.

Broadus gave a little bow and made introductions. The burly dwarven cleric was Kord; the black-haired sorceress, Talia; the wiry thief, Maurelio.

Holly was beaming. "My grandmother told many stories about the Legion of Light. She spoke very highly of you."

Broadus turned to Holly and seemed to study her face for several seconds. Then his expression softened. "The likeness is striking. The hair, the eyes, everything."

Holly smiled warmly. "You pay me a gracious compliment, sir. My grandmother was a great woman."

The Legionnaires exchanged troubled looks.

"Your grandmother saved my life," Broadus said, and then gestured to his companions. "All of our lives."

"I am pleased to learn this," Holly said, her face growing wary as she scanned the Legionnaires' troubled expressions, "but I sense that you have more to tell me."

Broadus explained the day, months earlier, when the Legionnaires, investigating a gathering of dark forces in the Forest of Rothrock, had descended into deep catacombs, where they were overwhelmed by the powerful necromancer Griselda.

As the evil necromancer was preparing to kill them, Holly's grandmother had appeared. She and Griselda fought a terrible battle with an even more terrible outcome: both women died.

"We tried to warn the barbarian of the dangers, yes?" Broadus said.

Maurelio spoke up. "Of course, we did not know then who you were, Holly, or we would have chosen a different clue."

Broadus nodded. "Maurelio placed a tiny head in the boy's pouch. A hint, since he had not listened to my warning."

"I'm so confused," Dan confessed. "A hint? A hint at what?"

"A hint of the horror awaiting us behind that wall," Talia said. "You had seen the real head before, correct? It spoke with you?"

Dan nodded. "Yeah, but I still don't understand the hint... and how do you know this, anyway?"

"I saw you in the crystal heart," Talia said.

Goosebumps raced over Dan's body. "How?"

"I practice divination," Talia said with a small smile. "In the same way, I—"

"Wait," Holly interrupted, her face suddenly horrorstruck. "The head... does it belong to...?"

Maurelio put a hand on her shoulder and nodded, frowning. "I'm sorry, Holly. Again, if we had known—"

Tears welled in Holly's purple eyes. Dan went to her side. She didn't seem to even notice him. Despite the tears, there was steel in her voice. "Where is my grandmother's head?"

*Her grandmother's head?* Dan thought, shocked.

Holly glared at Broadus, her knuckles white around the glowing staff. "My grandmother's head disappeared the day that she died saving you. This is how you repaid her sacrifice? By taking her head?"

"We did not take the head," Broadus said, "and we do not have it."

"Griselda has it," Talia said.

Turning to the sorceress, Holly said, "That's ridiculous. Griselda is dead."

"Some wizards are too ambitious for death," Talia said. "Through dark sacrifices and the foulest magic, they carry on after death, as undead abominations of unfathomable evil."

"Griselda has returned?" Holly said.

Talia nodded. "Several months ago, I began to see horrific images in the crystal heart. Night after night, the images returned, becoming increasingly detailed until I understood two things: Griselda had returned from the dead, and she was planning to strike here, today, at the conclusion of Campus Quest."

"Here?" Holly said, scowling. "My grandmother's murderer is here, now?"

The sorceress nodded. "Griselda plans to spread darkness over the world, to blot out light and life forever, and then to rule over a dark and lifeless planet, worshipped only by her death cult, The Acolytes of Eternal Darkness."

*Those assholes?* Dan thought. But that meant…

"Griselda is the Mother of Darkness," Holly said.

"Yes," Kord said. The dwarven priest's voice was deep. "That is why we're here. To stop Griselda and defend the light."

"We could not tell you earlier," Broadus said to Dan. "Too much risk, yes? The crystal heart showed us this time, this place. What if we told the barbarian, and he told the world? Then Griselda would not come. She would cast her spell some other place, some other time. And maybe the Legion of

Light would know nothing until it was too late, and darkness had already destroyed the light."

Holly stepped forward. "I will help you."

Dan stepped up beside her. "Me too."

Nadia glanced longingly at the glowing chest and the stairway to glory. Then she stepped up alongside Dan and Holly, her green eyes hard as emeralds. "If they're in, I'm in."

Everyone turned then to Zeke.

The old wizard scratched his beard for a second, then shrugged his shoulders. "Griselda sounds like a real bitch. I'm in."

Broadus smiled grimly. "Very good, my friends. We can use all the help that we can get."

The dwarven priest spoke up for the first time. His voice was deep as a war horn. "I must warn you all. For as powerful and evil as Griselda was in life, death has only made her more powerful and more diabolical. We must coordinate our attacks to have any chance at defeating her."

They quickly laid out a battle plan based on the addition of the Noobs.

As soon as Griselda appeared on the football field, they would make their move. Talia, the black-haired sorceress, would make them all invisible, and she would cast a circle of silence around her to muffle their approach.

The wizards would attack Griselda, doing their best to keep her on the defensive.

Maurelio, Nadia, and Holly would surround the wizards, protecting them from the Acolytes of Eternal Darkness.

"You and I will fight alongside Broadus," Kord the priest told Dan. "We will battle our way to the stage, where Broadus will finish the necromancer."

Broadus nodded and unsheathed a shining dagger.

Dan shielded his eyes, then squinted at the weapon, which appeared to be made not of metal but of liquid fire.

"The Blade of Light," Broadus said, his voice thick with reverence. "I will plunge it into her dark heart and return her to dust and memory."

"Sounds good," Holly said. "That bitch killed my grandmother."

"The necromancer is waiting for the trumpets to blast," Talia the black-haired sorceress said. "She and her acolytes will rise up at that point."

"We need every advantage we can get," Maurelio said. "When Griselda is distracted by her big moment, we will attack. Not from the champions' exit but from behind."

"In the meantime," Talia said, holding out her crystal heart and motioning for the Noobs, "gather around and behold the future... and in it, our enemy, the Mother of Darkness."

Dan stared down into the crystal.

Within the sparkling heart, he could see the football field above them. He watched with clenched fists as dozens of acolytes in dark blue cloaks marched onto the field.

At their center, several huge acolytes bore a black palanquin upon their shoulders. Whoever rode within the litter was hidden behind black curtains. But what really rattled Dan was the size of the bearers. They had to be nine feet tall!

The acolytes marched onto the victors' stage, much to the confusion of Campus Quest officials waiting there.

Then the crystal blurred out of focus.

When the streaming images returned, those confused officials lay dead upon the stage. Acolytes surrounded a sacrificial altar of black stone, atop which was strapped a struggling elven woman, naked and incredibly beautiful, with silver hair and amber eyes.

*A grey elf,* Dan realized, and then rage rose in him, replacing the simple determination he'd been feeling. *That's why the Acolytes of Eternal Darkness tried so hard to kidnap Holly.*

They had wanted her as a sacrifice.

*Crom,* he prayed, *let me kill every last one of them—twice!*

Beside the altar, a small figure stood hidden in a hooded robe so black that it looked like a hole in the universe.

*It's her,* Dan thought. *It's the necromancer, Griselda.*

Griselda thrust her skeletal arms held overhead, holding a wicked, black dagger aloft.

Below her, the bound elf screamed in terror.

Griselda threw back her head with laughter, and her black hood fell away to reveal a skeletal face, a large pair of black sunglasses, and a crown of bright white hair.

Dan gasped. "That's my professor, Dr. Lynch!"

## 53

## DR. LICH

"**D**r. Lich is more like it!" Zeke said, pointing as the hideous necromancer removed her sunglasses, revealing not eyes but yawning sockets filled with red fire.

Maurelio turned abruptly, staring across the room at a heavy door. His pointed ears twitched the way Holly's did when she was listening hard. "The gnolls are approaching," he announced.

Everyone spread out to either side of the door, weapons at the ready.

The door swung open, and the three surviving gnolls burst into the room, bloodied and battered. They yipped and snarled, pointing at the dead hydra.

Then froze, as blades appeared beneath their throats.

Dan was pleased to find himself holding the edge of the crappy goblin sword to the jugular of none other than his lifelong tormentor, Grady.

Broadus and the Legion of Light explained the situation much as they had for the Noobs.

"You will help us, yes?" Broadus finished.

"What happens if we say no?" Grady asked. "You cut our throats?"

Broadus frowned. "No. You are free. But we need your help. All of those people out there? They need your help. The world needs your help."

The gnolls burst into keening laughter, pushing the blades from their throats.

"Screw the world," Grady said. "Boys," he said, pointing at the Chest of Champions, "grab the treasure."

The gnolls jogged away, laughing nastily, grabbed the golden chest, and started up the stairs.

At the last second, Grady turned around, made eye contact with Dan, and shouted. "So long, suckers!"

*I should've slit his throat!* Dan thought, and was just getting ready to yell after him when Nadia tugged at his hand. The Sell-Swords and Noobs were moving the tapestry aside and disappearing into a secret corridor.

As Dan followed them into the hallway, sounds of the stadium echoed behind him. He heard trumpets and thunderous applause, the wild cheering of 80,000 spectators, and the booming voice of the announcer declaring, "The champions of this year's Campus Quest, *Alpha Alpha Alpha!*"

Dan growled, hurrying through the dim corridor at the back of the pack, thinking, *There goes my shot at gold and glory... and my hopes for staying in school.*

They emerged into a large corridor, where Dr. Lynch and the acolytes had apparently been waiting.

Dan and his friends hustled up the ramp toward the field. They couldn't attack yet, however. They had to wait until the powerful necromancer and her forces were completely distracted.

The Campus Quest announcer laughed. "And now, coming onto the field," he said, speaking choppily, clearly confused. "Some kind of surprise, I think. By the looks of this procession, I'd say we're in for a treat, ladies and gentlemen. A special guest is making his or her way across the field in a royal palanquin."

The crowd buzzed with excitement.

Holly wrapped her arms around Dan, squeezing hard, then gave him a kiss. "Take care of yourself, husband. I love you."

"And I love you, my wife. Let's kill this evil bitch."

Then he took Nadia in his arms.

He was surprised to find that Nadia was quivering with fear.

"Be safe," he said. "I love you."

"I love you, too," Nadia said, and Dan could hear that his tough thief was close to tears. "No matter what happens, no matter what I do, even if you can't love me afterward, even if you hate me, know that I loved you and will love you forever."

Dan drew back to stare at her, confused.

Now Nadia was wiping tears from the corners of her eyes.

"What are you talking about?" Dan asked. "I love you. No matter what."

"All right," Broadus said. "It is time. Preserve the light."

"Preserve the light," the Legionnaires echoed.

Talia cast her spells. Dan and the others faded into invisibility, and although he could still hear everyone, he knew that the entire party was encased within a sphere of silence that would block their sound from anyone beyond the area of effect.

They jogged up the ramp.

On the towering jumbotron, Dan could see that the acolytes had already reached the stage. The small, dark figure of Dr. Lynch floated from the palanquin, settled upon the stage, and lowered the microphone to the dark hood that obscured her face.

Dan and his invisible friends charged onto the field.

The handful of Campus Quest officials upon the stage clucked with consternation.

Then they fell to the stage, dead.

The crowd gasped.

The AAA gnolls sprinted past, fleeing center field and heading for the nearest exit. Grady's eyes were huge with terror.

*Pussy,* Dan thought, charging in the other direction.

"Greetings, vermin," Dr. Lynch's voice hissed over the speakers. "I am Griselda, the Mother of Darkness."

Then her face disappeared on the jumbotron, replaced by a screen of purple static.

"Whoa!" Broadus shouted.

A wall of sizzling purple electricity had leapt up before them.

Dan slammed to a stop mere inches from the wall. All around him, others cursed and clanked, slamming to a stop.

The crackling wall stretched up and up, arching across the field in a massive dome-shaped shield of purple energy. Center field, the stage, and the acolytes had disappeared, hidden behind the buzzing dome.

All across the stands, spectators shielded their eyes, muttering with confusion.

"Don't touch it," Talia's voice said. "Griselda has erected some kind of force field."

Campus security and vigilante spectators attacked. Numerous arrows, javelins, fireballs, and lightning bolts impacted the dome and vaporized like so many moths against a bug zapper.

"Behold the coming darkness!" Dr. Lynch's voice screeched over the speakers.

80,000 spectators cried out. Overhead, a second sun had appeared in the sky.

A black sun, like a hole in the sky. As Dan watched, the sun grew larger.

"That evil bitch has opened a gate to the Plane of Ever-Shade," Zeke said. "She's trying to flood our world with pure darkness."

"We have to get inside," Broadus said.

Dan knew that the Legionnaire was right. Only Broadus and the Blade of Light could vanquish Dr. Lynch. But how could they possibly breach the deadly dome?

## 54

## MAYHEM AND DARKNESS

Overhead, the black sphere in the sky swelled, losing shape. Its edges flared, going ragged in a lion's mane of darkness.

"I will tunnel underneath the shield," Talia said. "The acolytes might not notice the hole on this side, but they will probably notice when the tunnel opens on the other side."

"We will move quickly," Broadus said.

"Yes," Talia said, and though Dan couldn't see her face, he could hear the concern in her voice. "I will burrow as quickly as I can."

Then the invisible sorceress began mumbling incantations.

"We don't have much time!" Zeke said. "Look at the sky."

Particles of granular darkness flowed from the black hole and spread across the sky like a plague of locusts, buzzing back and forth, dimming the light of day, bringing dusk to noon.

80,000 fans murmured with confusion and burgeoning fear. People jammed the exits, everyone trying to leave at once.

At Dan's feet, a large, circular section of turf twisted and wrenched away from the ground. Grassy chunks tumbled aside, revealing topsoil. This raw earth began to churn, coming apart and spinning as if an invisible auger were drilling into it.

The circle became a hole. Loosened soil piled up around the rim.

"Spectators!" Dr. Lynch's voice boomed out of the speakers. "Don't just sit there. This is an interactive event, and you must all get involved," Dr. Lynch said. "Where is your school spirit?"

Several acolytes jogged out of the crackling purple shield and onto the football field, carrying torches overhead. The torches burned an odd green color and smoked heavily, sending plumes of green fog into the air.

One of the running torchbearers slammed into an invisible wall, dropped his torch, and flew into the air, obviously under attack by someone in the crowd. The acolyte tumbled up and away through the air, hit the crackling purple dome, and...

*Zap!*

The acolyte popped in a flash of light, incinerated against the shield. His boots spun away from the explosion and fell like dead birds to the turf, where they lay smoking.

*So,* Dan thought, *the shield allows safe exit but no reentry.*

The torch that the incinerated acolyte had dropped also lay on the turf, gushing heavy plumes of strange green smoke.

More sorcery, Dan knew. No natural torch could produce that much smoke.

Across the field, acolytes dropped, struck down by spells and arrows, but their torches likewise burned on, emitting heavy clouds of eerie green fog. These clouds billowed, swirled into the air, and broke into waves of green mist that drifted into the panicking crowd.

When the green fog misted across the stands, the stadium filled with the terrible sound of tens of thousands of people screaming in excruciating pain.

Dan gasped, seeing a wall of green fog drifting in his direction.

But Zeke's voice whispered nearby, and a light wind kicked up out of thin air, stopping the fog and pushing it away from where they stood, waiting for the tunnel to open.

The tunnel was deep now. An incredible amount of dirt and rocks had piled up to either side of it.

By some miracle, the acolytes hadn't spotted the soil piling up. Maybe the sphere obscured their vision. More likely, the evil bastards were too caught up in their big moment to notice.

All at once, the spectators stopped screaming... and started laughing.

Horrorstruck, Dan watched as the laughing spectators started to dance. They jerked and twisted, hopped and shook, leapt and spun, waving their arms crazily and laughing, laughing, laughing.

"Beautiful," Dr. Lynch said. "And now, all of you watching at home, you see what lies in store for all of you. Mayhem and darkness!"

"Darkness eternal!" chanted the acolytes. "Eternal darkness!"

Then the cackling spectators turned on each other, pushing and shoving, kicking and punching, drawing blades and plunging them, still squealing with laughter, into their neighbors.

Dan stared in horrified disbelief.

Then Talia announced that she had successfully burrowed to the other side.

Dan and the others charged into the tunnel, which Talia had carved through turf, soil, and bedrock. The passage opened on the other side of the shield.

Broadus crawled out first. Dan couldn't see him, of course, but he could see dirt kicking away beneath the Legionnaire's efforts and, since they were within the same sphere of silence, he could hear Broadus pulling himself up.

"All right, barbarian," Broadus whispered. "Lift Kord up to me. Kord, find my hand, and I will pull you up, my friend."

After a few awkward seconds, Dan found the invisible dwarven priest and hoisted him up.

One by one, Dan hoisted the others up through the hole. He moved quickly, knowing that at any second, the forces of darkness might notice the strange hole that had just appeared inside their defensive shield.

Despite their invisibility, Dan could identify each person whom he helped through the hole.

Maurelio scampered up, light as a feather, needing very little help at all. Holly, he knew instantly, because her touch was so familiar to him. The same was true for Nadia.

From one end of the tunnel came sounds of insane laughter and mass murder. From the other end came the chanting of the acolytes.

"Darkness eternal… Eternal darkness! Darkness eternal… Eternal Darkness!"

Finally, Broadus helped Dan scramble to the surface. From within the dome, Dan could see Dr. Lynch and her acolytes upon the stage and could see beyond the shield to where the stadium boiled with insane violence.

Luckily, Dr. Lynch and her acolytes were so focused on the swelling black sphere and the mass psychosis caused by the green fog that they hadn't noticed the invisible adventurers climbing up out of the tunnel.

"Everyone ready?" Broadus asked.

"Change of plans," Zeke's voice responded. "Talia, you'll have to attack Griselda on your own. I have to concentrate on closing that gate, or we're all dead."

Dan heard the rustling of the old wizard's robes. Zeke uttered a burst of gurgling nonsense.

At least the words sounded like nonsense to Dan, but an instant later, a beam of silver light leapt away from where the invisible wizard had spoken them. The silver beam passed without resistance through the force field and shot directly into the black sun, which seemed to flinch on impact.

Dr. Lynch screeched and turned in their direction, following the beam of light back to its invisible source.

"Now!" Broadus shouted within their sphere of silence. "Griselda knows we're here. Attack!"

## THE NECROMANCER'S FURY

"Meddlers," Dr. Lynch said, and her red eyes flared. "Death to you!"

As Dr. Lynch's eyes settled on them, Dan froze in place, paralyzed with primal fear, like a rabbit frozen by the cry of a diving hawk. His muscles seized. His eyes bulged, and his sphincter slammed shut. His heart hammered and lurched in his chest like a wild beast trapped in a cage. A low moan rose involuntarily from his throat.

His legs crouched, ready to sprint away, ignoring his brain, which, fear-struck though it was, screamed at his body to stand and fight. But his legs backpedaled, carrying him several steps toward the tunnel.

*No!* he thought. *Stand and fight!*

But his body was in full revolt, a terrified animal eager to bolt away.

Dr. Lynch swept her arm through the air, and suddenly Dan could see himself and his party members. Holly and Nadia had retreated as well and both looked to be fighting the same losing battle as Dan.

Dozens of acolytes howled with fury, leapt down off the

stage, and charged, their hands filled with Slivers of Darkness.

Then, with a loud crack, a bolt of lightning jumped from Talia's hand and slammed into Dr. Lynch with an explosion of light and sparks.

The necromancer disappeared in the flash. Acolytes who had been standing near her spun away through the air, their dark cloaks smoldering.

Dan roared and shook like a dog coming out of an icy lake, shedding the unnatural fear that had been upon him.

"With us, barbarian!" Kord shouted, waddling after Broadus, who charged straight at the onrushing wall of acolytes, including the giant palanquin bearers.

Dan hurried after them, hoping against hope that Talia's lightning bolt had finished the nefarious necromancer.

Then Dr. Lynch rose, stiff as a board, once more into a standing position, her red eyes flashing above a terrible, inhuman smile.

Dan charged on, undaunted.

The sorcerous fear that had gripped him was gone, broken by Talia's attack. Now, Dan had returned to himself, and he would happily die and burn in Hades with a broken back before he would abandon his friends.

"Amusing," Dr. Lynch said. Her skeletal arm lifted with superhuman speed, and a rope of black liquid rushed from her finger and struck Talia.

The raven-haired sorceress screamed in terror and raised her arms defensively. The black liquid struck her hand, enveloped it, and corkscrewed up her arm. Beneath the black coil, Talia's arm shriveled instantly, the flesh shrinking away, the skin cracking and peeling away like shed snakeskin.

Talia wailed in pain and terror.

Reaching her shoulder, the devastating black vine split into a dozen tendrils, which spiderwebbed across her torso, wound up her neck, and plunged into her screaming mouth, her nostrils, her ears, and her eyes, silencing her, ending her, leaving in her place a rigid mummy in red robes.

All this in a single second.

Dr. Lynch's skull-like head rocked back, her bony jaws parted, and horrible, rasping laughter filled the stadium, muffling even the tens of thousands of laughing spectators now fighting to the death along the bleachers.

"Forward!" Broadus shouted, hammering into the fray, a sword in one hand and an axe in the other, downing acolytes with every swing.

Beside the Legionnaire, Kord swung his glowing hammer mightily, batting acolytes away, two at a time, tossing them aside like men made of straw.

Dan sprinted to catch them. That was his duty, helping Broadus reach the stage.

"Kiiiiiiiill!" Wulfgar roared.

Dan swung the two-handed sword as hard as he could. The blade carved through three midsections, splitting dark cloth and flesh alike, and the front wall of Dan's would-be attackers stumbled, their legs tangling in their own entrails.

A detachment of acolytes rushed past, charging Zeke.

Dan glanced back over his shoulder.

Holly and Maurelio stood their ground, doing their best to defend Zeke, who continued to fire the magical beam through the dome and into the black sphere overhead.

Momentarily, at least, the sphere of darkness had stopped growing.

Where was Nadia? Where was Dan's dark-haired beauty?

Then he saw her, streaking away, her black cloak flapping behind her as she abandoned the fight, abandoned Holly, abandoned him. Without so much as a backward glance, Nadia dove into the tunnel and disappeared.

*Nadia... no... How could you?*

And Nadia's voice returned to him in memory, sad and serious, telling him, *You don't know me, Dan. You can't. And someday, after you really know me and can't love me anymore, you'll understand my reluctance. Please remember then that I still love you and always will, no matter how hard that might be to believe.*

Had she anticipated this moment, knowing that she would someday, during a dangerous moment, abandon Holly and him?

Dan felt a part of him crumble away inside his chest.

*Nadia...*

Maurelio parried and lunged, spun and sidestepped, thrusting his thin sword with all of the grace of a dancer in a choreographed confrontation. But there were too many assailants. Three, four, five... and he was losing ground, backing ever closer to the concentrating wizard.

The bulk of the acolytes, however, rushed Holly. She, too, fought furiously, striking with blinding speed, dropping attackers left and right with her glowing staff and leaping side to side, dodging would-be tacklers.

"Yessss," Dr. Lynch hissed over the loudspeakers. "Bring me the grey elf."

Holly's staff smashed into another acolyte, but before she could sidestep, another dark-cloaked assailant dove forward, hitting her with a low tackle.

Holly jerked backward.

Holding the staff in both hands, she hammered the hooded head with the butt of her weapon. Had that acolyte been her only attacker, she would have finished him, but several acolytes surged forward, and Dan watched his beautiful wife disappear beneath a wave of midnight blue.

"Holly!" he screamed, and started to turn in her direction.

Then a piano fell out of the sky and pounded Dan to the turf.

At least, that's what it felt like to Dan when the wall of force slammed into his face and neck and shoulder, smashing him to the ground, jarring his bones and knocking the breath from his lungs.

He had paid a steep price for taking his eyes off the battle. Something had happened to his hearing. Everything sounded strangely muffled and indistinct beneath the loud ringing in his ears. His jaw was broken, his mouth filled with metallic blood and bits of shattered teeth, and his eye on that side burned, swelling fast, threatening to close.

Now a gigantic boot was rushing toward his face.

There wasn't time to roll. Dan jerked his head to one side, and the massive boot pounded the turf an inch from his face.

The monstrous palanquin bearer towered over him, drawing back a fist as big as a boulder. The massive acolyte's hood peeled back as he leaned forward, and Dan was staring into a face so huge and primitive and unbelievably misshapen that it could only belong to an ogre.

"Pig-face motherfucker!" Wulfgar yelled, plunging into the raging ogre's solar plexus.

The ogre froze, hunching as the steel skewering him through the middle, and reflexively grabbed the blade. The big hands squeezed, spraying blood, and the ogre yanked its huge body backward, off the sword.

Dan scrambled into a crouch.

The ogre lumbered toward him and tried to roar, but all that came out was a hollow bark of pain and hatred. Blood drained from the corners of the monster's open mouth, and gray foam bubbled from the chest wound.

Unable to straighten, the ogre leaned forward and shambled toward Dan, who stayed low and swung hard.

Wulfgar sliced through a thick ankle.

The ogre spilled forward, coughing with rage and reaching for Dan with its massive arms.

Dan rolled sideways, tumbling out of the way just as the ogre slammed to the ground where he'd been crouching.

Dan didn't bother to finish his prone assailant. Instead, he leapt to his feet and charged forward, racing to the left, where several acolytes carried Holly's limp form toward the stage and Dr. Lynch, who cackled approving laughter.

A wall of midnight blue, the far flank of the main battle, shifted, blocking Dan from Holly.

Dan barreled into them, his curses joining Wulfgar's. The barbarian and his sword moved as one, chopping limbs, gutting torsos, and slicing through necks, sending hooded heads tumbling through the air.

Opening his broken jaw to bellow a guttural battle cry, Dan skewered an acolyte's guts, then ripped his sword free again, spraying blood.

But there were too many acolytes here. Alone, he would never cut his way through to Holly in time.

So he changed directions, charging again into the heart of the melee, where Broadus and Kord, temporarily stalled in their assault of the stage, now fought back-to-back against a dozen attackers, including three ogres.

Dan surged forward, barely aware of the deep cuts striping his body or the blood draining into his swollen eye.

None of that mattered now.

All that mattered now was reaching Broadus and Kord, carving a path to the stage, and killing Dr. Lynch before she could harm Holly.

He charged straight at an ogre standing with its back turned, attacking Kord. Dan raised Wulfgar overhead and swung downward with both hands, aiming to split the skull of the ogre.

At the last second, however, the oblivious ogre shifted its weight, sending Kord tumbling with a swipe of its arm.

Dan's sword missed the gigantic head, carving into the

monster's muscular shoulder instead. Wulfgar crunched through the ogre's clavicle and plowed through another foot of flesh, parting the giant from neck to mid-chest.

The ogre shuddered with impact and roared, wheeling around to face Dan, but its shoulder and arm sagged away, opening the yawning wound even farther, sending jets of black blood gushing into the air and throwing the hulking acolyte off balance. It staggered, glaring at Dan with burning hatred, and opened its mouth to roar.

The ogre's roar was cut off, however, along with the top of its head, when Wulfgar sliced through the giant skull in a straight line from ear to ear.

As soon as the ogre fell, another ogre rushed forward, roaring, and slammed into Dan like a charging bull.

Concussion shocked though Dan's entire body as he left his feet and crashed into a mob of acolytes.

Dan shifted into a red frenzy.

Everything erupted in a mad roar, his bellow joining the shouting of the acolytes and the inhuman battle cry of the ogre, who pressed forward, swinging his thick arm overhead even as several Slivers of Darkness plunged into Dan's back and gut and chest.

These were bad wounds, deep and devastating, but Dan ignored them, launching himself forward again to meet the ogre's attack.

As the giant swung its massive fist, Dan sidestepped, keeping Wulfgar tight to his body and running the blade across the ogre's stomach as he lumbered past.

Then Dan turned, wheeling around as quickly as he could, and almost fell, weak from blood loss and the bone-breaking attacks of the ogres.

Growling, he forced himself into position, ready to meet his attackers.

Both sides paused for a few seconds, panting for breath.

Meanwhile, a terrible battle raged between the sorcerers.

A river of black electricity poured from Dr. Lynch's hands and collided in midair with a rush of yellow electricity flowing from Zeke's hands. The opposing rivers of sparking force pushed back and forth, showering the ground with sparks, the necromancer and the wizard locked in a deadly stalemate.

A wavering silver circle appeared behind Zeke.

A gate to some other dimension?

High above them, the black sphere was swelling again, as Zeke could no longer work against its expansion. With every passing second, the sky grew dimmer as the Plane of Ever-Shade spilled into this plane of existence.

*Bam!*

With an explosion of black sparks, Dr. Lynch's river of force overwhelmed Zeke's, and the old wizard blasted off his feet and disappeared through the wavering silver circle, which snapped shut behind him.

Dan had no time to mourn his lost friend. He had tunnel vision now.

The ogre was bigger than him, but Dan was faster. And in this clash of microseconds, speed was king.

"Pukefaced shitsucker!" Wulfgar yelled, plunging into the ogre's eye.

No sooner had the huge acolyte toppled forward than half a dozen acolytes scrambled overtop him, charging Dan with black steel.

There were too many of them, and Dan was too damaged to beat them all.

How many hit points did he have remaining?

He pruned an acolyte's arm at the shoulder, but then the others were on him, hissing as they punched their blades into his flagging body.

Dan stomp-kicked one opponent in the chest and sent

him sailing away. Then Dan swung sideways, opening a long cut through another dark-cloaked back.

But the other acolytes grabbed at Dan's cloak and lunged for his legs and sliced at him with their Slivers of Darkness, pulling him this way and that and opening more burning, bleeding wounds.

Dan struggled for breath. His vision blurred, the edges darkening. He bellowed in defiance, willing himself into another rage, and bulled forward again, thrusting and chopping and smashing skulls with the pommel of his sword.

When the acolytes rushed again, crowding him so that he couldn't swing Wulfgar, Dan reacted like the wild savage that he was, kneeing crotches, elbowing heads, and sinking his teeth into whatever he could, chomping down hard and spitting out fingers and ears and noses as the acolytes howled with pain and fear and broke beneath his barbaric counter assault.

He ran them down as they fled, chopping them to meat, but then fell to his knees. His legs had gone to water.

He had nothing left. Nothing at all. He could feel his life force ebbing away and unconsciousness settling over him like a killing frost.

He wobbled as he kneeled there, trying not to fall flat onto the ground. Pain gushed up inside him, filling his dying body like a crimson fountain.

He was so tired, so weak.

*Have to keep fighting,* he thought. *Have to kill Dr. Lynch. Have to save Holly.*

But a rushing wind filled his ears, deafening him, and the blackness at the edges of his vision tightened, reducing the world to a small, dim sphere at the end of a long, dark tunnel.

*I've failed,* he thought. *I'm dying.*

## 5 6

## HEART

B ut then the rushing wind died, Dan's vision cleared, and the crushing weight of pain and fatigue and confusion lifted away, all at once, expelled from his body by a warm flood of pleasure and energy and an incredible sense of instantaneous and complete wellbeing.

He straightened with a laugh and stared in disbelief as his terrible wounds knitted together, smoothing to perfection in mere seconds.

"Rise, barbarian," Kord the priest said. "Rise and rejoin the fight."

Kord had healed him.

Completely.

Dan jumped to his feet. Yes, he'd just come face-to-face with death, but that wouldn't stop him, wouldn't even slow him down.

Because Dan was a barbarian, and he had *heart*.

Before Dan could even thank the dwarven cleric, however, Kord shouted, "This way!" hoisted his silver hammer overhead, and charged toward Broadus, who had battled his way to the edge of the stage.

Dan hurried after Kord.

Then a loud whipcrack split the air, and a line of black energy, pulsing and fluid and clotted with barbed black knots, lashed across the cleric, slicing through his magical helmet and armor like so much wet paper, splitting the man from crown to crotch in the blink of an eye.

The armored remains of the cleric split and fell to the ground like the halves of a broken mollusk, the flesh within the ruined mail boiling with black corruption, rotting to a dark soup in a fraction of a second.

"No!" Dan screamed, and charged the stage.

Dr. Lynch cackled, pointing at the festering remains of the dwarf who only seconds before had saved Dan's life.

Behind her, two black altars had appeared. The silver-haired elf from Talia's crystal prophecy lay naked upon one altar, Dan saw. His heart leapt with panic as he recognized Holly stretched out atop the other.

Dr. Lynch turned in the direction of Broadus, who hauled himself onto the far end of the stage. The brave Legionnaire was an incredible fighter, but a terrible red mouth yawned on his back, drooling blood.

Broadus had lost his helmet in the battle, and his bare and bloodied head slumped forward now. His jaw hung low. He gasped for air.

The Legionnaire stared at Dr. Lynch as he dragged himself slowly toward her, pawing at his beltline, trying, no doubt, to unsheathe the Blade of Light.

Dan charged the stage.

Dr. Lynch flicked a glance in his direction, raised her arms, and hissed, "Rise."

All around Dan, dead acolytes stirred, coming groggily off the ground and lurching to their feet. Many of them were missing body parts or leaking entrails. Their bloodless faces turned toward Dan, fixing him with empty stares. Then they lurched toward him, groaning, arms stretched out before them.

"Crom!" Dan bellowed, hating this dark sorcery.

He charged the stage, cutting his way through clumsy, growling acolytes who grabbed at his arms and face and cloak, trying to pull him down. They wanted him on the ground, wanted to pile on top of him, biting and pulling, wanted to pull him to pieces and eat him alive.

But Dan was young and strong and alive, and he carved a path through the undead, determined to kill Dr. Lynch and save his beloved Holly.

On stage, Dr. Lynch hissed, "Stun."

Broadus fell to the stage like a dead man. Then he floated into the air, drifted across the stage, and settled onto a third black altar, which appeared out of nowhere, Dr. Lynch's whim come to life.

She was so incredibly, inexorably powerful.

But ensconced in her power, the necromancer had underestimated Dan. He was, after all, merely a stupid barbarian. Assuming that her undead acolytes would finish him, Dr. Lynch didn't bother to turn his way and was therefore oblivious when Dan vaulted onto the stage, fueled by desperation and loathing and the need for vengeance.

Nor did Dr. Lynch hear Dan as he raced forward, rushing ahead silently in the way of his hunter-gatherer clan, drawing back his mighty two-handed sword and calling upon every ounce of his remarkable strength as he prepared to strike.

Dr. Lynch spread her withered arms, speaking, telling the murderous crowd, "Three perfect sacrifices to hasten eternal darkness!"

Dan swung Wulfgar in a powerful downward strike, nailing the necromancer at the crown of her hoary skull as Wulfgar roared, "Say goodnight, you filthy cock goblin!"

The sword bounced away.

Dan roared with surprise.

It didn't even make sense. He'd watched as the sword connected with the top of Lynch's skull…

Only it hadn't.

A hair's width from her white hair, the blade had slammed into an invisible something and slipped away, never reaching the skull and throwing Dan off balance and into instant confusion.

He'd had her dead to rights, with her back turned, completely unaware.

But then, in a moment of dawning terror, he remembered.

This world was based on T&T.

A game where some creatures were so powerful that they could only be hit by special weapons.

Magical weapons.

And apparently that class of weapon did not include talking two-handed swords with no additional attack bonuses.

Dr. Lynch spun to face him without even moving her legs. One second, she was facing away, not even flinching from his attack. Then she was facing him, her horrible face stretching into a terrible grin, paralyzing him with shock and fear and that awful breath, which rushed once more into his mouth and nose, making him gag and sputter.

The inhuman red eyes flared, and Dr. Lynch cackled, recognizing him. "You," she crowed. "So stupid!"

Dan swung at her again and again, hacking and slashing, chopping and thrusting, but nothing slipped through her invulnerability, nothing touched her, nothing stopped her mocking laughter.

Dr. Lynch's bony hand shot out with inhuman speed,

grabbed hold of Wulfgar's blade, and ripped the sword from Dan's grasp.

"You thought you could harm me–*me*–with this ridiculous sword?"

"Who you calling ridiculous, you dried up old—"

Dr. Lynch snapped Wulfgar in half, and the bellowing voice of Dan's mentor sliced off into the silence of death.

"No!" Dan screamed, and grabbed her throat, meaning to finish her with his bare hands, determined to snap her scrawny neck and rip the cackling head from her wasted body.

But her flesh was cold.

So cold, so very cold.

As soon as Dan's fingers touched Dr. Lynch's throat, his entire body seized, rigid with paralysis. He couldn't move, couldn't even scream...

Dr. Lynch wheezed laughter, shaking her shriveled head with disdain. "So stupid," she hissed one more time. Then she plunged a bony hand into his chest, tearing effortlessly through bone and muscle.

The last thing that Dan heard was Holly's cries in the distance as Dr. Lynch's icy fingers closed around his heart and ripped it from his body, killing him instantly.

57

## ALL IS LOST

**D**an woke to the sound of a tremendous crash. Shards of glass flew everywhere. Surprised voices cried out.

Looking down, he saw the smashed remains of the display case. Among the shards lay the decanter and its lid.

Alive again…

Back in the library.

Whipping his head in the direction of the screaming and seeing a librarian hurrying in his direction, Dan raced across the room and bolted down the stairwell.

Two flights down, he stumbled and slammed into a cinderblock wall.

It hurt. Big time.

What hurt even worse was the terrible realization that he'd lost everything. Dr. Lynch had killed him, and now he was back in the old world, right where he'd left off.

Hearing footsteps pounding down the stairwell after him, Dan hurried downstairs.

Gone were his incredible dexterity, his superhuman strength, and, as he discovered by the time he fled the library and charged out a path packed with students, his endurance.

Gasping for air, he bolted off the path, angled toward the back of the library, and dove under a hedge of heavy bushes.

Gone, too, was his barbaric disdain for pain. Just this simple action, diving to the ground hurt. His hands scraped across the ground. His knee banged into a rock. Stiff branches scratched his neck and back and arms as he scrambled into hiding.

He lay there, curled on his side, hugging his knees to his chest, trying to make himself as small as possible and fighting to catch his breath.

He'd lost everything!

Not just his barbarian skills and physical abilities. He'd lost Holly and Nadia, Wulfgar, and an awesome life.

All gone.

But not really…

*He* had gone.

The world that he'd left was still there.

Holly was still strapped to a sacrificial altar, probably screaming with grief and terror.

Nadia was wherever she'd run, hating herself for abandoning Dan and Holly as she had apparently always known that she one day would.

Wulfgar had been destroyed.

Zeke was missing, blasted into another plane of existence.

Talia and Kord were dead, along with tens of thousands of innocent spectators.

And everyone else would be dead soon enough, all because he had failed. All because he had foolishly attacked Dr. Lynch with brute strength and a sword lacking the necessary enchantments.

Dr. Lynch had conquered the Noobs and the Legion of the Light. Now she would open wide the gate to the Plane of

Ever-Shade and flood the world that Dan had lost with eternal darkness.

Dan's heart ached.

*Holly and Nadia...*

He had failed them, and now he would never see them again.

And what of their real-world counterparts?

Every time he saw Holly from across the hall, his heart would burn. Those girls would have nothing to do with him. They didn't want him. Never would. They didn't even know him.

And truth be told, despite how much he loved their otherworldly counterparts, he didn't know anything about these girls.

He didn't know them, didn't love them, didn't even want them.

He wanted his women.

But they, along with everything else, were gone.

And that's when Dan learned that he'd lost something else.

His barbarian's ability to hide in foliage.

"Come on out, kid," a voice said, and six uniformed legs appeared, all wearing similar, highly polished, black shoes.

A radio crackled.

One of the people surrounding him spoke into the radio, saying, "We've apprehended the suspect."

Dan didn't bother to fight campus security, even when they pulled his hands behind his back and snapped cuffs around his wrists.

The questions started. Who was he? Why had he destroyed the display? Why had he run?

Dan mumbled responses, vaguely aware of the gawking students crowding around.

Campus security led him to a waiting car. "Watch your head," one of the cops said, helping Dan into the back seat.

Then the door closed, and Dan sat alone in the back seat of a police cruiser, while the officer paused beside the car, talking to the other cops. They laughed and stole glances at Dan through the car windows.

*My life is over,* Dan thought.

He was right back where he'd left off, only now things were even worse.

He was sitting in the back of a police car, about to be charged with crimes. They would force him to pay for the display case, and they would probably send him to court and make him pay fines there, too. Worst of all, they would tell his parents. He would move home, deep in debt and even deeper in shame and regret.

If only he could go back.

But no.

He'd messed it all up.

And it struck him how absurd his failure had been. Really, he'd had the same problem all along.

Pretending.

Old-world Dan had blown off school and pretended that everything would be okay. Pretended that he could play T&T instead of studying and still keep his scholarship. Pretended that the problem with Grady would just go away on its own. Pretended that he could somehow get a girlfriend without ever mustering the courage to actually speak to females.

In the other world, he had misinterpreted the problems of old-world Dan as a problem of timidity. Feeling contempt for his former self, he had charged ahead, acting like Wulfgar. Swing first, scratch your head later. To hell with half-stepping and consequences. Thinking kills action!

Bullshit.

All bullshit.

And the same bullshit that he'd been feeding himself all along. Just a different flavor.

It was all pretending.

In both worlds, he had been in denial, pretending that things weren't what they were. Meanwhile, he couldn't get good grades, a bully-free life, or a girlfriend without actually working for these things. Nor could he, as a second-level barbarian, ever defeat a powerful necromancer with only brute strength and decisive action.

Sure, boldness was good. But if he could go back to his other life, he would do a lot more than just charge mindlessly into combat. He would think first, quickly and decisively, then jump in without hesitation. He would be what he should have been all along: a thinking barbarian.

Now, here in this shit-show version of the old world, he would have to apply these lessons as best he could.

Reality was staring him right in the face. It's tough to ignore your circumstances when you're sitting in the back of a police car with handcuffs on.

Dan squeezed his eyes shut. *I wish I could go back...*

When he opened them again, the front seat of the police car had disappeared.

In its place wavered a circle of shimmering silver, which dilated rapidly into a hole in reality, a doorway into another dimension, a gray nothingness with only one variation: an ancient wizard in a colorful poncho and ridiculous cowboy hat, grinning like a madman.

Zeke leaned forward, his head popping free of the gate, and glanced around the police car and out its windows.

"Weird place," Zeke said. "Never visited before."

Dan beamed. "How are you here?"

"I'm a quantum mage. I specialize in traveling the planes of existence, remember? That bitch blew me into The

Between so I saw your spirit fly here. I'm going to head back and try to settle her hash for good. Want to come with me?"

"More than anything!" Dan said, but then, thinking, he hesitated. "But wouldn't I be dead there?"

Zeke shook his head. "I just happen to have a Wish spell that could fix that. What do you say? You still have some fight left in you, barbarian?"

Dan hesitated for only a second, trying to live his promise to think before acting, but a second was all it took.

Yes, he wanted to go back.

Not because he hated this world, but because he loved that world.

"Take me back!" he bellowed, climbing through the gate…

## BRONAN THE BARBARIAN

Trumpets blasted, and everything–the gate, as well as the realities to either side of it–stopped.

Time had frozen again.

"Congratulations, you crazy son-of-a-barbarian!" Wulfgar's voice shouted. "You just leveled up!"

"Wulfgar?" Dan said, looking around. There was no sign of the two-handed sword. Just the frozen realities and Wulfgar's disembodied voice. "I thought you were dead!"

"Likewise, compadre," Wulfgar said. "Until this crazy-ass sorcerer came to get you. The good news is that you're third level now."

Dan felt a jolt of excitement. Third level? That would mean an additional eighteen hit points... just what he needed right now.

"Last time we talked experience points, you were sitting at 9005, basically 3000 points from third level," Wulfgar's voice said. "You get 500 points for that barbaric threesome with Holly and Nadia, 212 points for the goblins you slaughtered, 175 for your share of one big-ass hellhound, 234 for wasting the acolytes, not counting the ogres, which earned you another 460 points. Tack on another 500 points for the berserk rages, general decisiveness, and having the balls to attack that undead bitch, and you're sitting at 11086 experience points."

"But I need 12000 to reach third level."

Wulfgar sighed. "Here we go again. What are you, complaining? You get another 1000 for having the balls to come back. I mean, you were sitting there safe and sound, with no worries about somebody trying to kill you, and you decided to throw yourself back into a fight for your life. Barbaric!"

"There are worse things than death," Dan said.

"Truth," Wulfgar's voice said. "Reaching third level means you'll have 54 hit points and better chances with everything from attacking to saving throws. Oh–and you can use magic potions now."

"What about you?" Dan asked. "Are you coming back, too?"

There was a brief pause. Then Wulfgar's voice said, "Don't be a pussy! What, you need me to hold your hand? No, I'm not coming back. That stupid bitch snapped me in half and disenchanted me. The only time you'll hear from me is moments like these, basically when you level up. Keep leveling up, and I can give your sorry ass some pointers down the road."

Dan laughed. "All right, man. I just want to—"

"Spare me the sappy farewell, cream puff. I gotta go back to non-existence, and you have an evil, ugly-ass bitch to kill. Fare thee well, Bronan the Barbarian."

And time rushed back in.

## 59

### BETWEEN TIME AND SPACE

Behind Dan, the door of the cop car opened. People shouted in at him, confused and afraid. "Get the hell out of there, kid!"

But Dan plunged ahead, through the gate, which snapped shut behind him, leaving him face-to-face with Zeke in a bizarre gray nothingness.

Zuggy popped his head out of the front of Zeke's poncho, grinned, and extended a furry fist in Dan's direction.

"Sorry to leave you hanging," Dan said, realizing that he couldn't give the monkey a fist bump. "Zeke, you think you could remove these handcuffs?"

"No time," Zeke said. He dropped a lasso of silver light over Dan's shoulders, and they started flying through the gray nothing. "The shackles will disappear once we get back to the other reality."

Looking around at the endless gray void, Dan asked, "What is this place?"

"Welcome to the Between," Zeke said.

"Between my old world and the other?"

Zeke laughed. "That's a piece of it. A very small piece.

Imagine countless worlds, countless universes, arranged in a grid."

"All right."

"Now picture each universe–each plane of existence, if you will–as a square on a sheet of graph paper. The top of the page is goodness and pure light. The bottom of the page is evil and pure darkness."

"Okay," Dan said, picturing it.

"All the way to the left is complete order," Zeke said. "To the extreme right, total chaos.

"The upper third of the page, called the high planes, is dominated to varying degrees by good but split more or less evenly between order-dominant and chaos-dominant planes."

Dan had a hazy memory of Willis drawing up something like this for T&T. He remembered the sheet of graph paper and remembered his little friend being really into it, but their campaign didn't end up spilling into other planes, so Dan hadn't paid much attention.

"The bottom third of the page, called the low planes, is dominated by evil but also vary between order and chaos."

Dan nodded. "So the middle third is neutral?"

"Not exactly," Zeke said, "but there is a degree of balance between good and evil… and constant struggle. In the upper middle planes, good is slightly more powerful. In the lower middle, evil has the edge. Understand?"

Dan nodded. "I think so."

"There is a similar struggle between order and chaos at the vertical center of the page, from top to bottom," Zeke said.

"Makes sense," Dan said.

Zeke gestured with his arm at the gray space around them. "This is the Between. On that hypothetical sheet of graph paper, we're cruising along the lines between the squares. This is generally how I travel from plane to plane. There are ways to open gates directly from plane to plane, as Dr. Lynch has done, but it's very risky.

"Your two planes of existence are very close to the center in terms of both latitude and longitude. They both reside near the center of the graph, so there is a constant struggle between good and evil and order and chaos."

"But Dr. Lynch is trying to change that," Dan said.

"Exactly," Zeke said. "She opened a gate to one of the lowest planes, the Plane of Ever-Shade, and is flooding our world with darkness. If she has her way, we'll all die, the entire reality will fade like a dying star, and our square will reappear on the lower planes."

"We have to stop her," Dan said. He cared about the world, the universe, and everything, but mostly, he wanted to save Holly and Nadia… and destroy Dr. Lynch. "How much farther?"

"We're almost there," Zeke said. "Now shut your beer hole so I can cast the Wish spell and bring Dan the Barbarian back to life, all right? And try not to get yourself killed again, all right? I don't have another Wish spell in my back pocket. Also, because I'm using a Wish, your two selves might meld."

"Meaning?"

"Meaning, if you die again, I don't know if you'll reappear in your old existence."

Dan nodded grimly. "I'm all in. Let's go."

"Relax," Zeke said. "Time here is not tied to time there. Only the amount of time that you spent in the other world will have elapsed in ours. That's it. Events that occur here in the Between occur outside of time."

Dan nodded. How much time had they lost, then?

He had fled the library, hidden in the bushes, gotten cuffed and stuffed, and sat there feeling sorry for himself for a couple of minutes… maybe fifteen minutes, all in?

An eternity.

What had Dr. Lynch done in those fifteen minutes?

With no opposition, had she moved forward with the sacrifices?

*Stop worrying,* he told himself. *Worrying is worse than worthless. Now is the time to plan.*

"So what do we do when we get there?" he asked.

"There's only one way to stop her now," Zeke said. "I have to pull her out of that reality and transport her to the high planes, where her magic won't be so strong."

"How?"

"I don't want to fight that crazy bitch in the Between," Zeke said. "I need to open a gate directly to a high plane, with just a sliver of Between, so I can lasso her and pull her through."

"Will it work?"

Zeke cackled, that familiar less-than-sane glimmer returning to his eyes. "We'll see."

"And what do I do?"

"Buy me time to open the gate. But don't be an imbecile and rush her again, okay? Unless you enjoyed having your heart ripped out."

"No," Dan said. "That sucked."

"Well, then," Zeke said, and shuffled his feet in the gray non-space, shadowboxing with his scrawny arms, "you had better stick and move, sonny. Hit and run. Do just enough to keep her busy."

"Won't she blast me with one of her spells?"

Zeke shook his head. "I'm creating an anti-magic shell around you. It'll have a ten-foot radius. No magic in, no magic out. Just keep your distance and do not let her inside, or her spells will work. All right… we're here, kid. Time to cast that Wish spell and bring you back. You ready to rock and roll?"

## 60

## TOO STUPID TO DIE

D an opened his eyes and saw darkness spreading across the sky. He lay upon the stage, where he'd fallen.

There was no pain, no weakness. In fact, he felt stronger than ever.

*54 hit points now,* he thought. *Let them be enough, Crom.*

Dan sat up and grabbed the snapped half-sword that had once been his friend and mentor.

Undead acolytes crowded the stage, swaying back and forth and groaning a wordless chant.

"And with this sacrifice," Dr. Lynch's voice boomed from the loudspeakers, "I summon thee, Darkness."

Dan couldn't see the necromancer through the wall of undead acolytes, but her scrawny arms rose into view, as if reaching toward the darkness.

Reaching up toward the darkness with a gift.

A sacrifice.

A bloody heart…

"No!" Dan shouted, scrambling to his feet. "Holly!"

The undead parted as if shoved aside by invisible hands,

and Dr. Lynch glared at Dan from the other end of the stage. She stood beside the first altar, which was now a gory nightmare, topped as it was in the steaming remains of the naked, silver-haired elf.

Holly lay atop the second altar, closer to Dan. "Dan! You're alive!"

Broadus lay atop the third altar, closer still. "Here!" he shouted to Dan.

"Annoying little gnat," Dr. Lynch said. "What are you, too stupid to die?"

Dr. Lynch pointed in his direction. A trident of purple lightning leapt from her gnarled finger and exploded ten feet from Dan, shattering into a thousand spidery lightning bolts that sizzled over and around him, dissipating along the invisible dome that Zeke had cast around him.

"How cute," Dr. Lynch said. "An anti-magic shell."

Dan glanced over his shoulder. *Come on, Zeke! Hurry!*

"Acolytes," the Mother of Darkness called to her undead children, "kill the barbarian."

"Shit," Dan said, ripping the crappy goblin sword from his belt.

Groaning a collective battle cry, the acolytes shambled toward him across the stage.

Behind them, Dr. Lynch raised her bloody hands once more to the sky. "Come forth, darkness! I birth thee into this world! Come forth, fill this place, come!"

The gate to the Plane of Ever-Shade vomited darkness, further dimming the day. Icy wind swirled over the stage. Dan's cloak fluttered behind him, and windblown grit made him squint.

With a subpar short sword in one hand and a broken two-handed sword in the other, he rushed forward. He had to free Holly before Dr. Lynch sacrificed her!

"Barbarian," Broadus called weakly as Dan hurried past the Legionnaire's altar. "Here."

"I'll come back for you," Dan called, rushing past. He wished that he had the time to free Broadus. He could certainly use the Legionnaire's help, but there wasn't time, and if he couldn't save Holly, he didn't care about saving the universe.

As he drew back his swords, a line of light appeared in the air behind Dr. Lynch. Against the gathering gloom, the bright line looked like someone cutting through dark steel with a blowtorch.

Occupied as she was with the gory remains of the silver-haired sacrifice, Dr. Lynch didn't notice.

Then the acolytes were on Dan, groaning, grabbing, and gouging. They hammered him with overhand strikes and tried to bite his hands, his arms, his face.

Dan slid into a barbaric rage, fighting in the way of his people, leaping in and out, using his whole body, chopping with both swords, landing elbow strikes and head-butts and blasting one acolyte with a powerful kick that pitched the hooded zombie into the air and bowled over several would-be attackers.

Dan broke free of clutching hands, rolled with punches, and dodged biting teeth. With every mighty swing, his swords severed hands and arms and heads or sliced bellies open, spilling cold guts onto the stage.

And through it all, he battled forward, pushing across the stage, inching his way toward Holly while Broadus called weakly to him from behind and Dr. Lynch, beyond the wall of risen dead, coaxed forth eternal darkness.

But severing hands and arms did little good, regardless of the tremendous hit point damage these forms of trauma obviously delivered. The animated corpses pressed on, down a hand or an arm but completely undaunted, beating at him with stumps and snapping at him like vicious dogs.

Dan leapt back.

*Think, you stupid barbarian. Think!*

These were special zombies, animated by a high-level necromancer. The only thing that seemed to stop them was cutting off their heads.

*But you don't have time to decapitate all of them.*

Behind them, Lynch waved the bloody heart overhead with a flourish. "Mother has more for you, darkness," she shrieked. "More sacrifices."

Behind her, the bright line was beginning to widen from top to bottom, spreading like a slowly opening, fiery eye.

Still focusing on the problem at hand, Dan thought, *You don't need to kill all of these assholes. You just need to get past them, rescue Holly, and buy time for Zeke.*

The zombies lumbered mindlessly forward. An ogre staggered at the front, stumping toward him on its severed ankle.

*They're relentless, but they're clumsy,* Dan thought. *Even the ones with both feet. Knock them over. Use them against each other.*

"Barbarian," Broadus called again. "Here. Take—"

But Dan launched into the air and nailed the ogre with a flying side kick, smashing his boot straight into the hulking zombie's bloodstained chest.

In life, the ogre would have absorbed the shot and kept coming, but Dan's gamble paid off, and the undead giant toppled backward, flattening several acolytes.

Dan landed on his feet and sprung forward. Using the fallen ogre as a bridge, he charged ahead, running up the massive body. He stomped down on the ugly face and vaulted into the air, his strength, dexterity, and determination launching him in a high arch over the wall of groaning acolytes.

He tucked forward as he flew, bringing his head down and twisting into a mid-air flip. His boots arched overhead then dropped, and he stomped down on both feet, sticking a landing on the stage beyond the zombies.

Standing over the bloody sacrifice, Dr. Lynch showed him her terrible grin.

A hand closed on his shoulder.

Dan shrugged the paw and spun, dipping under the zombie's arm and bringing the goblin sword around in an uppercut that drove the blade up through the jaw and out through the top of the skull. The zombie toppled backward, ripping the jammed sword from Dan's hand.

Slow as they were, most of the zombies hadn't managed to turn in his direction yet. He made the most of this advantage, changing tactics again, hacking at their necks, chopping off head after head, piling their corpses in a battlement of ruined flesh before him.

The other zombies stumbled forward clumsily.

They were easy targets as they wobbled, tripping over the fallen dead, and Dan worked with cold efficiency, resisting the powerful urge to slide again into a red rage and instead striking with short, calculated chops, taking heads and dropping corpses.

Soon, the zombies were dead or down, flailing beneath their toppled comrades.

Gasping for breath and bleeding from a dozen scratches and bites, Dan cursed the remaining zombies.

He had to get to Holly!

Wild with desperation, he spun...

And froze in place, paralyzed by the icy hand that closed around his throat.

## 61

## THE LAST GASP

D r. Lynch had swept in behind him while he was battling the undead.

Now she had him.

Dan could still think, could still hear, could still see, but his muscles had turned to stone beneath her paralyzing grip.

"So stupid," Dr. Lynch said, spitting the word *stupid*, spraying his frozen face with a foul and choking mist of decay. "What made you think that it would work this time?" She split the air with a terrible cackle.

Meanwhile, behind her, the bright eye had opened further, and Dan could see a vague shape forming at the center, like an emerging iris coming to the surface.

"No, Dan, no!" Holly screamed.

Dr. Lynch's red eyes burned brightly, and a cruel smile came onto her face. "Oh… is it love, then? Sweet, stupid love?"

The necromancer threw back her shrunken head in a peal of terrible laughter.

"Well, your little sweetheart is special, that's for sure," Dr. Lynch said. "How I loathe grey elves, and none of them are as loathsome as grey elf *druids*, with their dusty libraries and conceited neutrality. The protectors of field and forest, defenders of balance, too smug for good or evil, order or chaos. The keepers of knowledge. Such proud and ignorant fools!"

As Dr. Lynch ranted, her ice cold fingers tightened on Dan's throat, choking off his air.

"I had instructed my bumbling acolytes to bring me your sweet sacrifice before this event, but they failed, of course. You can imagine how pleased I was when you fools and the Legion of the Lame actually brought her to me!"

Dr. Lynch threw back her head with another cackle.

Broadus's voice carried to Dan then, barely audible over the howling wind and Lynch's terrible laugher.

"Blade," Broadus called. "Blade of Light."

Dan wanted to scream, to cry, to smash his own face. How had he been so stupid?

In his fury, he had forgotten about the Blade of Light, the magical weapon specially crafted to destroy necromancers.

Ever since Dan had returned to this life, Broadus had been calling to him, trying to arm him with the one weapon that could've given him a chance against Dr. Lynch.

But Dan had ignored the Legionnaire, charged ahead, and stumbled straight into Dr. Lynch's diabolical trap.

Now it was too late.

"Your sweet grey elf will make the perfect sacrifice," Dr. Lynch said. "All of that balance and neutrality and longevity and especially the grey elves' hallowed tradition of keeping the past alive, of fading not into oblivion but stretching out into their 'great conversation' with the generations before and after them. Such utter nonsense! And now, I will cut out her heart and lift it up to the darkness, and your precious little elf will help me destroy balance and light, erase the past and the future, and usher in the age of oblivion and eternal darkness!"

The day darkened with her crazed soliloquy, and the wind blew harder and colder.

*Come on, Zeke!* Dan thought, but the bright gate had yet to open, and Dan, Holly, and the whole world had mere seconds left.

Lynch lifted him from his feet, smiling terribly, her eyes glowing like pits of hellfire. "I was going to save her for last," Dr. Lynch said, "but for you, my stupid barbarian, I will make an exception. I will carry you to her and let you watch as I rip out her pretty heart."

Inwardly, Dan raged with desperate, impotent bloodlust.

"Stupid children!" Dr. Lynch hissed. "You will suffer for challenging the Mother of Darkness!"

Turning with Dan and carrying him toward the black altar, where Holly lay squirming against her restraints, Dr. Lynch threw back her head with one more triumphant cackle...

Which cut off abruptly, as a dark shape rushed past Dan, growling. Its black muzzle snapped shut, sinking into Dr. Lynch's throat as it passed, and the head yanked, tearing.

The beast landed and wheeled with amazing speed and dexterity, spitting a mass of ruined gray flesh to the stage.

It was a wolf.

A huge wolf with chestnut fur and green eyes as bright as liquid emeralds, familiar eyes that turned for a split second to Dan, sad and soulful, piercing him with revelation.

*Nadia?*

The wolf leapt again, sailing at Dr. Lynch, who dropped Dan and lashed out with superhuman speed, slapping the wolf with a powerful backhand that batted the beast away like a puppy. The wolf hit the stage, slid several feet, and lay in an unmoving heap.

Dan gasped for air.

*That wolf... its eyes... Nadia... How?*

But he couldn't just stand there, thinking. He had to hurry, had to—

Dr. Lynch appeared before him, grinning terribly. She worked her jaws, meaning to mock and threaten him, but her torn and ruined throat only wheezed malevolently.

Then Dr. Lynch smiled and pointed past Dan toward Holly, conveying her plans perfectly without a single word. She would force him to watch her sacrifice his love.

But then a lasso of silver light fell over the necromancer's head and tightened around her neck.

Dr. Lynch's red eyes swelled with surprise.

Dan glanced over his shoulder.

A circle of light now burned against the gathering darkness like a window into summer. Zeke crouched in the opening, pulling hard on the rope, trying to drag Dr. Lynch into the high plane where he could hopefully overpower her.

Dr. Lynch's mouth opened in a silent scream, and her red eyes glared up at Zeke with burning hatred. Her hands closed around the silver rope, trying to pull Zeke out of that plane and into this one.

Zeke hauled back on the line, dragging Dr. Lynch several scraping inches nearer to the bright gate.

Dan sprinted across the stage. Not toward Holly but toward Broadus.

"Beneath me," the Legionnaire gasped, clearly fighting against unconsciousness. "Small of my back."

Dan lifted Broadus as much as he could with one hand and searched for the knife with the other.

Glancing across the stage, he watched in terror as Dr. Lynch released the silver rope and shot a line of terrible black energy into the bright gate.

Zeke screamed as the black corruption struck his chest

but held tight to the silver rope, yanking the necromancer toward him.

Dan's hand closed around the handle of a knife. He pulled it free. A dagger of shining fire burned in his fist.

The Blade of Light!

He charged.

Zeke tugged weakly. The black corruption wound around him like a constrictor snake, and as Dan watched, his friend began to wither beneath the mortifying coils.

No longer sliding forward, Dr. Lynch raised her bloody hands triumphantly overhead.

And that is how she was standing when Dan slammed the Blade of Light between her shoulders, driving it into her with all his might, sinking the fiery dagger to the hilt in her undead flesh.

A flash of blinding light exploded in Dan's hand, forcing him to release the blade and stagger backwards, shielding his eyes.

Then the flash died away.

The handle of the buried dagger glowed brightly now, tendrils of light stretching out and away, spreading across the necromancer's form, wrapping her in a bright web as she raged and writhed.

Dr. Lynch's flesh was peeling away and smoking. Her robes caught fire as the light enveloped her. Then she started zipping across the stage again, dragged by the silver rope.

Looking up, Dan saw Zeke, as withered and wasted as a mummy, hauling hard on the rope.

Lynch's burning form lifted into the air. Then she zipped up and way, flew past Zeke, and disappeared into the bright gate.

Zeke tipped his hat toward Dan.

Then the gate slammed shut.

Zeke and Dr. Lynch were gone.

The icy wind whooshed away to join the retreating darkness, carrying with it the evil green fog that had turned the spectators into butchers. A second later, only a dark spot remained in the sky. Then that, too, popped out of existence.

The bright day returned. The stadium cried and wept and shouted, survivors coming to their senses and waking to an unfathomable nightmare.

Dan raced across the stage.

Not to Holly, whom he would free momentarily.

But to his other love, Nadia, who lay naked upon the stage, still as a corpse.

## 62

## AFTERMATH

S everal days later…

"ENOUGH," HOLLY GASPED. "NO MORE, YOU INSATIABLE barbarian!"

Dan rolled off of her and stood beside the bed, smiling down at her gorgeous, naked body and beautiful face. "Just trying to get in a little fun before we visit your family."

He caught himself before reflexively glancing across the room at the elegant wooden box that authorities had discovered in Dr. Lynch's office and surrendered to Holly so that she might return its contents to her family. Soon the head of Holly's grandmother would rejoin the rest of her at the heart of the grove.

The mission filled Holly with both pride and sorrow.

So Dan forced himself not to glance at the box.

The last week had been very, very difficult, and he was

relieved to see Holly coming around at last, returning to herself.

Yes, things were looking good again.

*Speaking of looking good,* Dan thought, shifting his eyes.

"Don't even think about crawling back on top of me, you savage," Nadia said. She was sprawled out on the bed beside Holly, shimmering with perspiration. "I'm spent."

"I would've expected more stamina from a werewolf," Dan joked.

"And I would've expected that by now you could go at least fifteen minutes without mentioning my lycanthropy," Nadia said.

"I can't help it," Dan said. "It's sexy as hell!"

"You seriously are a barbarian!" Nadia laughed, then lay back, twirling a chestnut lock around one finger.

Dan knew that it would take some time for Nadia to be really comfortable with discussing her lycanthropy, but he also knew that she was happy to finally have it out in the open.

That secret had been weighing on her since they had met. All this time, Nadia had been hiding the truth, afraid that Dan and Holly would both reject her as a monster and a liar and a freak.

But of course, they hadn't.

They loved her.

Besides, Nadia had been in werewolf form when she had saved everyone by attacking Dr. Lynch at the right moment.

Overwhelmed during the initial assault, Nadia had turned and run, not to abandon the Noobs but to hide in the tunnel while shifting. Then, filled with the patient cunning that accompanied her full wolf form, Nadia had lain in wait until it was time to attack.

Dan had a million questions, and Nadia promised to answer all of them in time.

Dan was fine with that. If Nadia needed time, he would give it to her.

But he wanted no more secrets between them. The three of them were a family now. They would support each other no matter what, and they would share everything.

So much had happened. So much had changed.

Yes, they had defeated Dr. Griselda Lynch and saved the universe from eternal darkness but at great cost.

Nearly twenty thousand people had died that day, most of them in the stadium.

Was Zeke among the dead?

Dr. Lynch's diabolical mortification spell had ravaged the wizard and withered his flesh before he and the necromancer had tumbled away, fighting like cats, and vanished into a different plane of existence. Had the spell finished him?

No one had seen or heard from him since.

Dan hoped that Zeke was all right. Zuggy, too.

Sorcery still raised Dan's hackles, but Zeke had saved his life, had saved all of their lives.

And more to the point, sorcery had brought Dan to life again. Yes, he was a barbarian, but he needed to rethink some of his superstitions.

So much to think about. So much to do.

He was thankful for the break, anyway.

The university had suspended classes for the next month, through Thanksgiving.

In even better news, Dan's independent study with Dr. Lynch had been struck from his record.

Of course, if the university truly understood the role that Dan and the Noobs had played in defeating Dr. Lynch, they would award them all with honorary doctoral degrees in Heroic Ass-Kicking.

But Dr. Lynch's magical shield had blocked out their heroic actions.

In fact, the authorities had interrogated the Noobs. But seers had verified their testimonies, along with the testimonies of the surviving Legionnaires, Broadus and Maurelio.

The wiry thief almost hadn't survived to tell his tale. He'd been unconscious for most of the fight, bleeding to death. But luckily, Broadus had been carrying healing potions, which saved Maurelio and Nadia.

Eventually, the authorities had quietly thanked Dan and the others for their roles in stopping Dr. Lynch, but there would be no public recognition.

The university wasn't running a coverup, precisely, but they certainly weren't celebrating the catastrophe. The sooner that Campus Quest could leave the headlines the better.

Besides, university officials explained, not everyone would be pleased with the actions of the Noobs and the Legion of Light. A necromancer as powerful as Dr. Lynch had formidable allies, and dozens of acolytes lived on.

Dan stepped into his jeans and pulled them up.

"Where are you going?" Holly asked.

"I have to pick up my sword," Dan said. Having Wulfgar reforged was costing him what little money he had left. Not that it would be Wulfgar anymore. Now it would just be a sword that fit him perfectly.

"Why bother getting the thing fixed in the first place?" Nadia asked. "You could've gotten a perfectly good used sword and saved a few gold pieces."

Dan shrugged his shoulders. "I'm polygamous with women only. With weapons, I'm a one-sword man."

"Speaking of polygamy," Holly said, "when we get to the grove, dozens of unwed girls will be drooling over you. Let me know if you see one you like." She smiled brightly, mischief glowing in her purple eyes. "Maybe we'll bring home a pet."

"A pet, huh?" Dan said. Reflexively, his mind conjured the lovely image of tangled limbs and sweaty bodies, but in truth, he couldn't imagine bringing on another wife. At least not yet. Talk about complications…

"I'm allergic to grey elves," Nadia joked. She gave Holly's shoulder a playful shove. "And why does the idea of sharing our man excite you so much?"

"I want our husband to be happy," Holly said. "He's a powerful barbarian. As he grows stronger, he'll build an amazing harem, bringing his wives wealth and power."

"Whoa, whoa, whoa," Nadia said. "Enough with the husband stuff."

Dan laughed. "But you're fine with the harem thing?"

Nadia shrugged. "I've always wanted a big family. So, maybe? I would probably be all right with it as long as I got a say with every choice."

"Of course," Dan said.

"And," Nadia added with a sly grin, "as long as these women really do bring me wealth and power."

"Um," Holly said, "the harem will bring Dan's *wives* wealth and power… not his concubine."

Nadia gave her a shocked smile, mock offended. "Oh no you didn't, elf! Who are you calling a concubine?"

"If you refuse to join us in marriage," Holly said, "that's the only title you get." Then she stuck out her tongue and crossed her arms over her perfect breasts.

Nadia rolled her eyes and sprung from the bed, her lovely body bouncing in ways that made Dan want to drop his jeans again.

"You know what?" Nadia said, looking back and forth between Dan and Holly. "You're both *my* concubines!"

Holly and Dan laughed.

The girls decided to go into town with Dan. They would grab some last-minute supplies while he picked up his sword.

They got dressed and headed out the door together.

The day was crisp and beautiful. Dan smiled up at the hard blue sky, flanked by his two loves.

Nadia elbowed him as they were passing the AAA frat house. "Look who it is."

Holly groaned.

Dan glanced across the street, and saw Grady standing on the frat house lawn, drinking a beer with his buddies and grinning down at a semicircle of girls trying to talk to him. He and his team were celebrities now.

Looking at his former rival, Dan couldn't help but remember Grady's bulging eyes as he had fled Dr. Lynch and the acolytes.

Now Grady looked up from the girls and saw Dan looking at him. Grady's grin drooped. Not into a sneer, though. Grady merely frowned and looked quickly away, pretending that he hadn't even seen Dan.

Dan chuckled and kept walking.

"What?" Holly said.

"Nothing," Dan said, understanding then that Grady would never dare to look him in the eyes again. "Nothing at all."

They strolled downhill into town. The streets were fairly empty. Most of the students had already gone home.

"It's good that we're stocking up this afternoon," Holly said. "That means that we won't have to stop on the way out of town tomorrow. I want to get on the road early. I'd rather not run into the monster that Mother talked about."

Holly had already told them about the letter she'd received. According to her mother, some mysterious and deadly monster had made nighttime travel through the forest impossible.

"Whatever the monster is," Dan said, "I'll kill it if that will win over your family."

Holly laughed but made no such promises. Apparently, her dad was a total hard-ass, her brother was both a hothead and an expert swordsman, her mother was off-the-charts intelligent and tough as nails, and her little sister was as wild as the forest itself. And the rest of the community tended to kill any outsider that trespassed within their secret grove.

"Don't worry," Holly said. "I'll keep you both safe."

"I'm excited to meet your family," Nadia said. "Besides, if they kill us, at least I won't have to deal with Gruss when I come back."

"I will deal with Gruss when we return," Dan said, anger rising in him. According to Nadia's street urchins, the mobster was getting impatient and making vague threats.

"For the thousandth time," Nadia said, "forget about Gruss. He's big time. Seriously. He's—"

"Anyone who threatens my family—"

"Enough!" Holly said. "You two can argue on the trip. Preferably while I'm sleeping."

Reaching Calder Way, Dan kissed them both goodbye. He would pick up his reforged sword from the blacksmith and find Holly and Nadia in the shops when he was finished.

He didn't go straight to the blacksmith, though. Instead, he paused on the sidewalk and enjoyed watching the petite elf and dark-haired thief walk away.

Holly hip-bumped her friend, and Nadia's bright laughter streamed back to Dan as the pair disappeared into the alley.

Tomorrow, they would leave for the grove. It would be a dangerous trip.

The forest teemed with bandits and marauding humanoids. Random monster encounters were a distinct possibility. He expected serious trouble with Holly's family and the other xenophobic grey elves. And of course, they might run into whatever monster was gobbling up nighttime travelers.

*Better get my sword, then,* Dan thought with a smile. He was happy. Very, very happy. He didn't know precisely which dangers they would face in the wilderness, but with two amazing women by his side, he was ready for adventure!

———

THANK YOU FOR READING *DAN THE BARBARIAN*!

DAN, HOLLY, AND NADIA'S STORY CONTINUES IN *DAN THE Adventurer.* GET IT HERE!

IF YOU ENJOYED THIS BOOK, PLEASE CONSIDER LEAVING A review on Amazon. I know my stories aren't for everyone, but by sharing your opinion, you'll help the right readers find this book. Thanks so much for your time and help!

WANT TO KNOW WHEN NEW BOOKS ARE AVAILABLE?

JOIN MY LIST!

MANY THANKS TO THE HAREM LIT FACEBOOK GROUP, WHERE I enjoy talking books with other fans of the genre. Come join the discussion!

## ABOUT THE AUTHOR

Hi, I'm Hondo. I'm a lifelong fan of Dungeons & Dragons, fantasy, and science fiction. Though I write crazy adventure stories about kicking ass and building harems, I'm actually just a regular guy blessed with a great wife, a beautiful daughter, and a dog with two different colored eyes.

If you'd like to connect, swing by HondoJinx.com.

Thanks again for reading *Dan the Barbarian!*